RUBY BASU lives in the bea~~~~~~~~~~~~~~~~ with her husband, two children, and the cutest dog in the world. She worked for many years as a lawyer and policy lead in the Civil Service.

As the second of four children, Ruby connected strongly with *Little Women*'s Jo March and was scribbling down stories from a young age. A huge fan of romantic movies, Star Wars, and Marvel, she loves creating new characters and worlds while waiting for her superpowers to develop.

Also by Ruby Basu

The Twelve Wishes of Christmas

The Love Arrangement

RUBY BASU

ONE PLACE. MANY STORIES

HQ
An imprint of HarperCollins*Publishers* Ltd
1 London Bridge Street
London SE1 9GF

www.harpercollins.co.uk

HarperCollins*Publishers*
Macken House, 39/40 Mayor Street Upper
Dublin1
D01 C9W8 Ireland

This edition 2022

2
First published in Great Britain by
HQ, an imprint of HarperCollins*Publishers* Ltd 2022

Copyright © Ruby Basu 2022

Ruby Basu asserts the moral right to be
identified as the author of this work.
A catalogue record for this book is
available from the British Library.

ISBN: 978-0-00-847139-2

To Beej
Love you and miss you. Always.

Chapter 1

The man sitting across the table from me is intelligent, articulate, interesting, attractive … and looking for a serious relationship. In other words, he's completely unsuitable. Unfortunately, all the men I've spoken to this evening so far have been the same.

I mentally heave a sigh. What possessed me to think I would find someone who could help me with my scheme at a South Asian singles event? A bell rings, signalling it's time for the man to move on and for another to take his place. Luckily, there are only two more moves before my first round of dates is over. As my latest 'date' sits opposite me, I give him a bright smile – I can try to be engaging, but not overly interesting, until then.

Finally, it's break time and, as I make my way into the main reception area, I try to relax my cheek muscles after the effort of maintaining my fake smiles. I look around for my friend, Tinu Banerjee, but she hasn't come through yet. Because of the large number of attendees, the speed dating tables are set up in two separate break rooms. We've all been assigned a number and put on some kind of rota for the speed dating, so even when we're not at the tables, we're still able to socialise with others in the reception room. I'm completely impressed by whoever's organised this event. I could do with having people with their skills working for me on my projects.

As I wait for Tinu, I look round the room, noticing the decor I hadn't fully taken in when we arrived. The theme for the event is spring, but I think they've taken some inspiration from Holi with flower garlands over every doorway, lamps and pendants in vibrant reds, purples, yellows and turquoises, an equally colourful large mat designed as a rangoli and even large bowls filled with wrapped sweets that resemble the coloured powders usually thrown over each other for the occasion.

I spot Tinu coming out of the side room in the centre of a group of people and move into her line of sight but I don't interrupt her. She's here for genuine reasons – she wants to find a potential partner – and I don't want to risk possibly interrupting a conversation with her *One*. When she notices me, she says something to her companions then walks over.

'Any luck?' I ask her. 'Have you met the man of your dreams yet?'

'Who knows? I can't judge whether someone's my soulmate in five minutes of speed dating. But there've been a few prospects. Still, plenty more men to meet. How about you?'

I grimace. 'No, you were right. Everyone here is looking for a relationship. Nobody's likely to agree to be my pretend boyfriend.'

Tinu laughs. 'I still can't believe you thought it was even a remote possibility.'

I tut. It's not that funny. And she knows I'm desperate. 'I guess it was wishful thinking. But if all the stories we hear are true, wouldn't you think there was a small chance someone's parents forced them to come along tonight?'

'Those people are more likely to hire matchmaker aunties than to sign up for an event like this one. Typical of you not to think this through.'

'Okay, Tinu,' I say, holding up my hand in surrender, 'you were right. A singles event isn't the right place to find someone to help me with my scheme.'

'That's not the only thing I'm right about, Annika. You know I

2

think it's a bad idea for you to lie to your parents about being in a relationship. This is what happens when you rush into something. If you'd thought through the consequences before you lied to them, you wouldn't be in this situation in the first place. You're always so impulsive, leaping before you look.'

I press my lips together, not quite pouting, but annoyed by her patronising tone. I want to argue but I can't deny there is an element of truth to what she said. I know she means well. And she's right, I don't want to lie to my parents but it's for a good cause. 'If you could have seen Dad's face when I told him I'm in a stable relationship. The relief on it. I was right that my single status was causing him additional stress.'

'So why don't you take this evening seriously? Look for someone you *can* have a relationship with.'

'Because I'm not looking for one right now. You know that!' I've had this conversation with her and others so many times now I feel like I'm reading from a script.

'Yeah, yeah. You need to be single to travel the world for your work.'

'What can I say?' I shrug. 'I'm an independent, professional career woman through and through.'

'You can still be a career woman and have a partner and family.'

If only it was that simple. It's not like I'm against marriage or family per se but they don't fit in with my current life plans. I'm not ready to settle down – I don't know if I ever will be. There's still so much that I want to do, so many places I want to see. Maybe it's possible to do that with a partner or children but I don't want to make it harder on myself.

I can live without romantic love.

'It doesn't matter,' I continue. 'I already told my parents I've been with this boyfriend for a few months. I don't have time to meet someone for a real romance, even if I wanted to. Which I don't,' I add, perhaps hoping that constant repetition will convince people I mean what I say.

3

But Tinu isn't paying attention as suddenly her gaze goes beyond my ear. Someone has obviously caught her interest. I watch in complete fascination as Tinu looks down demurely, then looks back at that person through her half-closed eyelids before she takes a sip from her glass and licks her lips. I am clearly witnessing an expert at work. Well, I have no intention of getting in the way of my friend's attempts at finding her soulmate.

'Look, I think I'm going to go before the next session,' I say.

'Go?'

I nod. 'I'll find somewhere to wait for you. Text me when you're done. But if you do chat to someone you think could be up for a little family deceit, pass on my deets.'

I go to one of the hosts to ask for my number to be removed from further speed dating rounds. Luckily, I know I'm not the only person to have asked for this, although I suspect the others weren't for the same reasons as mine.

I leave the ballroom and head towards the main lobby on the ground floor. I need to find some place where I can kill time while I wait for Tinu to finish but since this is my first time at this hotel, I don't know what facilities I can use. I remember seeing signs for a business conference and, if the conference has evening events, I don't want to accidentally find myself listening to people talking over drinks and nibbles about how well their equity portfolios are performing.

After a quick chat with the concierge, I make my way to a small bar on the mezzanine level. A few older gentlemen are seated at one of the tables, but otherwise it's empty. Hopefully, that means service will be quick.

I take a stool at the bar and wait for the bartender to come over for my order.

'On your own?' he asks, handing me a menu.

'With a friend, but she's busy right now.'

'The singles event in the Marlborough ballroom, right?'

'Yes. How did you guess?' I laugh when he looks embarrassed.

4

It was a pretty good assumption when I'm one of the many South Asian people in the hotel that evening.

'You're not the first person who's ducked in here for a drink this evening,' he says.

'Really?' My eyes widen and I look around the room again. Nobody in here looks like they've come from the event, but from the sounds of it, there could be others who aren't really looking for a relationship. Perhaps this is the right bar to find them.

'So why did you leave?' he asks. 'Weren't you enjoying it?'

'Not what I'm looking for really.'

'Ah. I see. You have someone specific in mind then.'

'Kind of.' I open my menu and pretend to be completely absorbed in reading the drinks list before I'm tempted to spill out all the details of my scheme to the bartender. What is that saying about bartenders being like therapists?

Since the place is quiet and he doesn't have anyone else to serve, he stands by me, waiting for my order. I start asking him questions, to make it feel less awkward, and to prevent even the possibility of him digging any further into who I'm specifically looking for. He tells me he's Dac, twenty-six and working part-time while he completes his master's degree at the local university.

After the disaster this evening has been so far, I decide a cocktail won't hurt – it'll be the perfect way to improve my mood. I give Dac my order and inspect him as he goes to gather the ingredients for my drink. He isn't bad looking and his Eastern European accent is kind of sexy. Perhaps he would agree to pretend to be in a relationship with me.

I roll my eyes. Yes, that is definitely something I can bring up during small talk when Dac brings my drink over. And he has no incentive to agree to my scheme. Unless … I tilt my head as a thought begins to emerge. Could I pay someone to pretend to be my boyfriend?

Ugh, my desperation is rearing its ugly head. Even if I could pay someone, I can't ask a random stranger in a bar to help me and I have no idea how to hire an escort. Before I give in to temptation to throw caution to the wind and beg Dac to be my pretend boyfriend, I take my cocktail over to a small table for two by the window. The view isn't great, but I stare at it as if it's the path leading to the Taj Mahal rather than an ordinary London street illuminated by storefronts and streetlights.

I sip my cocktail slowly, enjoying the fruity flavours with the underlying hint of rum. I've drunk true daiquiris on a beach in Cuba but I have to admit a small preference for the frozen strawberry variety. Travel is one of the huge benefits of the work I do and in only a few weeks I will be in South America working on another project for at least two months. Usually, my projects are longer but I've limited the time I'll spend abroad this time because of Dad's health. Thinking of Dad brings me back to the predicament I've created for myself.

How am I going to find a fake suitor?

I finish my drink faster than I realise and wonder whether it's sensible to order another one when I catch a glimpse of someone familiar.

No, it can't be! But it is.

Rav Gohil.

Of all the places in the world, Rav's coming into this bar. He's with a group of businesspeople, and I studiously stare out the window hoping he won't see me. Not that he'd recognise me if he did. I can't believe my luck. Or lack of it.

I'd recognise him anywhere. He was the bane of my life growing up. And in some ways, he still is.

My parents always held Rav up as the epitome of the perfect child. And it wasn't just *my* parents. Nearly every person I grew up with complained that their parents used Rav as their shining example of what they expected from their children.

What made it worse was that my older brother, Nishal, and my younger sister, Shakti, manage to live up to the comparison. Almost.

Me, not so much. At least not in my parents' eyes.

Rav is only a year older than me – he's the same age as Nishal. They went to the same school and university, although different colleges. The comparison was never as bad for Nish since he was taking his exams at the same time as Rav. But because I was younger, I always had Rav's actual results and achievements to be judged against. Of course, I was also under the shadow of Nish's achievements, but they were somehow never quite as good as Rav's.

When Nish trained to be a doctor and Rav went on into finance, as some kind of venture capitalist, I thought the comparisons would stop, as we were all adults and taking different paths in life. But my parents simply changed their focus from academic accomplishments to personal ones, like when Rav earned his first seven-figure bonus, which his family somehow managed to casually drop into conversation at some event one day, knowing full well this piece of gossip would spread like wildfire within our community.

I vaguely remember hearing how Rav shocked everyone when he announced he was leaving his job to start his own business. I can't remember all the details. Over the years, I've managed to zone out of any conversation where his name is mentioned.

I hear the group walk past me to the tables at the back and expel a breath as a new worry enters my head. If there's the slightest chance Rav does recognise me, should I speak to him? I don't want to risk him mentioning to his parents that he saw me drinking cocktails alone in a bar. Although that would probably be better than telling them I was at an Asian singles event. Because if that information got back to my parents ... No, I reassure myself, there's no way Rav will recognise me.

Although I'd hear about him all the time, we didn't see each other that much. During our school years, we only met at functions our parents dragged us to, usually an annual medical party since both our mothers are doctors, and occasionally at a large community wedding.

The last time I saw Rav was at Nish's wedding five years ago. We did speak then, but if I remember correctly, it was mostly Rav boasting about his achievements and either showing no interest or clearly being unimpressed with what I was doing. The conversation didn't last too long before he was dragged away by a woman, who I presume was his girlfriend since she didn't seem happy we were talking, much to my relief.

I wonder what had happened to that girl. Nish and my parents had been expecting a wedding invitation from the Gohils to arrive within weeks but I can't remember whether it did because I left for a project in Bolivia shortly after Nish's wedding. I'm sure I would have heard if Rav was married – my parents would definitely have mentioned it; the same way they casually bring up that Nish and Shakti are both happily married and giving them grandchildren.

At least if Rav is single, we have that in common. I suspect it could be the only thing we have in common.

If Rav is single, then perhaps he could ... No! I stop that train of thought immediately. It's ridiculous and I can't keep inspecting every male as a potential candidate to play my fake suitor.

To distract myself from my thoughts, and Rav's unexpected presence at this hotel, I walk over to the bar to order another cocktail and briefly chat with Dac. He is definitely flirting with me, but that could be because he's hoping for a generous tip, which I give him anyway. I'm not interested in a flirtation otherwise. On my way back to my table, I can't resist glancing over at Rav.

The lighting is subdued, casting a shadow over his face, but it doesn't matter. I don't need the light. I know how flawless his sharp, intelligent features are. Despite his unwitting role as my nemesis, I've always found him handsome, in an arrogant, knows that he's good-looking, way.

When he catches my eye, I look away hurriedly, and return to my table, my breath coming fast. There is no way he remembers who I am.

I scroll through my phone, deliberately trying to tune out the groups chatting at the tables behind me, hoping Tinu messages me, sooner rather than later, to let me know me she's ready to leave.

'Sorry for disturbing you.' A voice interrupts me. I look up and swallow. Even though I know the voice, I'm still surprised to see Rav standing next to my table. 'Aren't you Nishal Nath's sister, Shakti?'

'Yes, I'm Nishal's sister, but my name's Annika,' I reply with a bright smile. So I was right, he doesn't remember me but he remembers my sister. Typical. 'Shakti's our younger sister.'

I awkwardly put out my hand and he clasps it briefly. When he lets go, I surreptitiously wipe my hand along my dress, something I probably should have done before I offered to shake his hand, as my palm suddenly feels hot and clammy. Could Rav be making me nervous?

'Of course,' he says. 'Sorry. You may not remember me but we grew up in the same area and I went to school with Nishal. I'm …'

'I know who you are, Rav.'

His eyes widen as if he's surprised. Surely Rav's aware of how well known he is in our community? It's more likely he was trying to be falsely modest in suggesting I wouldn't remember him.

'Are you here for the conference?' he asks.

For a moment, I'm tempted to pretend I was attending whatever conference he's talking about, not that I'm embarrassed about being at a speed dating event; it's just not something I want to admit to Rav. But there's the risk Rav might want to talk about some of the presentations at this conference, and I'll end up looking like a fool.

'No,' I reply, trying to dredge up a smile. 'I came here with a friend. She's going to join me in an hour or so.'

'Do you mind if I wait with you until she arrives?'

I blink in surprise. Why would Rav ask to sit with me? I don't have any stories about Nish to share, and Rav doesn't strike me as someone who wants to ask about mutual acquaintances or old hunting grounds.

I twist my neck to look over at the table he'd been sitting at with his colleagues. It's now empty. I didn't even notice the others leave. There's only one couple in the bar, other than Rav and me, and they look completely engrossed in each other. Perhaps he's waiting for someone and doesn't want to sit alone. Not that it matters – it's not like I'm going to ask him.

I can't come up with a good enough reason to refuse so I incline my head to let him know it's fine.

He takes the seat opposite me and lifts his finger at Dac, which apparently summons him over. Wait, there's table service here?

Since Rav is offering, I order another cocktail. It'll be my third, so I probably shouldn't drink anymore, but I'm going to need the liquid courage to get me through this conversation.

'Where did you say your friend is?' he asks. 'Apart from the conference, I only saw a spring singles event at the hotel this evening.'

Of course, Rav would have seen the boards advertising the event. They were front and centre in the hotel lobby.

For a moment I consider denying that's where I was, but who really cares if Rav knows. The only risk is him telling someone who might know my parents. But if my parents do find out and ask me about it, I can always add another lie to my growing list and tell them I came to support a friend.

I nod. 'That's right. I was there for a bit. Then I left and my friend stayed.'

'Not your kind of thing?' he asks with a small smirk.

I bristle at the implication there's something wrong with a singles event. Or maybe I'm overreacting to a simple question. I take a calming breath. I don't usually look for the hidden meaning behind what people say.

What is it about Rav that is rubbing me the wrong way? He hasn't done anything to me specifically. And it isn't his fault my parents used to compare all their children to him. I don't even know if he's aware that he was held up as the perfect child – which automatically made him my nemesis. But perhaps that *is* it. All

10

my accomplishments were compared to his and found lacking. And there's that saying about comparison being the thief of joy. I frown. Even with my muddled thoughts, I know that doesn't sound right. Is it even applicable to this situation?

I straighten and take a deep breath to clear my head. He's looking at me with the politest expression on his face as he waits for an answer.

I can't remember what the question was. Oh, the singles event.

'On the contrary,' I reply, 'it was very pleasant. Just not what I'm after right now.'

He raises a single eyebrow. How does he do that? I've practised in front of the mirror and can never raise only one eyebrow. Of course, he's able to do that better than me too.

'May I ask what you are after?' he says.

I'm definitely feeling a little buzzed after those cocktails. That's the only explanation for why I blurt out, 'I'm after a suitor, and it's all your fault.'

His eyes widen. With a light laugh, he asks, 'How is your needing to find a husband my fault?'

'Because everything in your life is so perfect. Perfect student, perfect career, perfect partner.' My tone becomes more sarcastic with each repetition of *perfect*.

'You shouldn't believe everything you hear.' His expression hardens. I've offended him.

'It doesn't matter. If you weren't so perfect, then Nishal and Shakti wouldn't feel the need to be the same. And if they weren't so perfect, I wouldn't seem like a loser for not having the stable job, house, and husband and children.'

He blinks. 'Are you okay? Do you want some water?'

I shake my head at his offer. 'I just don't know how to change my family's mind. For some reason, my parents are convinced I can't possibly be happy and live a contented life if I'm single.' I don't understand why I'm spilling my guts to Rav, of all people, but now I've started, I can't seem to stop.

'It's not unusual for parents to worry about things like that.'

'Yeah, I know. But recently, my dad has taken it to a whole other level. He seems genuinely concerned about my future. Which, of course, is stressing out my mum. And I can't cause them any more stress. Not after Dad's—' I break off. I don't like thinking about my dad's health, and it's still difficult to voice aloud.

He tilts his head in sympathy. 'I was sorry to hear about your dad's heart condition. Everyone was very worried for a while. But I heard he's recovering well.'

'He is. Which is amazing. It's wonderful. But it was touch and go for a while and I think the experience has made him question his own mortality. And of course, he's convinced he won't be able to—' I clear my throat. 'He's convinced he needs to see me settle down with a husband, seven kids and a mortgage in the country.'

'And that's not what you want?'

'Last thing I want.' A glass of water appears before me, with a basket of bread and some dishes with olive oil and balsamic vinegar. When did Rav order those? I didn't see him talk to Dac. But I reach for a slice of bread and dip it into the dishes. Tinu and I ate before we came out but that seems like hours ago and I'm a lot hungrier than I realised.

'Why did you come to a singles evening? You say you want a suitor but you don't want to get married. Are you looking for someone or not?'

'Oh, I *am* looking for someone.' I almost laugh at the confusion on his face. 'But I have someone very specific in mind,' I say, trying to clarify it.

'Isn't that the whole point of the event though?'

'No!' I bang my hand against the table, making the dishes jump, spilling some of their contents. 'You don't get it. See, I already told my dad I was in a steady relationship.' I put my hand over my mouth as if I could take back the massive lie I told my parents.

He blinks again. 'Why?'

'So he wouldn't stress about my relationship status.' I shake my

12

head and exaggeratedly roll my eyes. Rav is supposed to be highly intelligent. Why is he having so much trouble understanding the situation?

'Then why did you come to speed dating?'

'To find someone who'd pretend to be my suitor.'

Rav throws his head back as he bursts into laughter. 'Why did you think you'd find someone here? No, forget that question. Why did you lie to your father?'

I sigh deeply. 'I didn't want him to worry. I made up the lie months ago because I was hoping my dad ... all my family ... would stop stressing about me being single. I guess I was expecting Dad to be back to his old self by now, so things would return to the way they used to be, when my parents were more subtle about their concerns for my unmarried status and weren't offering to set me up!'

I shake my head. 'Perhaps I should have taken a long project abroad to avoid all their fussing – it would have been the easiest solution. I don't know if you know this but I work overseas a lot. But I didn't want to be abroad for too long when my dad wasn't fully recovered. But now they keep asking me when are they going to meet him, when am I going to introduce them?' I say in a sing-song tone emphasising how often I've heard these words uttered. 'I don't want to ... I can't disappoint my parents. I've been able to put off making the introductions so far but I can't put it off for much longer. There'll be no excuse for them not to meet him when I return from my next project. Perhaps my parents will be less concerned about me settling down by then, but I don't hold much hope for that. So the alternative is to find someone who wants to play the part and then train him to be a suitable partner for me.'

It occurs to me that I've said a lot and I'm not entirely convinced anything I said makes any sense. I am not making a good impression on Rav and I've probably come across as slightly strange. For a brief moment, I consider laughing heartily and pretending everything I said is a joke. I take a long drink from the glass of water, waiting for Rav to speak.

'That is the most ridiculous scheme I've ever heard,' he says finally.

How rude! 'Excuse me, it's foolproof.'

'Apart from the fact you don't have someone to introduce to your father.'

I open my mouth, then close it again. 'Apart from that.' I cover my face with my hands. 'I know it doesn't make any sense. But I was trying to do a good thing. Dad really did stop worrying when I told him I'd found someone, which made my mum feel better, and if Mum is happy, Nishal and Shakti are too.'

The water and bread must have done the trick because my head is suddenly clear and the enormity of what I've just told Rav bears down on me. If I beg hard enough, maybe, just maybe, Rav won't tell Nish or anyone else connected to my family what I've just admitted.

'So what you're saying is that you're worried your dad will become stressed if you tell him you don't have a boyfriend?'

'Yes. If I come back and tell Dad and Mum my boyfriend and I broke up ... well, they may figure out I've been lying to them, but, in any event, I would be back to square one – unsettled with no prospects – and I don't want to risk what it could do to my dad. They wanted to meet my boyfriend before I leave for my project but I said there wasn't time. I'm only here for another two weeks before I fly out. But I said I'd introduce them if we're still together when I return. It's unlikely that I'll find a suitable partner while I'm in Guyana – I won't have the time to search for one thing – so I need to find one before I leave. Which doesn't give me much time. Everything could be perfect, if only ...'

'If only you can find a suitable man to agree to your plan.'

'That has always been the biggest flaw.' I rub my hand across my forehead. Rav's right. It *is* the most ridiculous scheme. 'I don't suppose you have any single friends who could help me out?' The alcohol has definitely made me a little more relaxed – more brazen.

Rav barks out a laugh while shaking his head. 'Why the deception, though?' he asks. 'Why don't you look for a boyfriend? A real one, not a fake one.'

I narrow my eyes and harden every muscle in my face.

Rav laughs then clears his throat to cover it. 'I've heard looks can kill,' he says, 'but this is the first time I've believed it could happen.' He holds his palms up in an apologetic gesture. 'I see that was the wrong thing to say.'

'The whole point of my scheme is because I don't want a relationship. It may surprise you to know, Rav Gohil, but not everybody wants a partner. We can be perfectly happy single.'

'I never—'

'We don't need a man to make us whole. Why is that so hard to understand? Do you think this is just lip service because I can't find a man?'

'No, I—'

I'm about to continue with my rant when my phone buzzes. I pick it up and read the text from Tinu.

'My friend's finished. I have to go. Thanks for the drink.'

'Are you staying in the hotel tonight?'

I scrunch my face trying to understand his concern. 'No.'

'Will you be okay to get home, or would you like me to escort you both?'

I'd probably laugh at his old-fashioned gallantry if I wasn't so embarrassed at everything I've disclosed to him. Instead, I shake my head and tell him we'll be fine before walking out of the bar and deliberately not looking back.

Why, of all the people I could have spilt my guts to, did it have to be Rav Gohil?

Chapter 2

'Annika, do you have a moment?'

I glance up from my laptop, where I've been working on my weekly status report to see Pete, one of the newest team members, standing in my doorway looking nervous. I've been in Guyana for four weeks and, until this moment, everything has been running smoothly, but I can tell from Pete's expression that it's about to change.

I smile to put him at his ease. 'Of course, take a seat.'

'Something's come up. I thought you should know about it,' Pete begins.

'Okay, what it is?' I ask, giving him my full attention.

Pete explains one of the problems they're having with another organisation, who seem to be ignoring some of the concerns from the Indigenous people and it's having a ripple effect on our team's work. I try hard not to roll my eyes but this isn't the first time this has happened. Too many organisations come into the area determined to impose their visions on the communities without considering whether they would work for the people they are trying to help.

After I leave this project, one of Pete's main roles will be to act as a community liaison, so I need to guide him on how to handle the issues when I'm not around. I carefully coach him into offering suggestions that we discuss together before we settle on an option Pete is happy to implement.

After Pete leaves, I go back to my status report. Because I've done this so often I've already made substantial progress – it's almost like a copy and paste job. But it means if no other problems arise, I'll be finished within a couple of hours. Although I would never wish for problems to arise, the day-to-day work activities can feel a little repetitive when everything goes according to plan. It's the location that makes it all worthwhile.

I haven't had a chance to explore the country yet. I glance at my watch. I should be done in time to take the minibus, which our company arranges for the project team every Friday to take us into the capital if we want. The journey only takes a few hours and it'll be my first time visiting Georgetown since I arrived in Guyana. I quickly speak to one of my colleagues to check there's a seat available, then go to my room to pack a bag with some clothes and toiletries, which I take back to my office with me so I can work until it's time to leave.

Later that evening, I'm in my hotel room, washing off the travel weariness. I change into a loose-fitting kurta and light cotton trousers. It's the perfect casual outfit for relaxing with the other team members when I meet with them later. Usually, I'm happy to stay in a hostel with the others, but I've splashed out on a hotel room with Wi-Fi on this occasion. I've only had the chance for quick phone calls with my parents, and I want to video-call them. Make sure everyone is okay.

It's so wonderful seeing their faces in front of me. My dad looks better each time I see him but it is hard to know for sure how he really is without seeing him in the flesh. Once again, I'm pleased I decided to take on a short project this time.

They don't mention *the boyfriend* on the call and, naturally,

I'm not going to bring him up myself but I do need to find a solution to this predicament I'm in – preferably one that doesn't cause Dad any unnecessary stress or worry.

I should probably sign up on some dating websites but I don't want to risk someone I know recognising me and the situation getting back to my family. Logically, I realise the prospect of that happening is exceedingly slim but sometimes our community is surprisingly small. Besides, online dating would have the same problems as the singles event – I would have to find someone prepared to pretend to be in a relationship. And how many people sign up and create a profile for that reason?

But there isn't much time left on this project before I return to England.

I could possibly pretend that my 'partner' works abroad too and is simply unavailable. I immediately discard that idea. It's too unbelievable, and if that was the reason, I would have mentioned it before. Besides, it wouldn't even help reassure my parents that I'm thinking about settling down.

I'm about to do an internet search for escort services but I stop myself because I know that's probably taking things too far, so instead I decide to check my emails to kill some time before my plans later on.

I scroll through my inbox, then frown as my eyes land on the subject heading 'FAKE SUITOR'.

Apart from Tinu, there is only one person whom I used that term with. I look at the sender. It is from Rav. For a moment, I wonder how he got my personal email address but then realise I'm just delaying opening the email and click on the message.

I skim through his polite greeting until I come to the line:

If you're still looking for someone for a pretend relationship, let me know. I may have a solution.

What does that mean? What solution can he possibly have?

I still can't believe I told him all my schemes for subterfuge. I remember that evening more clearly than I would like to and, occasionally, I still feel guilty for the tongue-lashing I gave him after he suggested I look for a real relationship.

I pause for a moment. I do vaguely remember asking Rav if he had any friends who could help me out. Perhaps he's found someone.

Half excited, half convinced it's a really bad idea, I reply to Rav's email because I don't have anything left to lose at this stage. I add that I only check my personal emails once a week at most because my work site has limited Wi-Fi, so if he doesn't hear from me, it's not because I'm ignoring him.

* * *

The following weekend, I'm back in Georgetown, and I log on to my emails, looking out specifically for one from Rav. Nothing.

I don't know whether to feel relieved or disappointed. It's one thing thinking about, or even planning out, a deception and another thing to actually go through with it.

I have my usual video call with my parents, pleased that both of them are looking well. Perhaps I should just admit the truth to my family. Or at least tell them the relationship didn't work out. Surely that wouldn't be enough cause for Dad's health to worsen? Still, it isn't something I should say over the phone or on video call. It can wait until I'm back in England again.

As the next week passes, things are very busy and I get so wrapped up in the project that I can't make the trip to Georgetown, needing to work through the weekend. The minibus is a lot emptier than usual. Many of us are giving up our free time to ensure the work we're building is a success.

I love the kind of work I do. Not just because I get to travel the world with it. I love collaborating with different team members and the local communities. But more than that, I also believe we're genuinely helping the communities we work in; that we're making a difference. I wish my family understood that. They're all in professions that help others – doctors, scientists, teachers – but for some reason, they don't see my job in the same light.

I go to the shared lounge on site to see if one of the communal computers is free. But as I expect, there's a long waiting list and I decide not to add my name. Instead, I put in a request to use the phone – my parents don't expect to hear from me each week, but since Dad's illness, I choose to check in more regularly.

After another busy week, I decide against heading into Georgetown but to hang out with some of my colleagues at a nearby ecolodge instead, where we can go boating and swimming and relax after a stressful couple of weeks at work. Once I'm there, I finally get a chance to check my personal emails and notice there's one from Rav, which was sent around ten days ago. I click his message, eager to know what it says.

I have a business situation. For reasons I don't want to go into fully until we meet in person, I need a partner at a series of work events I have coming up over the summer. I think we could help each other out. I'll pretend to be a potential suitor in front your family if you will agree to act as my partner at these events.

Let me know if you're interested in my proposition.

I blink then reread the email several times, trying to make sure I understand it properly. It is businesslike and formal in tone, but there's no denying the content of the message. Rav Gohil is seriously offering to be my fake suitor.

I can't imagine why Rav would need to pretend he has a girl-friend for business but it doesn't matter. He would be perfect for the role. Even more so because my parents would be over the moon. I couldn't find a better suitor. I'd even briefly thought about asking him when we met at the hotel but I didn't in my wildest dreams think he would be willing.

I quickly fire off a reply.

As soon as I press send, the doubts began to set in. Rav *would* be the perfect boyfriend from my parents' perspective. They know him. They adore him. He is beloved in our local community. And that's part of the problem.

It makes sense that I would have kept the truth about dating Rav from Mum and Dad until we were a more established couple because there would be gossip and interest about us as soon as we become public. Which means if we start a pretend relationship, it would also be the subject of a lot of gossip. And there will be big repercussions when the time comes to call things off. I already know, regardless of the reason we give for ending our relationship, I'm going to bear the brunt of the blame.

Could Rav pretending to be my boyfriend potentially cause my parents more stress in the long run?

Perhaps I was too hasty agreeing to his proposition. It reminds me of Tinu at the singles event, cautioning me to look before I leap. Well, it's not too late. We haven't committed to anything. After exchanging a couple of emails, we'll most likely realise we aren't compatible and, realistically, it isn't going to work. It would mean I'd be back square one, but I can cross that bridge later.

The words from Walter Scott's play about tangled webs being weaved come to mind – as they often have since I first lied to my parents.

As another week flies by, I barely have time to think about Rav's suggestion, but then I'm in the minibus on my way to the capital and I'm already a ball of nerves.

Rav writes:

This is good news. It's a relief you're amenable to my suggestion. We will need to discuss arrangements. In my opinion, it will be better if we can wait to talk about specifics until you're back in the country. For now, we should share some background information.

The rest of his email is effectively like a CV. Is he this formal with everyone? I'm starting to get the impression Rav likes order and planning and isn't prone to spontaneity, so he must have given our arrangement a lot thought before contacting me. Maybe Rav is deliberately writing to me as if he's conducting business.

What we are proposing to enter is more like a business relationship after all.

But no one in my family will believe I'm dating someone with a stick up his behind. It's not looking hopeful.

I write back:

Thanks for the data. I will have it memorised in case anyone wants to test me. I've attached my stats.

If we're going to pretend we're in a relationship in front of my family, it's a good idea for us to get to know each other better; get an idea of what makes us tick. So, tell me. What was your favourite subject at secondary school? Did you have an imaginary friend growing up? Did you want siblings, or do you like being an only child? What do you do to relax? What's your favourite constellation? If you could retire anywhere in the world, where would it be? What's one, as yet, unfulfilled dream of yours?

If you're wondering – I loved geography and languages. My friend's name was Bonuni – he was a pink elephant/whale. I've wished many times that I was an only child, but you've met Nishal so I'm sure you understand. I like socialising with friends or exploring new places. Pavo. I'm still exploring the world and will let you know once I've visited as many places as possible. That's one of my unfulfilled dreams as well. I would love to go on a working sailing trip in the Indian Ocean, perhaps as part of a research programme. I have my sailing licence but the opportunity hasn't come up yet. Still, I dream …

After I press send, I think about how Rav would respond to my email. He probably thinks I'm quite flighty and I can't hold my alcohol. My parents know me, and I can't imagine they'd be so desperate for me to be in a long-term relationship that they'd want me to be with someone serious or cheerless all the time, even if Rav has always been their golden boy.

I rub my face. If they think Rav isn't right for me, they'll just start suggesting I meet other men – other men they can introduce me to. I humph. If Rav is going to be my boyfriend, I'm really going to have to loosen him up.

The following week I receive his reply.

Economics and politics. No imaginary friend. I liked being an only child but sometimes I wished I had a sibling to deflect attention away from me. I enjoy reading or going to the theatre but I don't seem to have time to relax. I don't have a favourite constellation. I like living in England – I'd be happy to retire here. I can't think of any unfulfilled dreams, only ones in progress.

Well, at least he answered my questions, although they are the blandest things I've ever read. But I'm determined to get him to open up more in our emails. Rav asked some more questions. All practical, of course. I answer those, then I add:

Do you have any pets? I don't. If I did have a pet, it would definitely be a dog, preferably lots of dogs. I think I'd be too needy to be a cat owner. But since I'm never in one place long enough, sadly, pets aren't part of my life.

Where did you go on the most successful date you've been on, and what's your most successful chat-up line? If we were dating for real, what line would you have used on me?

Now favourites – film, book, band, TV show, drink? Favourite flavour of ice cream? I should warn you, the only correct answer to this question is butterscotch but other choices are acceptable such as mint choc chip. However, do not, under any circumstances, reply with rum and raisin because that's not a flavour – it's an aberration. I would not like to meet the mind of the person who came up with that idea.

Even as I type, I'm almost certain Rav's favourite ice cream flavour will be rum and raisin. No, it has to be basic vanilla.

Then I end the email with one last question – what's the most trouble he's ever been in with his parents? But, because it's Rav, I'm not holding out too much hope he'll have a response. Probably that he didn't study hard enough for an exam and ended up with an A minus instead of an A once.

Over the next few weeks, we exchange more emails. Rav's responses are more well thought out, covering more practical topics about our arrangement, whereas I ask any random question that pops into my head. Although I've heard all about Rav and his many accomplishments over the years, I've never got to know what he's really like. I'm not entirely sure our online conversation has helped me to better understand him as a person, only that we might be polar opposites. But I don't have any other options, and there's still time for us to get to know each other once I'm back in England, before I have to introduce him to the family.

Besides, it's not as if I need to actually like the person I'm pretending to date.

Chapter 3

It's strange being back in my family home in my own childhood room. Nothing has changed since I left for university – not even the bedding. I run my hand over the desk. I used to sit there for hours studying or pretending to. There are still textbooks on the bookshelves next to the desk from when I was taking my A levels. It's like being in a museum of my life. I almost expect to see my secret stash of 'unsuitable' books in its hiding place, only those were the first things I'd taken with me when I left home.

Usually, when I'm back in England after one of my projects, I spend a lot of time visiting friends, couch surfing at their houses until I've decided which town I want to rent in for the brief time I'm in the country. As much as I enjoy travelling the globe, I want to explore the UK and Europe too, so on past occasions I've done short-stay rentals in places like Rome, Paris and Barcelona. Of course, my parents can't understand why I don't have my own place with its accompanying mortgage and responsibilities. They know I have the savings to put down a substantial deposit but there are so many wonderful places where I could live, and with no partner or job to restrict me, how can I decide where I'd want my permanent home to be? This time, however, I've decided to stay at my parents' house for as long as possible.

Dad was taking a nap when I arrived home so I haven't been able to see him yet. Before his operation, it was unusual for him to sleep during the day. I can't help but worry something's wrong and I'm not being given the full picture of Dad's health, even though Mum has assured me a nap is part of Dad's new routine.

As I sit on my bed, I think back to that awful day last winter when I received the call Dad was in hospital. It doesn't matter that I'm an adult in my thirties; when I visited Dad in the hospital after his heart operation, I was a scared toddler again, wanting my daddy to hug me and tell me everything was going to be okay, not for him to be hooked up to monitors with machines breathing for him.

I'm so grateful I was between projects at the time. I'd only been visiting friends in Bath and was able to make the one-hundred-or-so-mile journey back to Sutton Coldfield in a few hours. I don't even like to think about what would have happened if I'd been abroad when it happened. My projects are usually located in places where there's decent infrastructure to get around fairly quickly, but on many occasions, I've had to travel further away from established towns and communities into less inhabited areas. It could have been a different story if I'd been at one of those places where I had to rely on satellite phones to even get messages let alone try to organise transport back to England at short notice.

I was due to start a project in November last year, but a colleague took over for me because I didn't want to leave my family while Dad was in hospital. I returned the favour by taking over my colleague's project in April, which is the only reason I went overseas when I still wasn't one hundred per cent sure Dad was fully recovered. Before I leave for my next project, I want to ensure that Dad's health is good and continually improving. I do have work lined up in September – it's meant to last until the end of the year, which is longer than I wanted while I'm worried about Dad, but it's the shortest project I could find.

And that's why I'm back here living at home – because I want to see for myself that Dad is well. I know something happened to him, health-wise, while I was in Guyana but nobody's told me anything yet.

At the same time, I really hope I won't regret moving back home. I don't want to set a precedent – or create the expectation that I'll be living there in the future.

I know being in the same house as my parents will give them plenty of opportunities to nag me about settling down and buying my own place instead of wasting my money on rent, or even save money by living at home. Although, of course, I'm fully aware their real preference would be for me to find a husband and my own home and be 'settled'.

I shake my head and release a long breath.

If I could find a man who would be happy with me being away for long periods of time, travelling to other countries for work and for pleasure, who also enjoys travelling the world, then I would be more than happy to settle down.

But I'm not going to hope and wish for the impossible. From experience, I know that I will inevitably be the one who has to sacrifice my job if I want to maintain a relationship and it's too painful for me to ever want to put myself in that position again.

Rather than dwell on unpleasant thoughts, I pick up my duffel bag. I don't have much with me, I always travel light, so it doesn't take me long to unpack and by the time I'm finished, Mum's calling up to me, telling me to come into the kitchen to help. I suppress a laugh. Nothing has changed.

I go down to the kitchen where Mum is beginning to prepare dinner. Almost by habit, I start emptying the dishwasher and setting the table, the same chores I did as a child.

'Chandnipishi called,' Mum says. 'She wants to know whether you're bringing anyone to Rohit's wedding.'

'Chandnipishi wants to know?' I smirk.

'We would like to meet this boy you have been seeing at some point. That's not us being nagging parents, Niki.'

I breathe in, mustering all the patience I can manage. 'I know, Mum.'

'You can at least tell us his name. Why does everything have to be so secret-secret with you?'

'I'm not trying to be, but we both agreed to hold back as of yet because we want to make sure we're in a place where we're ready for our families to be involved.'

'You already told us this. But how long will you keep us waiting for?'

'Yeah, we're beginning to think you made him up,' my brother says, coming up behind me.

'Charming as always, Nishal,' I say rolling my eyes before giving him a brief hug. For some reason, I've missed everyone a lot more than I usually do. 'Are your better half and mini-mes with you?'

'Not this time. I only popped in to say hello and see how Dad's doing.'

That puts me on alert. 'Why are you worried about Dad? Has something happened?'

'No, I come by every week. You know that.'

'Of course.' I mouth 'perfect son' at him as I sit back down.

He grins, happy to be referred to that way. 'Anyway, don't change the subject. When will we meet this guy who may or may not be real?'

I throw him an exasperated look. 'He's real! I'm going to see him soon and I'll definitely suggest he meets you all. I promise.'

'Sorry to disappoint you, Mum,' Nishal says, 'but it looks like we're never going to meet this man.'

'What?' Mum looks confused.

'Annika's always easier to get along with when you don't have to see her that often. Now they're in the same country, this mystery man is bound to realise he's made a mistake.'

I hear movement in my parents' bedroom, which prevents me from answering back. Not that there's any point. Nishal spends his whole life teasing us, his sisters. I've learnt over time that

28

engaging with him only encourages him more. But you would think now we're in our thirties, and he has his own wife and family, his need to needle me would lessen.

I leave the kitchen and go upstairs and knock on my parents' door. My dad's voice tells me to enter. He's standing in front of the mirror combing his hair but his head is turned to see who it is.

'Niki!' His smile is wide as he opens his arms. I go in for the hug – Dad feels thin and frail.

'Dad, how have you been?'

'Good, Annika,' he replies, patting my back. 'I'm glad to have you home. I've missed you.'

'I've missed you, too,' I reply. We have this same conversation each time I return from one of my projects, but I don't think I've ever meant it as much as I do this time.

He asks me about my latest project while he finishes getting ready.

Dad has always taken an interest in my work, even though he doesn't fully understand what I do. He definitely didn't understand why I stopped working as an employee of a company to start up as a freelance consultant, only to have my original employer as one of my clients.

But he was supportive anyway. He even offered to loan me money to keep me afloat when I was between projects before I told him I made a lot more money working on a couple of projects a year than I did when I was employed. Since I have hardly any expenses when I'm abroad, I've accrued a comfortable amount of savings, which I use when I'm between projects.

I always thought my parents supported me, even if they didn't really understand why I wanted to travel rather than settle down. That's why it came as such a shock when Dad asked me, while he was still in hospital, if I wanted their help in arranging a marriage. It made me realise how serious seeing me married and settled down is for them.

'Come on,' Dad says when I finish telling him about the

Guyana work, 'we'd better go downstairs. Your mum will be waiting for us.'

Dad grabs my hand tight for support as we walk downstairs. I close my eyes against the tears threatening to form.

My dad has always been larger than life. The life and soul of the party with a big laugh and a big appetite. Now he seems ... smaller. At five foot seven, he has never been the tallest person, but to me, he has always been a giant among men. As much as I was hoping he would be, I can tell he isn't back to his former self. If anything, he's more fragile than when I left two months ago. I made the right decision to live at home, for now.

I help Mum serve tea and biscuits, just like old times. Our kitchen has always been the hub of our home. Any time we spent together as a family was usually in this room. We only use the dining room when we have guests round for dinner – which was fairly often since both my parents love to cook. And we only used the living room when we wanted to watch TV.

Whenever I think of home, I picture the five of us sitting around the kitchen table, talking about what we did during the day or discussing what was going on in the world, sharing stories and jokes. The room was always filled with the smells of food. Mum loves making Bengali curries, but Dad has always experimented with cuisine from around the world.

I chew my bottom lip. When was the last time Dad felt strong enough to cook? I glimpse the look of love and concern on Mum's face as she pours more tea for him.

Mum had barely retired before Dad's illness. My parents had so many plans to travel the world during their retirement. Now those plans are on hold, possibly shelved for good.

Another reason I know – despite my parents' concerns – I'm right to seize the opportunities for travelling while I can. Because nobody knows what can happen down the line. I'm young, healthy and privileged. I'm not going to turn my back on what possibilities the world has to offer because of some antiquated expectation that I should be married with children – settled – now I'm in my thirties.

'Annika.' Nishal's voice breaks into my thoughts.

'What?'

'Dad was talking to you.'

'Oh sorry, what was that, Dad?' I ask, embarrassed that I wasn't paying him full attention.

'I said I'm looking forward to playing against you at carrom. I haven't had a good challenge since you were last here.'

'Well, prepare to be defeated as the reigning Nath champion,' I reply. 'We'll have to dig out the board and counters and have a proper tournament.'

I catch Nish mouthing the words 'imperfect daughter' to me. It's always been our joke that he's the perfect son, I'm the imperfect daughter and Shakti is the 'darling daughter', but I also know, behind the humour, Nish thinks my desire to live my life in a way that makes me happy, without worrying about how it affects others, is a bit selfish. As if my decision to work abroad robbed my father of some joy in life. Although I hardly think playing a simple strike and rebound table game was the biggest priority for my dad.

'Kaya texted,' Nish says, referring to his wife. 'She wants to know when you can come round for dinner, spend time with your nephews.'

'Soon. Very soon. And I'm available for babysitting any time while I'm here.' I may not want children myself, but I love kids and enjoy spending time with them, especially my nephews. 'Actually, I have something for the kids. Can you come with me for a second, Nish?'

Nish gives me a puzzled look – he knows I would rather give my nephews their presents myself – but he follows me to the living room anyway where I use the opportunity to ask him if anything happened with Dad while I was gone.

At first, Nish tries to wave away my concerns, but eventually, he tells me Dad had a minor setback and was in hospital overnight.

'Why didn't anyone tell me?' I ask, unsure how to process the feelings from being left out of the situation. 'I would have come back.'

'Would you?' Nish asks pointedly.

'I can't believe you'd doubt me. I know you think I'm selfish, because my lifestyle takes me away from you all a lot of the time, but this is about Dad's health. There's nothing more important.'

Nish sighs. 'The parents didn't want to worry you. That's why they never mentioned it. Dad was only there for the night, and by the time you would have got on a flight and arrived in England, Dad was already back home.'

Nish tries to reassure me that there's nothing to worry about, that Dad is recovering, albeit slowly, and he's on the mend, but I'm pleased I'm home for four months. If things haven't changed, and I still feel concerned by the end of August, I can always withdraw from the project. It won't be ideal but that's one of the benefits of being a consultant – I can pick and choose when I work, to an extent. And right now, my family is my priority.

'It would be better if you pretend you don't know,' Nish says.

'Why?' I don't see why we can't be open about things now I'm back.

'Because that's what Mum and Dad wanted and we should respect their wishes.'

I agree not to say anything, even if I don't like it. But who am I to argue, given the lies I've been telling my family? We return to the kitchen.

'What are your plans while you're home, Annika?' Dad asks.

'Nothing set in stone yet,' I reply. 'The usual stuff. I hope to visit my friends around the country and spend some time in London.'

'That's where your boyfriend lives, isn't it?' Nish asks.

'That's right,' I say.

'And you've been together a year?'

I wonder whether my darling brother is trying to catch me out in a lie. For a moment, I think about telling him the truth and getting him in on my scheme. It would be nice to have someone on my side whom I can confide in. And despite our bickering, Nish and I have always got on really well. Since he married Kaya he's a lot more understanding of my need to maintain my independence – Kaya's influence. But then if I tell Nish, he will need to tell Kaya, and if that happened, I will feel bad keeping Shakti in the dark. And Shakti is pregnant and has more important things on her mind. Besides Shakti would want to tell her husband. And suddenly, everyone would know the truth. I can't expect them all to lie to our parents for me.

'Not quite a year,' I answer.

'But long enough that we should meet him now, Annika,' Dad says. 'I've been waiting for you to come back home so we can finally meet this man.' He beams at me. At least his smile is as strong as ever.

'Thanks, Dad, nice to know I've been missed,' I tease.

'Of course, we've missed you, Niki,' Mum says, 'but it would be nice to meet this man now. Your father has been looking forward to it. He talks about it all the time.'

Both of them look at me with excitement and anticipation. I still don't know why it's so important to them that I'm in a stable relationship, but I can tell it will only create stress if I tell them I don't have a boyfriend. I have to commit to this fiction that I have a suitor. I straighten my shoulders.

'I'm hoping to go to London next week,' I say. 'I'll be seeing him then and we can organise a date for you to meet him. I promise.' Both parents look happy and relieved at my assurances.

I may be creating a tangled web, but it's clear what I have to do – I need to message Rav and hope to goodness he isn't planning on backing out of our scheme.

Chapter 4

My stomach churns as I stand outside the Parisian-style restaurant in Covent Garden. I'm almost as nervous as if I'm going on a real first date – only if this was an actual date, I'd be excited about the possibilities, not dreading it.

I just have to remember it's not real – it's a business meeting where Rav and I are going to thrash out the details of our mutually beneficial arrangement.

As I expected, staying with my family means I have to deal with them relentlessly asking me when they will meet my partner. And if it isn't my parents, Nishal and Shakti are both adept at piling on the guilt by constantly reminding me of our father's ill health and telling me how much he has perked up since my return. I hope that's true, that my presence is lifting my dad's spirits, but I wish it wasn't solely due to the prospect of his middle child finally settling down.

I waited over a week after getting back, and only when I couldn't put it off any longer I contacted Rav. I know that was unfair of me because Rav obviously needs my help too.

I peer through the restaurant window, hoping Rav is already there. I catch sight of him in a semi-secluded area, talking to one of the waiters. He smiles and my heart skips a beat – with relief.

I'm relieved he's turned up. That must mean he's happy to go ahead with a possible pretence between us.

He does look amazing though. He's wearing a navy jacket over a Nehru-style white shirt, which emphasises his broad shoulders and a surprisingly muscular neck. It won't be a hardship having him around.

As long as he doesn't talk too much.

I briefly glance at the silk-blend midi-skirt I'm wearing to check it's smart enough, then I stop myself. I've never cared about what people think of my clothes and I'm not about to start now. I take a deep breath and enter the restaurant.

He stands as I approach the table. I can't help nodding with approval – my parents will love his manners.

As I draw up to the table, I step towards him but then hang back awkwardly. How do you greet someone you've barely met in person but who you're supposed to be in love with? Air kiss, shake hands, wave? In the end, I bob my head quickly then sit down before either he or a waiter has a chance to pull out the chair for me.

And then nothing happens. He just sits there with this half-smile.

'Well, this is weird,' I finally say, trying to break the tension.

Rav smiles as he inclines his head. 'It's one of the weirdest situations I've been in, that's for sure.' He hands me the wine list. 'I was thinking of getting a bottle of red. If you want red too, perhaps you'd like to choose one.'

I admit I appreciate the gesture. Even though it's been a few years since I was part of the dating scene and perhaps things have changed now, unfortunately, in my experience, the percentage of men who seem to think choosing a decent bottle of wine is beyond my capabilities is high. After I give our order to the sommelier, the awkward silence reappears.

I rub my palm along my skirt. Although the restaurant isn't particularly romantically lit, there is a definite date vibe in the

35

ambience. Perhaps I should have prepared an agenda so we can treat the evening like a proper business meeting – to be honest, I'm a bit surprised Rav hasn't sent me one.

I clear my throat, ready to dive into the necessary conversation when a waiter appears.

'How did your project go?' Rav asks after we've ordered our food.

'Well, thanks. I mean, obviously, the work involved is long term but my part went well. I think this could be one of the company's most successful projects in the country. Perhaps even in South America.' Suddenly I'm launching into a long description of what our work involves, only pausing for a moment to taste the wine, and I only stop when our appetisers arrive. I bite my lip. I've done it again. 'I'm sorry, I've been talking too much. I do tend to wax lyrical.' Which is clearly an understatement.

'Not at all,' Rav replies gallantly. 'You're obviously deeply passionate about what you do.' He gives me a smile of approval. 'To be honest, I'm a bit surprised.'

'Why?' I ask, trying not to feel wary.

'In your emails, you didn't go into much detail about your work beyond a job description, but it's clear you love what you do.'

My face brightens. 'I do. I love it. I can't give it up.'

'Which neatly brings us to why we're here.'

I take a moment to chew a mussel from my seafood casserole starter. 'I guess there's no reason to avoid the elephant anymore.'

'I presume, since we're both here, the situation is still the same and you're looking for someone to pretend to be in a relationship with you.' His words are clipped and his tone is formal. It's hard to believe we're about to discuss a potential romantic relationship. Then I remember I'm supposed to treat this as a business arrangement.

'Yes,' I reply. 'And I presume you still need someone to attend some events with you.'

'That's correct.'

'Can you tell me more about these events and why you need a partner?' I can't deny I've been intrigued about this ever since I read that first email from him.

He sighs. 'Of course, but I must let you know there's been a bit of a development since I first contacted you. I'm going to need more than someone to accompany me to business events. I have to ask if you'll be willing to pretend to be my long-term partner ... girlfriend.'

'Okay.' That doesn't sound like it will be a major problem. It's the same thing Rav's pretending to do for me after all. 'What's happened?'

'It's a complicated and delicate situation. But to put it simply, I'm hoping to buy out a family-owned company. We'd approached the owner to determine whether he was interested in selling and we were starting our negotiations. Unfortunately, we couldn't get an exclusivity period, and some other companies found out the owner is thinking of selling. Now the owner ... you may as well know his name since you're going to meet him, Rupert Bamford, has decided to accept proposals from all the interested companies and we've heard he's partial to selling to a family-oriented person because he believes they'll better understand the ethos of his business.'

'Sounds very traditional. Is he Indian?'

He laughs. 'No. English. But you're right, Rupert Bamford is a traditional man. My company is doing well, but it's only been around for a few years, and we get the impression Rupert is concerned that we haven't been in the business long enough to demonstrate the kind of commitment he's looking for. There are two companies I consider to be our main competitors and they've been around for at least ten years.'

'I see. So how would dating me help?'

He grimaces. 'Well, I'm hoping if he sees I have a long-term partner, it may convince him that I'm serious and show him I can commit on a personal level, even if I can't prove it professionally

37

yet. The people leading the negotiation for the other companies are married. Although I went to uni with one of them, Aiden Watson, and he's only been married for two years. However, his company has been in his family for generations, so they have a reputation to build upon. We don't have that.'

As Rav mentions Aiden Watson, I notice a hint of discomfort in his tone. I have this gut feeling there's something he's not telling me about this couple, Aiden and his wife. I wait to see if he'll tell me more but he doesn't say anything else.

'So I guess, the problem is you don't have a girlfriend at the moment whom you can introduce to this man.'

'That's correct. Even then, it wouldn't be enough. If I want to convince him I'm a family-oriented person, perhaps that marriage is on the cards soon, it can't just be a girlfriend I've been seeing for a few months. It needs to be someone who knows me through and through, whom I've known for a long time now. A partner rather than a girlfriend.'

I nod. I can understand that.

'What about your business partners?' I ask. 'Aren't any of them married or in long-term relationships?'

Rav grimaces. 'No. And my business partner, Greg, has the infamous reputation of being a heartbreaker with women. There's no way anyone would believe it if he suddenly announced he'd found a woman to settle down with. He would need to be married for it to be believable.'

'So this man, this Mr Bamford, knows about Greg's reputation? Is there some business community gossip network I don't know about?'

His mouth lifts in a half-smile. 'No. But unfortunately, our competitors have conveniently managed to bring up Greg's many girlfriends with Mr Bamford already.'

I roll my eyes at the idea someone's sex life correlates to how they work in business, but I don't fully understand the corporate world. 'So that's where I come in. I'm the proof you can do commitment and stability. I guess we'll both be going with the same story, which will be useful and easier.'

'That's right. We can say we've been in each other's lives since we were children but only got to know each other properly last year. Because you're out of the country a lot, we've been taking it slowly, but we're now ready to take it public. I want to show Rupert I intend to settle down and have a family.'

'And do you? At some point?' Which isn't really relevant to the discussion, but I want to know whether he avoids relationships for the same reason I do.

'Yes. I plan to get married and start trying for a family three years from now.'

'That's very precise.'

He inclines his head. I want to ask him how he can be so sure a woman will fall in line with his plans according to his schedule but that would be a diversion from our current discussion. I put it aside since now is not the time to ask, but I'm definitely going to bring it up at some point.

'So what kind of events are they? Are you going to be competing against each other in some tests, like an assessment centre? Rival businesses vying to take over a company in some epic battle? Last one standing takes it all?' My eyes flash with excitement.

'No,' he replies curtly, deflating my enthusiasm. I should know business deals will never be that exciting. 'There's an evening reception, which is mainly a networking event. Then Mr Bamford hosts a summer garden party for his company, which we've all been invited to, and then the final event in the late summer is at his home but we don't yet know what that will entail.'

'So why are all these events necessary?' I ask. 'Don't companies owe it to their shareholders to get the best deal? Why does it matter whether you've been around for years or you're in a long-term relationship?'

'It's a private company, wholly owned by Mr Bamford and

his wife. The financial aspect will be important but Mr Bamford thinks of his employees as part of his family and he wants to make sure he sells to the right kind of person.'

Rav's lips thin, which makes me wonder whether the right person is of a specific ethnicity. But I want to meet Rupert Bamford with an open mind so I don't go down that road.

'How long is this deal going to take?' I ask instead.

'We need to get our final proposals to him by mid-August and he said he'd make his final decision by September.'

'Okay. Do you have any dates for when you'll need me? I need to make sure I'm around and not travelling anywhere.'

'Yes.' He pulls his phone out of his jacket pocket and looks at me expectantly.

'You can text or email me the dates,' I say.

'Don't you have your phone with you?'

'Yes.' I beam at him. 'But I don't ever use my phone calendar. I prefer to write it in my diary, which I'm not carrying with me at the moment.'

He blinks. I suspect Rav wouldn't be able to exist if he didn't know his exact schedule every moment. 'Why not?'

'Because I find it easier to tell people I'll get back to them rather than commit to something right in front of them.'

'You don't like to make commitments? How do you stay organised?'

I roll my eyes. 'Obviously, with work it's different. I schedule meetings in advance and will meet any deadlines. And of course, I'll make sure I'm free for whatever dates you send me. But otherwise, I don't want to be restricted to a time or a place if I don't need to be. Most of my friends know I'll often make my decisions at the last minute and it's no reflection on them but on what I'm doing at the time.'

He shakes his head as if my lack of planning ahead is deeply problematic to him.

'Fine.' He taps on his phone, and I hear a ping on mine

indicating he's sent me a text. 'And what about your family? I presume you'll arrange a day to meet them in advance?'

'Yep. Sure. I guess weekends would be better for you. Any particular ones?'

'Give me a date and I'll make sure I'm free. I usually work weekends, so I don't have many social events to juggle. I am away the last weekend in July for my best friend's wedding, and there's a reception in August. I do have to prioritise those events, I'm afraid. Kesh has been a close friend since university.'

I nod in understanding. 'I'm sure my family will understand that. I don't think there are many events where they would expect you to be there. We have an end-of-summer get-together, usually over the bank holiday weekend. Then there's another family get-together with my extended family sometime in July but I don't think it's the last week, so it would be nice if you could come to that. I'll confirm the dates with my parents and let you know. Does that sound fair?'

'Of course. Otherwise, I would be getting a lot more out of our arrangement than you.'

I like that Rav calls it an arrangement rather than a pretence. It sounds more formal than what we're really doing – simply lying to people we know.

I rest my chin on my hand. His comment about what each of us gets out of the arrangement strikes a chord. 'Do you think we need to formalise this agreement somehow?'

'What do you mean?'

'Like having a contract that sets out that we agree to go to a specified number of events. Perhaps set a limit on how many we each have to attend, especially in your case, otherwise my parents will be expecting you to visit every week.'

'I'm not sure it would be legally binding,' he replies with a laugh. He makes it sound like that's the silliest thing he's ever heard.

'You know what I mean.'

41

'I'm happy to keep it open-ended.'

'I'm not sure, Rav. This is going to be awkward anyway. I'd feel better if we set out some guidelines.'

'Fine. Well, I know there are a couple of dinners I'll need you to attend and then there's the summer party, I mentioned. So let's say four, no, five since the party could take up the whole weekend and will be more demanding than a normal meeting. How about I agree to go to five family events with you.'

I grin. 'Agreed.' I definitely prefer it when Rav speaks to me as if we're negotiating a business deal. Without the formality, the conversation could get awkward at any moment … well, awkward again.

I hope this feeling of discomfort fades as we continue with our arrangement. It has to if we have any hope of convincing people we're a couple in love.

It's so much easier to be single, I think, only realising I said it out loud when Rav says, 'You know, you never told me why you want to remain single.'

He's right. After my slight rant at the hotel when he asked me why I didn't look for a real relationship, I've deliberately avoided going into the subject during our email exchange. Similarly, I haven't asked him why he doesn't already have a long-term partner, even though I'm incredibly curious after hearing him mention his plan. 'Is it something I need to explain?'

'Not really. But it's unusual for someone to know with such certainty they plan to be single for the rest of their life.'

'I don't plan on being single,' I reply, emphasising *plan*. 'It's just the way it's likely to be. I like my job. I like being able to travel around the world. Any relationships I have are invariably going to end because of distance – why put myself through an emotional wringer unnecessarily?'

'Why would that be? Why is distance such a problem? Couldn't you have a long-distance relationship?'

'In my experience, it doesn't work. It's not like the

long-distance thing would be time-limited. I love the work I do. I'm not giving it up.' He doesn't reply but stares at me intently. I recognise the question in his expression and take a deep breath. 'I've had a few relationships fail because of the nature of my work. My uni boyfriend didn't want me to take overseas jobs in the first place and another one asked me to cut down the travelling abroad – told me I had to if I wanted us to have a future together.'

'That's a lot to ask of someone.'

'Exactly.' Finally, someone who understands my position. I'm only surprised that it's Rav. 'Why should I give up what I love? It's not worth it.'

'What about in twenty or thirty years' time?' he asks. 'Do you think you'll be doing the same kind of work?'

'Are you suggesting I may want to settle down then?' I ask, not trying to hide my irritation. It frustrates me no end, how everyone thinks I will suddenly yearn for a home and family one day. It's not a case of me being adamant I'll remain single. I'm just realistic. The circumstances of my life don't allow me to have my work and a relationship without a major sacrifice that I'm not prepared to make.

'Simply a question,' he replies with a kind smile.

'I don't know. I don't know what the future holds. It's not like I can plan it.'

Rav makes a choking sound.

'Okay, it sounds like you've made plans to settle down some-time,' I said, finally letting my curiosity get the better of me. 'Is that why you don't have a long-term girlfriend at the moment?'

'Like you, my career is my priority at the moment. I don't want any distractions. I haven't had a girlfriend or been on dates for a long time – it wouldn't be fair to her. But I would like to marry and have a family in a few years. Thirty-five sounds like the optimum age for that.'

'The optimum age?' He speaks more dispassionately about

relationships than I do. How can he treat his future marriage so objectively?

'Yes. That's my plan anyway.'

'And, if I may ask, how do you plan something like that?'

He smiles and I think I see the barest hint of a wink but I must be mistaken because that's such an un-Rav action. 'Through singles events.'

My jaw drops. 'You're joking.'

'Partly.' He takes a few mouthfuls of his beef bourguignon before putting his knife and fork together. 'To be frank, I think my parents, and the people in our community, can help match me to a suitable bride.'

'Suitable?'

'Yes.'

'What would make a suitable bride?'

'I don't know,' he replies, but the way he avoids my gaze makes me believe he does know.

'Come on, you must have thought about it.'

He sighs. 'I haven't put a load of thought into it yet. It's not going to be for another few years and my requirements may change. I would like to marry someone intelligent, although she doesn't have to be formally educated. Someone I can discuss things with, even my work. Someone career-driven at the moment would be ideal, but I'd like someone who wants children in the future.'

'And will she have to give up her career once you have these children?' I ask.

'That's something we can discuss when the time comes. It's not a deal-breaker if she doesn't want to.'

I smile at his unknowing admission his preference would be for his wife to give up her career. 'And what would be a deal-breaker? Does she have to be of the same caste?'

He looks offended. 'That doesn't concern me.'

I raise a hand. 'Let's not pretend it's not an issue for some people in our community.'

'I'm not pretending that. I'm saying it's not a requirement for me.'

'And that's all you want from your future wife? You're not looking for the love of your life?'

'I don't believe in a grand love. I'm only looking for someone I can be compatible with.'

I'm at a loss for words – not a situation I'm used to or enjoy. Of course, I know matched, or arranged, marriages are popular in our community. My parents even suggested helping me find someone by arranging introductions for me, even though no one else in my family has married for anything other than love. That was one of the main reasons I resorted to lying about having a boyfriend.

But Rav is right. Compatibility is important, shared values and dreams are important. Love isn't enough to guarantee a happy future. I've learnt that the hard way – my heart's been broken more times than I care to admit.

In a way, it's good that Rav's corporate values are so different from mine. It minimises the risk of someone getting hurt by our scheme.

'Perhaps if I'm ready to settle down in twenty or thirty years, I'll follow your lead and ask people to look for a suitable groom for me,' I say.

'Well, it's always a possibility.'

We stare at each other for a while. I suddenly feel a shared camaraderie with Rav. We are so different in our approach to life and what we want from it but, right now, we are united in our desire to live that life on our own terms. For the first time since Rav suggested this arrangement, I am filled with a quiet confidence that it could actually work. I break my gaze when a waiter comes to clear our plates and ask whether we want to see the dessert menu.

'Well,' I begin after we've placed our order, 'it does sound like we're in perfect agreement that a real relationship isn't on the cards right now. So our pretence sounds like the right thing for both of us. Now the only other thing I think we need to agree on is when we call this off.'

'Yes, you're right. We never discussed how long you'll need our arrangement to go on for.'

'I'm afraid it's open-ended for me and I haven't come up with an exit strategy yet. I'm hoping my dad continues to stay in good health and, over the next few months, I can convince him that I'm perfectly fine if I'm on my own. But don't worry, it won't be forever. If the worse comes to the worst, when I come back from my next project we can tell everyone it didn't work out after all and call this arrangement quits.'

'When is your next project?'

'I'm waiting for a firm start date but it should be from mid-September to the end of the year.'

'That works for me. We should know Mr Bamford's decision by then and, if we do buy his company, the deal will be completed while you're away. There'll be no reason for me to see the Bamfords after that, but if I do, I can say the same thing about us not working out. So, what do you say?' He looks intently into my eyes and I'm hypnotised. I don't think I can look away even if I want to. 'Would you do me the great honour of being my pretend partner?'

'I would.' I laugh. 'Should we shake on it?'

He holds out his hand. 'To seal our arrangement.'

'Our fake-suitor arrangement? Absolutely.' I clasp his hand across the table. Shivers run up my arm, no doubt due to the excitement that we're actually going ahead with this huge deception we're about to perpetrate. I laugh. 'I can't believe how perfectly this is working out. The only thing that could go wrong is if you fall in love with me. So make sure you don't do that.'

'Ditto.'

I laugh again, even more heartily. There is absolutely no chance of that happening.

Chapter 5

The following Friday, Tinu and I are walking towards a wine bar in Soho, where we're meeting Rav and his business partner, Greg.

After Rav and I agreed to go ahead with our fake-dating arrangement, he suggested we should do a test run in front of our friends and get their feedback before we meet my parents or the man Rav wants to impress. We've already exchanged a lot of information about each other so I'm not sure it's really necessary, but I can tell Rav would feel better if we're more prepared – I guess it won't hurt for us to try to practise being a couple in a real-life situation.

We find some seats and get comfortable. I look towards the door. Perfect timing; Rav and his friend are just entering and beginning to scan the room. I get up and start waving to get Rav's attention.

Tinu gives a slow whistle. 'Wowsers! You never said he was such a hottie. And his friend too. Do you know if his friend's single?'

I shake my head, barely registering her words. Rav's dressed casually today but his clothes still look like they were made for him. His jet-black hair has a blue sheen in the light – something I've always wanted but never managed to have without using hair dye. I've always known Rav is a handsome, commanding man,

47

but it's always been in an objective, detached way because he's simply Rav. A classmate of my brother. Nemesis of my childhood. Not someone I ever thought about being in a relationship with.

Now he's *Rav*. My supposed-to-be boyfriend. Someone whom I'm expected to find physically attractive and should probably show signs of being attracted to. There are still parts of this scheme I haven't thought through properly. This test run is starting to feel more and more like a good idea.

Will we really be able to convince anyone, let alone my family, that Rav and I, who've known each other for a long time, suddenly grew close to each other? Are in love with each other? I push back my shoulders and straighten up. It's time to find out.

Rav introduces Tinu and me to Greg. I notice Greg holds on to Tinu's hand a fraction longer than is necessary. I throw a conspiratorial glance in Rav's direction – I see why he says Greg wouldn't be the right person to convince Mr Bamford he's in a serious, committed relationship.

I did suggest we meet at a restaurant but apparently, Greg said the setting would be too formal for a test run. Not having eaten since I got on the train before lunch, I already ordered some chips for the table and my food arrives while we're finishing the introductions. I quickly scoop up some mayo on a chip and shove it into my mouth when Rav clears his throat. He makes a face, which I hope isn't disgust, but he doesn't say anything and takes the seat next to me.

Greg goes to the bar to fetch drinks.

As soon as he gets back, he and Tinu begin asking Rav and me questions about our relationship. We can answer the basic questions about family, education and how we met fairly easily and I think the test is going well.

We can do this! We can convince my parents we're a couple. But then Tinu sighs loudly and Greg shakes his head.

'This will never do,' Tinu says. 'You two still act as if you've just met.'

Rav and I exchange surprised glances. 'But we answered all the questions correctly,' Rav says.

'But it's not enough to know little details about each other. You act like you're strangers,' Tinu replies, placing a lot of emphasis on *act*. 'Look, you've put as much distance as possible between yourselves while still sitting at the same table.'

'Yes, there's more chemistry between Tinu and me,' Greg adds, winking in her direction.

I look at the gap between Rav and me. Tinu's right – I have inched my chair towards hers and Rav's body is angled away from me. I grimace. It wasn't even a conscious action on my part and I doubt it was on Rav's.

Rav sits up straight, suddenly looking serious. I sometimes forget it's also important for him that this arrangement works out. Perhaps more important than my reason because I do still have the option of telling my parents the relationship didn't work out, whereas it sounds like this deal is important for his business. 'What are we doing wrong?' he asks.

'You're still nervous around each other. Very stiff. You're going to have to loosen up,' Tinu says.

'What do you suggest we do?' Rav asks. 'We should formulate a plan.'

'Okay,' Tinu says, 'that makes sense.'

I furrow my brows. *It does?* How are we supposed to come up with a plan to feel looser around each other? I feel like I'm missing something here in this conversation.

'Firstly, you should sit as close to each other as possible. And it would help if you practised holding hands and hugging and kissing,' Greg suggests.

I wave my hand in dismissal. 'Oh, my parents aren't going to want to see any public displays of affection, thankfully.'

Rav rubs his neck. 'That may not be the case for me, though.'

'What do you mean?' I tilt my head but Rav avoids my gaze.

'He means,' Greg answers for him, 'Mr Bamford is very

49

affectionate and open with his wife. If you're going to convince him that you're in a serious, committed relationship, you're going to have to perform some of those PDAs and look natural doing it. You'll need practice.'

'And how do we practise that, exactly?' I ask, drinking some of my beer. 'Hold hands for twenty minutes a day, like we're learning an instrument?'

'No,' Tinu says, 'but most couples always instinctively find ways to be near each other; they can't resist touching each other.' She taps her index finger against her lips. 'Come on, let's start. Move your chairs closer to each other and then turn your bodies to face one another.'

I look at Rav but he's already edging his chair over.

'Come on, Annika, move your chair,' Tinu says. I do as I'm told. 'Perfect. Now hold hands.'

'Put your hands above the table so we can see,' Greg says.

It's like Rav and I are in junior school and being reluctantly directed in the school play. But I know they're trying to help. And they're right – we do need to show some physical intimacy. I put my hand on the table and Rav covers it, linking our fingers.

'Great, now kiss,' Greg says.

Both Rav and I inhale sharply.

'Not here,' Rav says at the same time as I say, 'Baby steps.'

'Fine,' Tinu says. 'But I think you need to go on a practice date.'

'Or ten,' Greg adds.

I meet Rav's gaze again. 'It's not the worst idea.'

'Great,' Tinu says, clapping her hands together. 'Now you need to choose your dates carefully. Not any places like a theatre or cinema where you can't talk to each other.'

'And if you go out for dinner, make sure it's in a casual rather than a formal setting. You don't want to be sitting across the table from each other,' Greg added.

I watch in fascination as Tinu and Greg continue to ping-pong date ideas. Greg was right when he mentioned the chemistry between him and Tinu. I frown. Based on what Rav has told me about Greg, I'm worried Tinu could fall for Greg's charm and get her heart broken.

Thankfully, it's not something I have to worry about with the mutually beneficial and unromantic arrangement I'm entering into with Rav.

But I know if I want to have any chance of convincing my parents I'm in a loving, stable relationship with Rav, I need to commit to the idea wholeheartedly. No more looking for reasons why the deception won't work. I used to love acting. If I put my mind to it, I can convincingly play the part of someone fathoms deep in love.

From this moment on, I'm all in.

And it won't be a hardship to spend time with Rav. He's extremely easy on the eye. And in many ways, it's better our personalities are so different that in real life we wouldn't be at all compatible – I know, from books and films, the biggest problem with fake-relationship arrangements is when feelings develop between the couple. There's no chance of that happening with us.

'You know what,' Greg says, breaking into my thoughts. 'There's no time to waste. Tinu and I can leave and you two can have your practice date now.'

'Now?' I squeak. 'I can't now.'

Three faces frown at me.

'It's the opening night for my friend's bar,' I explain. 'I promised them I'd go there for moral support. Tinu, you said you'd come with me. There's karaoke tonight.'

'You arranged to go somewhere else tonight?'

I narrow my eyes at the annoyance in Rav's tone. 'Well, I didn't actually get a say on when Jaks had their bar opening. You said you couldn't meet any other day this week. This way, I can kill two birds with one trip to London.'

'We could come with you,' Greg suggests. I snicker at the look of horror on Rav's face.

'Wouldn't that defeat the purpose of a practice date? We won't get much talking done.'

Rav nods. At least we agree on something.

'It's about being comfortable in each other's company, remember,' Tinu says. 'This will be a good opportunity for that.'

'And you need as many practice dates as you can get. Tinu and I can join you for half an hour or so, then we'll leave you to it.' He gives her a flirtatious look and she smiles shyly in response.

I mentally roll my eyes.

Rav's phone, which he had out on the table, vibrates. He glances at the number. 'I'm sorry, I'm going to have to take this. It's a call from the States I was expecting.'

He walks over to a quieter area of the bar. After a couple of minutes, Greg suggests Tinu and I head to my friend's bar – he and Rav will join us later. I give him the address, then he and Tinu exchange phone numbers, which strikes me as unnecessary, then we leave.

'Are you sure karaoke night is the best place for my practice date with Rav?' I ask once we arrive at Jaks' bar.

'We didn't have much choice since you'd already arranged to come here,' Tinu says. I'm beginning to resent the slight chastisement in her words – as if making two appointments in one evening is a huge crime.

'It doesn't look like your friend needs that much support,' she continues. 'This place is heaving.'

I nod vigorously. I'm so happy for Jaks. They've wanted to own a bar for as long as I've known them and their dreams are finally becoming a reality. I see Jaks at the back of the bar, near a makeshift stage area and make my way over.

'Annika, you came!' Jaks hugs me.

'Of course, I did. I wouldn't miss it. But it looks like you've already drawn in a great crowd. You didn't need me to fill up the tables.'

'I honestly didn't expect such a turnout.' Jaks turns to Tinu, so

I make the introductions. 'When I saw it was filling up, I reserved a place for you. Follow me.'

Moments later, Tinu and I are seated at a table at the perfect distance from the stage that we'll be able to see the singers, but it isn't so close we'll risk our hearing. I have the most thoughtful friends.

'Here, take this.' Jaks hands me a gadget. 'You can scroll through the available playlist and select your song on this. Make your choice quickly because once it's been selected, it's gone for the evening. I'm not listening to the same song on repeat.'

'Fab. You have to promise to sing one with me. Is our usual here?' I ask Jaks.

'Of course. But I've already selected it for us.' Jaks squeezes my shoulder. 'I need to go and check on a few last-minute things. I'll send someone over to take your order. Catch you later.'

'Does Jaks know about your fake-dating scheme?' Tinu asks after they leave.

'No, they've been too busy for us to have a proper heart-to-heart chat. And I don't think they need to know.' I've already told a few friends about my scheme, even though Rav wasn't in the picture at the time, but I realise I probably should limit how many people I let in on the arrangement.

Rav and Greg arrive soon after. We've just ordered a bottle of wine for the table when Jaks picks up the microphone to start the evening and introduce the first singer.

We make several quickly aborted attempts at conversation but Tinu's right; the music is too loud for us to speak properly. Tinu gives me a knowing look.

Rav sighs, glances at his watch, and scrolls on his phone, probably going through his work emails. He couldn't make it more obvious he thinks this is a complete waste of his time.

When the current song ends and before the next singer begins, I'm about to suggest we postpone to another day when Tinu says, 'I've had a great idea. You and Rav should do a duet.'

Rav looks horrified at the suggestion.

'Why would we do that?' I ask.

'Part of being a couple is feeling relaxed in each other's company. At the moment, you're acting as though you're strangers. Perhaps singing will help loosen you up and make you more comfortable. Rav should sing with you when it's your turn for karaoke.'

'You're planning to get up there?' he asks me, gesturing at the stage.

'Of course,' I reply. 'It's probably too late for us to pick a song anyway. Besides, I'm already singing with Tinu and then with Jaks later – my friend who owns the bar. Two songs from me are enough to subject any audience to.'

'Rav can take my place,' Tinu says. 'You know "River Deep, Mountain High", don't you?'

Rav swallows. I'm sure I can see the blood actually draining from his face.

'I don't think that's a good idea, Tinu,' I say. 'It's not exactly going to help us feel more like a couple if we're doing something we don't want to do.' I chew the inside of my cheek. Rav is so different from the people I usually date. More reserved. I usually go for extroverts who love being centre stage.

It's not like I'm treating karaoke as a metaphor for our different approaches to life but for our relationship to be believable, I need someone who can leave their comfort zone and let loose a little. Not just to convince my parents but to be able to pull off the pretence in the first place. In return, I can be as strait-laced and conservative as Rav needs me to be in front of Mr Bamford.

We may not have managed a successful and proper test run – nonetheless, this evening has been enlightening. I can now tell our scheme *isn't* going to work.

'Come on, Rav,' Greg says, 'it's not like you've never done karaoke before.'

'Usually in a booth. Not out in the open, well, not since university.'

I instantly perk up. This is intriguing. It sounds like Rav's objections aren't about the activity in itself but the venue. I wonder why I'm so ready to jump to conclusions that our arrangement isn't going to work? Could I be hoping the deception will fail? That doesn't make any sense. I'm not usually so pessimistic. And I desperately need the scheme to work.

I recognise the opening bars of the next song. It's my turn to take the stage. I turn to Tinu. She looks at Rav but he shakes his head. With a shrug, we go up on stage while Rav and Greg remain at the table, still scrolling through their phones, even during our performance.

I know there's a saying that opposites attract, but it could be stretching the bounds of credibility too far to expect my parents to believe I'm in love with someone so different to me.

After we get back to the table, Greg and Tinu tell us they'll be heading off. She gives me a pitying smile as she puts on her coat. I can tell she doesn't have much faith in our scheme, but I put that to the back of my mind for now.

Once they've left, I try to engage Rav in conversation. He gives me curt replies but it's clear he'd rather be checking his phone.

I try again. 'So karaoke?'

'Hmm' is all the reply I get. He looks around the bar with disdain, and I'm immediately offended at the idea my friend's place isn't up to his exacting high and mighty standards.

I excuse myself and occupy a WC to gather my thoughts. I'm so tempted to sneak out. I wonder how long it will take for Rav to notice if I do – he'd have to look up from his phone first.

This is ridiculous. Rav is making no effort at all. Why should I be the only one trying?

If business is so important to him that he spends his evening on the phone, then I'd have thought it would be important enough for us to practise getting comfortable as a couple.

This is a huge mistake.

I return to the table to collect my jacket. 'I'm going to go. This is all a bit pointless.'

Rav gives me a startled look but I notice him glance quickly at his phone. That tells me everything I need to know. I shake my head and leave.

By the time I reach the entrance to the tube station a few minutes later, I regret my impulsive behaviour again.

My parents know I came to London to see my boyfriend. If I go home now and tell them we've broken up I'll be back to square one. All my concerns about my dad's health and the growing pressure from my parents to find someone to settle down with come rushing back.

If I end my arrangement with Rav, I'd just be cutting off my nose to spite my face. And I really don't have time to find someone else.

Right now I'm desperate, and Rav Gohil is my only hope.

Chapter 6

'Is something wrong?' I ask, looking up from where I've started to unpack the picnic basket I brought with me. Rav is just standing there looking uncertain. I pat the blanket I've spread on the grass and give him a bright, hopefully encouraging smile. It's been a week since our disastrous first practice date. I did send him a text that evening saying I would be in touch but, apart from an 'okay' in response I haven't heard from Rav so I travelled up to London, arriving by midday, and texted him from outside his building to come out for lunch with me.

He initially texted back that he was too busy until I threatened to come into his offices and drag him out. The fact he texted back within seconds, telling me he'd be right out, speaks volumes. Not only has it made it clear he doesn't want anyone in his office seeing me, but he also doesn't know me well enough to know I would never embarrass him in front of his work colleagues. Our situation is a private matter – even though he's in our arrangement for business purposes, I don't see any reason to mix the personal and the professional more than is strictly necessary.

'No, nothing's wrong.' He removes his suit jacket before sitting down, carefully folds it lengthways and lays it flat on the blanket. He brings his knees up and looks at his shoes.

'It's fine. You can keep them on,' I tell him.

He looks at my feet. I kicked off my sandals as soon as the blanket was on the ground, but now I wonder whether I should put them back on. I fold my legs beneath me to keep my feet hidden from view. I suspect having an informal picnic will prove to be another bad choice. Yet again, I'm filled with a sense of hopelessness. Maybe Rav and I are just too different after all, and we won't be able to convince anyone we're a couple.

'It's been a while since I've done this,' Rav says.

'Had a picnic?' I finish unpacking the food, pull out a wooden board and begin setting up a charcuterie platter.

'That too, but I mean, took a lunch break. Unless I have to go to the odd business lunch, I usually eat at my desk.'

I stop in the middle of unwrapping some cheese. 'That doesn't sound healthy.'

'You're right, it isn't, but unfortunately, it's all I have time for.'

On every project I've worked on, mealtimes have been a communal affair, with all team members and helpers eating and chatting together. No one's forced to attend. We all understand people need time on their own too but being away from family and friends for long periods can be lonely, and our meals are a way of making sure nobody is alone unless they want to be.

I understand my experience isn't common in the corporate world Rav inhabits, but I can't imagine enjoying that lifestyle.

'Well, since part of the reason we're having this practice date is to help you win the company, why don't you pretend we're on a business lunch so you can eat without feeling any guilt.'

'I don't think I could ever pretend you're only business to me.'

I tilt my head. That almost sounds like flirting. 'What do you mean?' I ask.

He glances at me quickly. 'Nothing much. I probably shouldn't think of you as business if we're going to pretend we're a couple. And a couple in love at that.'

'Good point.' I hand Rav a ceramic plate and mug and some

steel cutlery. He glances at them, then raises his eyebrows at me in a question. 'Oh I know they're more hassle than using disposables but it's better for the environment. Plus, I like the aesthetic,' I explain. 'Okay. What will you have?'

As well as the charcuterie board, I've brought an antipasto platter, different kinds of salad, crudités and dips and a variety of breads.

'What is there?'

I chuckle. 'I don't really know. I did ask the vendors but there was so much I can't remember each individual dish. Since I know you don't have any food allergies' – one of the facts we've shared already – 'I bought whatever looked interesting.'

He furrows his forehead looking sceptical at the prospect of trying food with unknown ingredients.

'I've made some plain cheese sandwiches if you prefer,' I tell him, with a disappointed sigh. I anticipated he'd prefer a safe choice.

Rav laughs. 'That's okay. I think I'll start with some bread, cold meat and salad, thank you.'

I prepare a plate to hand him.

'You've gone to a lot of trouble. Can I give you some money towards this?' he asks.

I wave his offer away. 'Not necessary but thanks for offering. You can pay next time if you want.'

I take a spoonful of one of the dips I bought and moan. 'This is amazing. You've got to try some.'

'What is it?'

'It's got aubergine but it's not quite baba ghanoush.'

Rav's face remains sceptical, but I place some dip on his plate anyway. I continue doing this each time I sample another dish. After he's finished eating his meat and salad, he picks up a small portion of one of the dips with his bread.

'Mmm,' he says, his mouth wide as he nods with approval, 'this is delicious.'

There's silence between us while we sample the food. But at least it's not an awkward silence.

'This cheese is amazing,' Rav says after biting into some white Stilton.

'I got it from a French farmers' market I read about near Tinu's place. Lots of fresh stuff. I went a little bit over the top.' I break off a chunk of bread and hand it over. 'Smell that. It's heavenly.'

He doesn't follow my instruction.

'I never asked you where you're staying while you're in London,' Rav says. 'That sounds like something I should know. It's a big omission.' He looks annoyed with himself.

'It's no big deal. My parents wouldn't know either. I'm staying at Tinu's until tomorrow and then I'm going to another friend's place afterwards, until the end of the week when I travel back home. I don't like to impose on one person for too long but I don't mind inconveniencing lots of different people for a couple of days at a time,' I say with a wink.

'I have a spare room. Perhaps you should stay at my place while you're in London,' Rav says, almost making me spill my drink. 'Don't you think your parents might expect you to stay with me, or do they have some traditional views about cohabiting before marriage?'

I shake my head. 'Both Nishal and Shakti lived with their now-spouses before they got married. I'd never really considered staying with you and what Mum and Dad would think.' I eat a few mouthfuls of salad, imagining all the other pitfalls and traps ahead of us as we continue our arrangement. 'We're not making a mistake, are we, Rav? We know a lot about each other, but we're still not very prepared for this.'

'It's an unusual situation. It's difficult to plan everything in advance.' It's obvious from the way he speaks that he's uncomfortable with this side of our arrangement. He puts down his plate and rubs his hands against each other to remove the crumbs. 'Annika, if you're uneasy about this, we don't have to go further. You can tell your family that we didn't get along after our time apart and we broke up. Or if you're worried that telling your parents you're single will cause more stress for your dad, you could tell them things are a bit rocky between us at the moment and you think it's best to try to fix things first before I meet them. That could buy you more time.'

I quirk my lips. 'Wow, it almost sounds like you've been thinking about ways out of our lie.'

His lips quirk so quickly I almost miss it. 'I get the impression you don't want to lie to your parents.'

I dip my head. 'You're right, I don't. But I have to keep telling myself it's for a good cause. I want my parents to be happy. And, since they're convinced I need a husband, right now the best way to do that is by making them think I'm in love. Trust me, I would use one of your excuses in a heartbeat if I could, but I just can't risk it at the moment.' I nibble at my inner cheek. Despite Nish's and my parents' assurances, I have a gut feeling Dad isn't making the progress I would have hoped to see. The last thing I'm going to do is make the situation worse.

Rav reaches over and puts a hand on my knee. I appreciate that he knows better than to try offering some platitude to comfort me. I briefly place my hand over his and give it a squeeze.

'Anyway, do you want anything else, or I can start clearing up?' I ask.

'I'm good. That was delicious. I liked the chutneys. I haven't tasted those before,' he says, helping me pack everything up. 'Thank you for getting me to try them. I've tended to stick to tried and tested meals in recent years, so it's nice at times to try different and new things.'

This whole situation must be completely outside Rav's comfort zone. I still can't believe he's the one who has followed through with my hare-brained scheme and suggested he pretends to be my boyfriend. But it's probably better to stick with safer topics for the moment so I simply reply, 'I love trying new food. I couldn't resist the smell when I saw those chutneys in the market.'

'What's your favourite dish?'

'How am I supposed to choose?' I exclaim as if he's asked me to choose my favourite family member.

'Not curries then?'

'Curries are amazing. And you can't beat the flavours of home and the smells you grew up with, can you? But there are so many sublime dishes. What about you?'

'Oh, I'm a simple lad. It would be my mum's mutton curry. For the same reason as you, it reminds me of home. Whenever I visit my parents, my mum will make it for me, and she'll always give me a tiffin to bring some home.' He grabs a handful of nuts and chews. 'What about if you could eat only one meal for the rest of your life, or the world is about to explode and everybody gets one last meal, what would you choose then?'

I'm taken aback by the unexpected flight of fancy in his question – he comes across as so down to earth and practical.

'Well, I suspect those would be two different meals. But if the world were about to explode, I would probably pick something my dad used to make. I think it was a Scandinavian dish of leftover meat and potatoes, served with a fried egg. It's not healthy or particularly nourishing, but it's simple and hearty and probably reminds me of home more than anything else.' My smile falters momentarily. How I wish Dad felt well enough for me to ask him to make the dish again. 'I think that's one of the best things about travelling – trying out a country's authentic cuisine.'

'Why is travel such a big deal for you? Don't you want to spend more time at home?'

'What is home? You know how people always say they don't want to regret not spending time with family on their death bed?' He nods. 'Well, I don't want to be on my death bed and regret not taking the opportunities I had in front of me because I followed the expectations of my family or culture and settled. I don't think I could truly be happy if I'm restricted to one place.'

'And you don't think your wanderlust, your need for adventure will end?'

'Why should it? I love my job because I get to explore the world with it. But even if I wasn't going to all these new places, I would still love the kind of work I do.' I know I'm beginning to sound like a broken record – I don't know how to make people listen to what I'm saying and actually hear it. 'At the moment, I have the best of both worlds and I can't see any reason I'd want to give that up. So, I guess if I wanted to commit to a relationship with someone who wanted me to be in the country more, my job is flexible and I'm able to remain in one place. But I could never really love someone who would ask that of me.'

'It sounds important to you.'

'It is.' I'm silent for a moment. 'My mum had a great job opportunity in the States,' I begin quietly. 'Great city, great standard of living. A promotion for her. She'd studied hard to get the opportunity and my dad was more than happy to emigrate but she couldn't take it because of me.'

'You?'

'Because she was pregnant with me. She had to sacrifice her career for her family. I know that it was her choice and she says she doesn't regret it. But I'd rather not be in that position in the first place. I don't want to have to choose between a partner and family and being independent somewhere down the line.'

I've never shared that with anyone before. I wonder why I opened up to Rav about it.

'I can understand why it's important to you then. Do you know …?' Rav begins, then he stops.

'What?'

'It's okay. It was an observation. Nothing important.'

'An observation about me?'

'Hmm.'

'Tell me. I won't be offended if that's what you're worried

about.' I turn to face him. 'Perhaps we should have a policy of being honest with each other, particularly if we're lying to nearly everyone else.'

Rav inclines his head. 'Sometimes it sounds like you want a relationship, but you don't think you can have one.'

'What does that mean?'

'You don't think you can have your work and travel while also having a supportive partner. Is that true, though? What about someone who does the same work you do?'

'I tried that. Years ago when I was still an employee. It was fine when we were working on projects together, but then he wanted us to decide in advance where we could go for our next job *and* how long we spent in England and how long we travelled. I didn't want those kinds of restrictions. That's around the time I moved to a consultancy role.'

Rav blinks but says nothing.

'What are you thinking?' I ask.

'It sounds like he was the wrong person for you.'

I sigh inwardly. With that kind of comment, there's always the unspoken assumption that if the right guy did come along, I'd be happy to give up my career for him. Not. Going. To. Happen.

'He *was* the wrong person,' I reply, 'but the chances of my finding the right person are slim, aren't they? And it hurts when a relationship doesn't work out. Why put me and another person through that?'

'I understand that. That's how I feel about dating at the moment. It's not likely to go anywhere because it isn't the right time for me. I can't give the time or commitment a real relationship deserves.'

'Doesn't that get lonely?' I ask, voicing the most negative aspect of my decision to remain single.

'At the moment, I'm too busy to notice.'

I have so many follow-up questions, I wouldn't know where to start. So, instead, I change the subject slightly and ask, 'So what else would this future bride of yours be like? You've already told me she'll be educated and want a family. What else?'

'I don't know.' He gives me the ghost of a smile.

'But won't you have to give your family or the matchmaker some criteria?' It's Rav. I can't believe he doesn't know exactly what he wants his wife to be like. 'Does she have to be tall? Beautiful? Curvy, slim? Child-bearing hips? Do you want someone with the same background as you, or born and brought up in India?'

'None of that matters to me. I don't think there's anything specific I need for me to find someone compatible enough to marry them.' He looks into the distance. Instinctively I know he's not ignoring me. After a few moments, he continues, 'I would like to meet someone I can talk to. Someone I can share my thoughts with. Someone who shares my values. And I can't define that through criteria.'

I'm surprised by the simplicity of his response.

'Well, I guess you still have three years before you need to worry about it,' I reply.

It's unexpectedly easy to talk to Rav, to open up to him. Perhaps it's because I don't have to hide anything from him the way I feel I have to with nearly everyone else, even some of my closest friends. Sometimes it's hard to articulate how I feel about marriage and family without sounding like I'm criticising or judging others for wanting things I don't. With Rav, I can explain my thoughts without trying to justify them.

Rav has relaxed over the course of our picnic. He lies back against the blanket lifting his face to the sunshine. I watch him for a few minutes.

I bite my lip, weighing up the wisdom of my next action. Part of the reason we're doing these pretend dates is to be comfortable and close to each other. But I don't want to make a move that can come across as too fast too soon. I take a deep breath and then lie down next to him, staring at the cloudless blue sky.

'So, have you given any more thought to your favourite constellation?' I ask.

'I think about it all the time. Just when I think I know, I hear about a different constellation and suddenly that one's my favourite.' He sounds serious, but there's a slight quirk of his lips. My heart soars at his light-hearted response – I hope it means our initial discomfort in each other's company is a thing of the past.

'Why is Pavo your favourite?' he asks.

'I don't know.' I shrug. 'Because it means peacock, and I love peacocks perhaps.'

'I wouldn't expect such an unromantic reason from you.'

I grin. 'I am captivated by some of the mythology behind the names. Did you know the peacock was said to be Hera's sacred bird and they drove her chariot? And of course, it's India's national bird.'

'So you love mythology and you love space. If space travel was possible, you'd be exploring the galaxies, wouldn't you?'

'Of course – wouldn't you?'

He is silent for a moment, giving the question more consideration than is necessary. 'I think I would. But out of curiosity rather than for adventure.'

'That's an interesting distinction.' Since Rav is relaxed, I press him on some of the answers he gave me when we were exchanging emails and he seems happy to respond. I didn't expect to laugh so much in his company.

This afternoon has been a revelation. It's the first time I'm seeing a less serious side of Rav and it's a side I wouldn't mind getting to know better. My family would believe I could be in a relationship with *this* Rav. We still need to have more practice dates before Rav's business events but I feel confident we can convince my family.

There's no excuse to put it off any longer. It's time for Rav to meet my parents.

Chapter 7

'Are you sure that's what you want to wear?' Shakti asks me as she looks up and down at my blouse and skirt. There's nothing wrong with what I'm wearing. The clothes are good quality. I think they suit me and most importantly, they're comfortable.

'I think the question is, why are you so dressed up?' I reply, similarly inspecting my sister's bright salwar kameez, her pregnancy bump looking larger than usual.

'It's a special occasion. Not every day my older sister introduces her boyfriend to the family.'

'I'm not sure it's salwar-wearing special. You didn't wear Indian clothes when you introduced Tony to the family.'

'That's because we were eighteen and nobody expected it to last past university. Besides, he's white,' she adds, knowing that's all the explanation necessary.

'Well, we don't want to give off the wrong idea. If Rav sees me in a salwar or sari, he may run for the hills, worrying that I'm expecting a proposal at any moment.'

'Rav? Did you say Rav? You don't mean Rav Gohil, do you? No, you can't!'

I bite my lips and raise my eyes to the ceiling – I could kick myself. So far, I've been careful not to tell Mum and Dad what my fake suitor's name is – mostly because to begin with I had no idea who would play the role and I was sensible enough to know, even when starting my lie, that it was better to keep details to a minimum.

'What are you talking about Rav for?' Nishal says, coming up behind me. I almost admire his uncanny ability to enter a conversation at exactly the wrong moment.

'Rav's her boyfriend. That's who Annika's dating.'

'You can't possibly be dating Rav,' Nishal says, looking at me directly.

'Why not?' I stick out my chin, automatically adopting the stubborn look I get whenever Nish annoys me.

'You're not his type.'

'Hmm, interesting. What is his type?' I'm genuinely curious to know the answer. I deliberately haven't kept up with the gossip about Rav, but I wonder if the women he's dated in the past are a similar type and how they compare to the 'criteria' he's mentioned.

'Determined career women, with ambition and definite plans for their future.'

'And you don't think I'm a career woman or ambitious.'

'Of course, you're a career woman,' Shakti says.

'But it's a different kind of career,' Nishal adds. 'You'll always work but you're not looking for a big promotion, or you'd stop being a consultant.'

My career choice has always been a mystery to Nish. He followed the expected path of becoming a doctor. I'm convinced he thinks I'm playing at a hobby rather than doing something important.

'I don't think this is the time to discuss my career ambitions,' I say. 'Rav will be here soon.'

'So you are dating Rav Gohil. I don't believe it. Dad and Mum are going to be ecstatic,' Shakti says.

'Yeah, I know. That's why I didn't want to tell them before. I know it's a big deal and I didn't want them to be disappointed if nothing came of it. Anyway, I'm going to help Mum. Where's Dad?'

'I'll go upstairs and check,' Nishal offers while Shakti goes to help her husband with their two-year-old.

I go to the kitchen where my mum and Nish's wife are preparing platters of food. Rav has agreed to come over for tea and biscuits but I'm sure he understands that's code for at least a meal, lots of snacks and mishti.

Both Mum and Kaya are wearing saris. I look down at my skirt and blouse again. Have I gone too casual for the occasion? Rav and I may not be dating for real but am I taking the wrong approach by not dressing up?

Ack, I hate this overthinking and second-guessing – it doesn't come naturally to me.

'Mum,' Nish says as he comes into the kitchen with Dad. 'Have you heard it's Rav Gohil?'

'What's Rav Gohil?' Dad asks, suddenly alert and upright.

'Annika's boyfriend. She's been dating Rav Gohil.'

Both sets of parental eyes turn to me with obvious delight.

'Yeah, I didn't want to tell you until we were more secure in our relationship. I know he's part of the community and things could get awkward if things went wrong.'

'No, no, Niki. Of course.' My parents speak over each other, trying to reassure me they understood my reluctance to introduce him before.

'But I always thought he'd be perfect for you,' Mum says.

'You did?' She has never once suggested I date Rav Gohil before. Mum did, however, suggest Shakti date Rav when Mum wasn't sure about Tony. But the important thing now is to know why she thinks Rav is perfect for me. We are so different. What could she possibly be seeing? Or is Mum trying to convince me she's happy with my choice?

'He's got his head on his shoulders. He would be a stable influence on you,' Mum tells me.

69

Stifling an internal scream, I force a smile. 'Yes, he's very down to earth.'

'And you'll be good for him too. His mother used to tell me she worried that Rav was too serious.'

'And I don't take anything seriously?' I mutter under my breath, rolling my eyes. I've always been accused of this. It was part and parcel of my family's concerns about me not settling down and not planning enough for the future.

Dad puts a calming hand over mine. 'You are serious about the important stuff, and that's what matters. But you know how to make the most out of life. That's all your mother means.'

'We haven't seen Rav in years. Not since Bobby and Karishma moved to Kent when they retired,' Mum says, probably deliberately changing the direction of the conversation.

'The Gohils never struck me as the type to live near the seaside,' Nish observes. 'I'm surprised they didn't move to India, at least part of the year.'

Dad laughs. 'That's more common for people who grew up in India before emigrating here or who have a lot of family there. Both Bobby and Karishma were born and brought up in England. Their parents came over in the early Fifties. Before my dad did.'

I notice my mum's smile fade away. Mum was born and grew up in India and came to England for a medical posting. Here, she met and married my dad and never went back to live in India but most of her family live there and I know there's a big part of Mum that still thinks of India as her home. Whereas my dad came to England when he was young.

For a moment, I wonder whether England would feel like home to me without my family here. Or, is my need to be on the move constantly, part of my search to find a place that truly feels like home?

'Have you seen the Gohils' house in Kent?' Shakti asks me.

'No, they uh—' I break off when the doorbell rings.

Rav.

This is it. From the moment the door opens, Rav and I are committed to going through with our fake-relationship arrangement. Dad goes to answer. There's no going back now.

Soon enough, Rav is seated on a two-seater sofa with five pairs of eyes on him. Luckily all the children are playing in a different room with Tony – very wise of him since that way he doesn't have to endure their scrutiny too.

I place a small table in front of Rav and bring over a plate with some pakoras, onion bhajis and samosas with sauces that Mum prepared. By which I mean, she heated them in the oven. Even for my potential suitor, Mum isn't going to spend hours wrapping up vegetable filling in individual pastries.

Luckily, Rav knows better than to try to refuse the food he's offered.

After helping Mum serve the others, I sit next to Rav as would be expected of his girlfriend. I'm not sure how close I should sit next to him. It's tricky because I would always want to be respectful in front of my parents but I don't want them to think I'm maintaining my distance because we're not used to each other's company yet.

I notice Dad lean back in his chair and take a deep breath. He steeples his hands and says, 'So …'

The inquisition is about to begin.

Oh, they're very subtle. I'm actually impressed by how seamlessly my family are dropping their questions about our relationship into the conversation.

Overall, Rav does an excellent job. Not only answering my family's questions and eating a lot of my mother's food but also acting the besotted boyfriend. He smiles at me often and touches me fleetingly but fairly frequently as if he can't resist even though he knows it isn't the 'done' thing to be overly affectionate.

I silently thank Tinu and Greg for encouraging our practice dates; otherwise I would have jumped out of my skin as every light contact sends shivers through me.

71

The shivers are unexpected. They never happened during our practices. It must be my nerves for needing this afternoon to go well, making my senses go haywire.

'And have you and Annika seen your parents since she's been back?' Mum asks Rav. 'Perhaps we should have them over for dinner soon. We were just saying we haven't seen them since they moved to Kent.'

The blood rushes from my face. Although Rav and I have discussed how much he would tell his parents, we didn't think about the possibility my parents would suggest a get-together.

'I'm sure they would love that,' Rav replies. 'But actually, we haven't told them about our relationship yet. I would have introduced them when we first went out but Annika wanted to wait.' He gives me a look of exasperated indulgence and I can swear the women in the room sigh. Me included. 'We're hoping to go down to Kent soon though, even if it's just for lunch. I'll mention that you suggested meeting up.'

Dad nods. 'It's not easy being with someone who isn't in the country much. Trying to fit everything in when she is here.'

Rav turns towards me, giving me a quick smile as he stares into my eyes. 'It's worth the effort.'

I frown, trying to warn him not to overdo things. I want this to go well. To give my parents a little peace of mind that I'm happy and in a settled relationship. The scheme isn't for my parents to become so convinced by our love affair they start making wedding arrangements.

'It's so weird thinking you're going out with my little sister,' Nish says.

Rav laughs. 'It was a little strange for us. I couldn't believe my eyes when I first saw her again.'

'Ah yes, tell us how it happened. Annika has been very secretive about you,' Mum says.

'Hopefully not because you're embarrassed by me.' Rav squeezes my hand.

I jerk at the unexpected intimacy of the action. Hopefully, if anyone notices, they'll put it down to my embarrassment at the show of affection in front of my family.

'Only a little bit,' I reply.

We will definitely have to work on the physical side of our fake relationship more. It's only a week until the first event in front of Rav's business colleagues and I need to stop being so jumpy around him before then.

It's going to be tight to find time to fit another practice date in, but Rav and I will make it work. We have to. I snort, hoping nobody heard. It's so unlike me to make even small plans in advance if I can help it. Perhaps Rav is already rubbing off on me.

Thinking about our need for another date and needing to be more affectionate with Rav, touching and kissing him, has made me miss some of the conversation because the next thing I hear is Kaya asking where we met up again and I automatically reply, 'At a hotel' at the same time Rav says, 'At a bar in Leicester Square' – which was the response we practised. Through my distraction, I've inadvertently given them the truthful answer.

They must have noticed our different answers. I feel the blood rushing from my face. I glance at Rav. Not surprisingly his face expresses his confusion but he doesn't look worried. Unexpectedly, that reassures me. There's no need to panic. I can make this right.

'We met at a bar,' I say, pretending I never mentioned the hotel. I then give them more details about how we recognised each other and started talking and how Rav asked me out for dinner before I left – just as we rehearsed before.

I give them so many details about our meeting that hopefully my brief slip of the tongue about the hotel is forgotten. It seems to work since no one mentions it again.

Unfortunately, we hit another small snafu a little later when Rav is answering questions about his apartment. Even though Rav suggested I stay at his place when we were on our picnic, I haven't seen it, and apart from knowing its location, I don't know anything about it, so I'm thrown for a loop when I'm asked what my favourite part of the flat is.

I take longer than necessary to answer because I worry whether giving an obvious response like the bedroom will give rise to innuendo and I begin calculating the likelihood of being caught out in a lie if I mention something that doesn't exist and the chance that one of my family sees his apartment and finds out I made it up.

Rav squeezes my hand. 'You always say how much you love the view. I think your favourite part must be the balcony.'

I smile with relief and gratitude. 'That's right. It has to be the view from the balcony. I haven't had many chances to go to your place over the past year, though,' I add, hoping it explains my overlong response time.

Unfortunately, it leads to Nish asking, 'So how do you manage the long-distance aspect when Annika is abroad for so long?'

'Well, I miss Annika when she's not around,' Rav says, quick to respond while giving me an adoring look. 'But I'm busy at the moment building the business. No doubt I would be accused of neglecting her if she was here all the time. While she's out of the country, I can put my head down and power through work without worrying about not being the best boyfriend and when she comes back, I make sure I have free time to spend with her.'

Yet again, he's given the perfect answer. If only my real boyfriends had felt the same.

'But what happens after you're married and have kids?'

I choke on my drink, tempted to throw a pillow at Shakti for her question.

'Jumping the gun a bit there, sis,' I say.

Rav nods. 'As Annika says, it's a bit soon to be talking about children. Annika knows that I don't want to start a family before the business is more established. I don't want to be so busy I

74

never get a chance to spend time with my children. But, as I said, it's too soon.'

'Yes, of course, there's plenty of time for you. You're both still young,' Mum replies, making my head whip round in her direction.

Since when did my mum decide I was young for children? I mentally roll my eyes. I know the answer to that one. It was since Rav spoke.

Nish asks Rav about his business. I release a breath, grateful the topic of our future children is dropped. Before I know it, it's close to six p.m. and time for Rav to head back to London.

The afternoon has gone well. My parents and siblings look convinced Rav and I are having the love affair of the century. Luckily, nobody brings up marriage or our long-term future again.

'I hope we see you again soon, Rav,' Mum says as Rav stands ready to leave, armed with leftover samosas and gulab jamun. Mum's also given him a container with biryani, so Rav doesn't have to cook this evening.

'I hope so too,' Rav replies.

'I have a wonderful idea,' Dad says as he walks with us towards the door. 'It's my nephew's wedding next month. You should come.'

'Of course,' Rav agrees. 'Let me have the dates. I'll come if I'm free.'

Mum gestures at Dad, not very subtly, clearly suggesting that he leave Rav and me alone to say our goodbyes.

When it's just the two of us left alone in the hallway, Rav and I stand grinning at each other. We know, without saying, we have to let time pass so the others can think we're being affectionate.

'I think it went well,' I whisper to him as I open the door. 'Only a few hiccups and we recovered well. Pats on the back for both of us.'

Rav gives me a thumbs-up sign and grins. The setting sun casts a golden halo behind him, throwing shadows, which chisel his cheekbones and jaw – my breath catches at one of the most beautiful sights I've ever seen. I blink rapidly to clear the vision.

'Bye, everyone,' Rav calls out as he leaves. 'Don't forget to send me the date for the wedding.'

I wince. Why would Rav bring that up? I know he's probably being polite, but the expectation now ... I pause. I'm being irrational – there's nothing for me to worry about here. There's plenty of time before my cousin Rohit's wedding for Rav and me to invent a reason he can't attend. The more people who meet Rav in his role as my pretend boyfriend, the more involved our deception grows and the more people will hear about our eventual break-up later on. As far as I can, I want to limit the boundaries of our pretence to my close family only.

Plus, a wedding creates even more incentive for people to ask about when you'll be settling down, and there's no way I'm exposing myself to that if I don't have to.

Chapter 8

The following Thursday, Rav meets my train when it arrives at London Euston station. I tried persuading him it wasn't necessary but he insisted, telling me he would always meet a real girlfriend when he could. One day he will make someone a real perfect boyfriend, but right now, he's being an excellent fake one for me.

Rav wasn't able to schedule any free time until this afternoon. The cocktail evening, our first event for his business, is the following evening so we have twenty-four hours to practise our story again. We managed to get away with the small mistakes in front of my family, but I don't want any mishaps in front of Rav's business colleagues.

We take the DLR to Greenwich then walk to his flat, barely saying anything on the journey. Each time we meet up, I feel like we're back at square one – uncomfortable and unsure around each other.

We don't have much time to snap out of it, so I put my hand on Rav's elbow in an attempt to get into the romantic mindset.

He looks down at my hand, then grins at me. 'That doesn't feel too bad, does it?'

'No, very natural.'

'Perhaps we should hold hands, though. Having your hand in the crook of my elbow makes me feel like I'm in the 1940s.'

'Sure.' I slide my hand into his. I'd forgotten how sensitive the palm of my hand can be and how safe and protected it can feel simply having someone walk by my side. I miss it. To change the direction my thoughts are heading, I ask, 'Are you nervous about tomorrow?'

'I find preparation helps the nerves. A lot is riding on this deal, but we're in a strong place from the business perspective.'

'So it's just a matter of convincing the owners that you're the right person. A family man.'

'That's right.'

'Well, you did a great job with my parents. I'm determined to do an equally grand job for you tomorrow. Coach me on what I should and shouldn't say.'

'Let's have something to eat and relax first.'

'Sounds good.'

'We're here,' he says after we've walked for a few more minutes. 'My apartment is in this block.'

I look up at the riverside development we're standing in front of. All glass and chrome, reflecting more buildings of glass and chrome. There are three blocks surrounding a communal garden area. The flats on the far side of the building must have exceptional views over the River Thames.

This is literally a world away from the place I stayed in Guyana.

As much as I admire the external architecture, I'm desperate to know what his flat looks like inside.

'You have parking here?' I ask as I notice a button on the lift panel saying P.

'Yes, underground. I don't find it necessary to drive around London, but it's handy to have the car if I need it.'

There are twelve floors, excluding the parking garage, and we get out of the lift on the tenth. It looks like each floor has four units, at least at this level. As I expect, Rav goes to open a door to a unit that gives him a riverside view.

Once inside, I automatically take off my shoes and leave them under the coat rail in the hall. The hallway is narrow and has a couple of doors and another narrow hallway leading off it.

'Why don't I show you your room?' Rav suggests.

He opens the door of a room to the left of the hall and gestures for me to precede him inside. The room is mostly white with a blue border below the ceiling. The soft furnishings are modern in matching blue and lime. I wonder whether he bought the showroom display or copied its style exactly.

Rav puts my bag on a storage ottoman next to the bed. 'The bathroom is directly opposite. Do you want to take a few moments for yourself, or would you like a tour?'

'Definitely a tour!'

The rest of the flat is sleek and modern. The main space is open plan with a small but fully functional L-shaped kitchen at one side with a round glass dining table and four chairs next to it. The living space is separated from the dining area by a low unit backed against a sofa and has an armchair, coffee table and wall unit.

I'm very used to a minimalistic lifestyle but if I had my own home, I'm not sure I would be so sparse with the decor. I would want my place to feel homely, although I have to admit that Rav's flat still has a warm, friendly atmosphere despite the whiteness of the kitchen units and the reflective surfaces.

There are large floor-to-ceiling windows, and behind the dining table are sliding glass doors that open onto a wraparound balcony overlooking the river.

I step onto the balcony and inhale deeply. What a breathtaking view! The river is calm, and I can see the London Eye in the distance. I could get used to living here – Rav is so lucky.

As he leads me back to my room, Rav tells me there is a gym in the basement and a communal space on the roof, although he hasn't had the chance to use them much. Rav shows me another bedroom that he's set up as a home office, although it does have a divan. He doesn't show me his bedroom, simply pointing to the door. I guess I'll never see the inside of that.

When we're back in the living area, Rav glances at his watch. 'I do have to do a couple of hours' work if you don't mind. I'll be in my home office if you need me. Feel free to make yourself at home. I thought we'd get a takeaway for dinner, but we can go out if you prefer. There are plenty of places to eat around here.'

'A takeaway sounds good. I think I'll spend some time out on the balcony. How about a cup of tea?'

'Sure, I'll make some.'

'No, you go start your work. I'll bring it through to you.' I hold up my hand when Rav is about to protest. 'I think I can work out where everything is.'

'You know, I could get used to you in this supportive girlfriend role.' He grins broadly. 'I may never end our arrangement if you play it too well.' He's still laughing as he heads to his office.

I spend the rest of the afternoon on the balcony, reading and surfing social media. There is a chance I won't want to end our pact either if it means I can stay in this apartment with this view. I love visiting places around the world, but something about London calls to my heart, even though I've never lived here.

A movement to my side alerts me to Rav's presence. He stretches as he steps onto the balcony, letting out the kinks from working at his computer. His shirt rises, exposing his stomach and an intriguing happy trail, which I find myself following all the way down. I blink and clear my throat, trying to restrain my thoughts.

I can look at Rav objectively and recognise he is a good-looking male. Of course, that's all it is; there's nothing more to it. If I was actually attracted to him, it could be uncomfortable for me when we have to put on our affectionate displays in front of the Bamfords, knowing Rav was just faking it.

This reminds me that we will need to practise kissing at some

80

point. I immediately look at this mouth. His lips look firm and lush, almost sensual. Can lips look sensual?

'Everything okay?' Rav asks. 'Do you have a preference for what we eat tonight?'

I laugh at the prosaic question, as effective as a cold shower in changing the focus of my thoughts.

I open up the delivery app on my phone. 'Is the local Jamaican food any good?'

'It is. Good choice.' After placing our order, Rav pours us wine and brings my glass out onto the balcony.

'I feel like you may have taken root out here,' he says as he hands me the glass and then takes the seat next to mine.

'You're lucky you get to live here. Well, I guess the reality is you worked very hard to accomplish all you have.'

'Yes, but I recognise a certain amount of luck comes from having two parents who supported me financially through school and university and encouraged my ambitions – offering me moral support. And my high school education gave me the chance to go to one of the best universities, which opened the door to my first job.'

I'm impressed. Not many people I meet would acknowledge the luck or privilege that went into their circumstances. The thought makes me frown. 'Maybe my parents think I'm ungrateful because I'm not making the best of all the advantages they gave me.'

Rav's laugh surprises me.

'How could they ever think that?' he asks. 'You're doing the work you love, with your skills, and are doing it very well from what I can tell.'

'But, in my parents' eyes, the end goal is to be settled, and my family consider my lifestyle to be anything but stable.'

'Then their definition of stable needs to change.'

My eyes lock with his. Having brown eyes myself, I sometimes ignore how many different shades they can be. Rav's eyes are dark, with golden flecks, his pupils large. His lashes are impossibly long.

I blink to break the connection finally. I cast around in my mind for some conversational topic to quickly change the subject. 'I'm sorry my parents put you on the spot about my cousin's wedding. I know you agreed you'd come, but you don't have to. It's not too late to say you're busy.'

'No, that's fine. If we're going to convince your parents of our relationship, I should go to these events.'

'Yeah, but you didn't agree to pretend in front of my extended family.'

'Believe me, you've got the worse end of the deal here.'

'Really? With you, I get to have cocktails at one of the most exclusive places in London, stay the weekend at a country club *and* attend a gala event. While you have to put up with my family.'

'I like your family!'

'Oh, I love them. But come on! You have to admit nobody's idea of fun is meeting the parents.'

'It went well. And I think it helped that I already knew them. Whereas you're meeting a group of strangers who are only interested in how far they can get ahead in business and, on top of that, you have to play the role of the doting, affectionate girlfriend.'

My brows furrow. 'Do you think that's going to be a problem for you?'

'Of course not. But we didn't talk about the physical nature of this pretend relationship when we made our pact. As you pointed out, it wasn't necessary in front of your family. It's only on my end.'

'Well, I'm happy to add this as an extra to our arrangement but I can understand if you feel uncomfortable. Anyway, it's not like we're going to have to have sex in front of everyone. It's a little handholding, arm around the waist and perhaps a kiss or two. Nothing to make a fuss about.'

'You won't mind if we have to kiss?'

'Not at all. Actors do it all the time. It only means something if you want it to.' He doesn't reply and I can't quite decipher his expression. 'What?'

'Nothing. I was wondering whether we ought to practise kissing.'

My mouth goes dry but I'm saved from answering by the door buzzer signalling the arrival of our dinner.

Over a meal consisting of goat curry, beef patties, fried plantain and rice and peas, we go over the details of the cocktail evening the following night. It's not technically a Bamford event, since a completely different company will be hosting, but all the people interested in the Bamfords' business will be attending, so it's a good time to get to know the competition before spending the weekend together at the Bamford garden party.

'I wasn't sure what to wear tomorrow. I've brought a couple of dresses. Do you want to pick out which you think is most appropriate?'

He smiles as he chews his mouthful. 'I'm sure whatever you've chosen will be fine.'

'I wouldn't be too sure about that,' I say with a laugh. 'I don't have a lot of dressy outfits. I'm hoping Shakti or Tinu will have something I can borrow for the gala – don't worry about that.'

'They're both shorter than you, though. If you want to buy something that would fit better, I'd be happy to pay.'

'Oh, no, I couldn't ask you to pay for my clothes.'

'It's the least I could do. You shouldn't have to be out of pocket because you're helping me.'

'The thing is,' I admit with a grimace, 'I don't really have occasion to wear those kinds of clothes. Since I practically live out of boxes, I only store what I'm going to need. But thanks for offering.'

'You can give the dress to someone after the weekend if necessary. But tell me more about living out of boxes. I can't imagine not having a place to put my things.'

'You're beginning to sound like my family.'

He holds his palms up in surrender. 'Sorry.'

'No, it's fine. I can live out of the bags I take on my projects with me for a few weeks. And my parents are great at letting me store most of my boxes at their house until I've decided where I'm going to rent. But I think it's also a constant reminder to them that I don't have a permanent place.'

'What do you take with you and what do you store? And how do you decide?' Rav asks as he refills my wineglass.

I chuckle. 'You sound fascinated by my nomadic lifestyle.'

'It's different from anyone else's I know. It must be very freeing.'

'Exactly.' I can't believe the sense of delight I feel that Rav sounds like he understands where I'm coming from. I would never have expected that.

'I don't think I could do it.'

I press my lips together. I had, however, expected that.

While we're relaxing together watching a crime drama later that evening, I end up sitting close to Rav on the sofa. After a few minutes into the TV show, I feel his arm go around my shoulders.

I raise my eyebrows.

'For practice,' he says in reply to my unspoken question.

I nod, then lean back, resting my head against his shoulder. It feels natural.

'Is this okay?' I ask.

'Perfect,' he replies.

Wondering how far I can go, I rest my hand lightly on his mid-thigh. 'Is this okay for you?'

He clears his throat. 'Yes.'

I tense. For a moment, I'm worried I've gone too far and he isn't pleased with my action, but then he places a brief kiss on the top of my head. I relax. This is working out much better than I'd hoped. I'm feeling more and more confident about Friday's cocktail evening.

Chapter 9

'Do you feel ready?' Rav asks the following evening as we're walking from the tube stop to the bar for the first of our business-related events we'll be attending.

'Let's see. I have to drink cocktails, eat canapés, listen to dull business talk and pretend I'm madly in love with you. I think I can manage that.' I quickly wink at him.

'Almost correct. It will be incredibly interesting business talk.'

'Sure,' I reply, raising my eyebrows. Although, if I'm being honest, I do find it fascinating when Rav talks about the kind of work he does. Perhaps it's because of the passion evident in his voice. It is clearly more than just a job or money to him.

It's strange putting Rav and passion in the same thought. He is becoming a contradiction in my mind – in many ways, he is still the strait-laced, formal man I've always known him to be, but he's also warm, kind and funny. His sense of humour – more so the way it meshes with mine – makes this situation much more bearable.

I can't imagine the paragon I'd created in my mind proposing this arrangement or going on practice dates with me.

Am I what he was expecting?

Not that he's likely to have any expectations of me. He barely knows me – I highly doubt his family have been singing my praises growing up or regaling him with my accomplishments.

'Are you sure this dress is suitable?' I ask, running my hands down my sides. Hoping to smooth out any creases and wipe off some of the sweat building up. It's unusual for me to worry about what I'm wearing or whether it is appropriate unless someone in my family makes a comment on my wardrobe choices. But this evening, I want to make sure I'm not letting Rav down. He's done such a wonderful job of playing the role of a besotted suitor in front of my family; I want to make sure I play my part equally well.

'You look beautiful,' he replies, picking up my hand and giving it a quick squeeze before releasing it. I'm glad I just wiped the sweat off.

I grunt.

'What's up?' he asks.

'Only problem with this fake relationship. I don't know if that was a genuine compliment or whether you're already in couple mode.'

Rav gives me an enigmatic look. 'Can't it be both?'

'I suppose.'

We reach the bar. I look inside through the floor-length windows. Many people are already there, but I wouldn't have said they look particularly like they're at a business networking event.

I follow Rav into the bar and we go straight through to the back, where there is a door blocked by a velvet rail. Rav gives our names to the woman standing next to it, which she checks off on her hand-held computer before letting us past. Of course, a financial company would have hired rooms for a private event. They wouldn't want to conduct business where anyone could overhear.

Greg is already there, standing at a tall table. He beckons us over.

'Annika, how lovely to see you again. You look beautiful.' Greg presses a kiss on my cheek.

'Thank you.'

I hear Rav mutter, 'Funny how you believe him.'

Ignoring Rav, I turn to Greg. 'It's good to see you again, Greg,' I reply. 'Are you on your own?'

'Yes,' Greg says, rolling his eyes. 'Better for the Bamfords to see me on my own at these events than with a different date each time.'

I nod at the reminder Greg's reputation is the reason Rav was the one who needed a fake girlfriend.

'Is Rupert here yet?' Rav asks.

'No, but Aiden is. And Marie is here with him.'

'Well, she is his wife,' Rav replies. His voice is calm, but I can sense him tense slightly when he hears her name. Aiden must be Aiden Watson; the man Rav went to uni with. As I suspected when Rav mentioned him at our first dinner, there is some history between them.

'We should make the rounds, Annika,' Rav says. 'Are you ready?'

'Definitely,' I reply eagerly. I've been exceedingly curious to meet all the people Rav's spoken about, especially Mr Bamford, who sounds like a man who doesn't want to sell his business at all.

Rav introduces me to several people as we walk around the room. He doesn't stop to chat with any group for long – it's just a blur of names, fleeting greetings and quick handshakes before we move on. I don't know if Rav is purposely staying away from Aiden Watson but, apart from Mr Bamford, they are the only people here I want to meet.

After about half an hour, I finally get the chance to meet Rupert Bamford and his wife, Moira. They are a lovely older couple, full of life and heart. I would estimate Mr Bamford is in his mid- to late sixties, whereas Moira is probably in her early sixties. I can understand why Greg believes Rav and I need to show affection in order to pull this charade off – the Bamfords have no problems with expressing their attraction to each other in public. In a way, they remind me of my own parents. Like the Bamfords, my parents share a strong connection, even if Mum and Dad aren't always showing affection, in front of others at least.

Naturally, the Bamfords are curious about our relationship. This time we could answer the questions without any difficulty – a big improvement from the interrogation my family gave Rav and me.

'I love how you two grew up with each other but never dated until recently. It's so romantic,' Mrs Bamford says.

Rav places a kiss on my hairline and I rest my head against his shoulder in response. It almost doesn't feel like an act, that we could be a couple so completely in tune with each other.

'Yes, I still can't believe it worked out,' he says.

'How did it change?' Mrs Bamford asks.

'I don't understand …' I falter, worried about how to answer an unexpected question.

'You've known each other for so long. One moment you're friends and then suddenly you want to be in a relationship. When did you realise you were interested in each other?'

I was right. We hadn't thought to prepare for this type of question.

'It's hard to say,' I begin at the same time that Rav says, 'At her brother's wedding.'

I have to cover my shock. That was fast thinking on Rav's part.

'I've always thought I'd love to get to know Annika better but it was at her brother's wedding when I knew I was attracted to her and wanted to try to take things further. Though I didn't get a chance to act on it until we met again last year.'

He sounds so convincing, I can't help staring at him, wondering whether he's telling the truth. He can't be. He has never once given me any indication he's attracted to me. And it would probably make our arrangement awkward if it was true.

'And was it the same for you, Annika?' Mrs Bamford asks.

'I've always found Rav handsome but I never believed he'd ever be interested in me until he asked me out for a drink last year.'

As I speak, I feel Rav stiffen beside me. I follow the direction of his gaze and see Aiden Watson and the woman who I presume is his wife, Marie, approaching the group.

My eyes narrow. Did Marie hold Rav's hand a moment longer than necessary? Aiden must have noticed from the way he quickly inserts his hand into hers to extract it from Rav's. Mr Bamford tells Aiden he'll catch up with them later but I can tell the Watsons are reluctant to leave.

At some point I'm going to have to ask Rav for the full story about Aiden and Marie and him. It's very clear to me now that they have history.

When the discussion inevitably turns towards business, Rav and Mr Bamford politely leave Mrs Bamford and me to go to talk to other guests.

Mrs Bamford smiles at me. 'You'll have to get used to this, I'm afraid, when you marry someone who's also married to their business. I chose not to work after marriage to support Rupert with his work, but I was in events management before I got married, so I've always organised the hospitality for his company. In a way, I look at it as if I'm dealing with one single client for the rest of my life.'

'What kind of events did you put on?' I ask, which seems to be the opening Mrs Bamford needed to regale me with her stories about their parties and travels. Even though she's probably closer to Mum's age, we chat as if we've known each other for years. It sounds like she shares my wanderlust, telling me she hopes to indulge that passion once they've sold the business. She has endless questions about my work and the places I've visited. As I reach out with my left hand to accept a drink from a passing waiter, Mrs Bamford says, 'I don't mean to be rude, but why don't you wear your engagement ring?'

I look at her with a start. What is she talking about engagement rings for? I glance at Rav but he's since left Mr Bamford and is now standing near the buffet table, deep in conversation with someone I haven't been introduced to. How in the world has Mrs Bamford got the idea Rav and I are engaged? Did Rav tell her that or has she misunderstood something?

I try not to panic. She's giving me a curious expression. I need to come up with an answer. If Rav and I are engaged that would probably help convince the Bamfords that Rav is the committed family man they're looking for to take over the business. But how to explain no ring? In the end I decide to stick with the truth.

'To be honest, I don't have one,' I reply. 'It's still an informal engagement.' Okay, so bending the truth slightly. 'We haven't wanted to make a big announcement because of my dad's health.' Mrs Bamford nods in sympathetic understanding. I send a silent apology. *Sorry for using you in my lie, Dad.*

'Oh, so maybe you want to choose one yourself then?'

I sigh and shake my head slowly. 'I'm not sure I will ever wear an engagement ring, mainly because it's not practical to have it on me while I'm working. Call me superstitious but I prefer not to get one in the first place than have to take it off for long periods.'

'Oh, I completely understand. Once my ring went on my finger, it was never coming off.'

As we chat, other people come to our table, where Mrs Bamford introduces me as Rav's fiancée, and I notice the curious looks on their faces before they move on. After half an hour, I excuse myself. I'm desperate to know what explanation Rav has for why the Bamfords think we're engaged, but first I make a detour to use the restroom.

On my way out, I bump into Aiden. It almost feels like he's been lurking there, waiting for me to leave the restroom. 'It's Annika, isn't it? You're here with Rav Gohil.'

'That's right.'

'I'm Aiden Watson. We met when you were speaking to the Bamfords.'

'I remember.'

'I have to say I was surprised when I heard Rav had a fiancée.'

Probably not as surprised as I was. I try to maintain my normal tone. 'Why would that be?'

'He hasn't had a serious relationship since my wife broke up with him a few years ago.'

'Yes, I know,' I reply, even though it's the first time I've heard about this. There is something odd in how Aiden speaks about Rav, particularly about his wife. This isn't simply business rivals competing for a contract, I don't think. But I'm not sure what it is.

'So he told you about them then?' he asks, arching an eyebrow. 'I'm surprised since it didn't end well. She left him for me. I don't think he likes that I'm the one she chose. That's why he's always going out of his way to try to beat me in business.'

I try to imagine how I'd react to Aiden if I were truly Rav's fiancée. I probably would be interested in what he's saying, wouldn't I? But I can't help feeling Aiden is intentionally trying to provoke a jealous reaction from me. I don't want to give him the satisfaction.

'He hasn't said much to me about it,' I say. 'He mentioned he had a relationship that didn't work out. I guess that was with your wife. But I didn't need to know any details. Rav's put that behind him now. We all have a past, don't we? It's the present and future that matter. Now, if you'll excuse me, I'm going to find Rav.'

I straighten my back and walk out the room, desperately wanting to know whether Aiden is watching me but determined not to give in to the temptation to turn my head.

But for now, I need to find my so-called fiancé and ask what the real story is.

Rav is talking to a group of people. I catch his eye before going to one of the free tall tables nearby to wait for him.

'Everything okay?' Rav asks when he joins me a few minutes later.

'Yes.' I take a sip of champagne. Then raising my eyebrows, I say with sarcasm dripping from my tone, 'I do wish you'd told me about our engagement. I think I would have enjoyed celebrating it.'

Rav has the grace to look ashamed. 'I'm sorry. That was all Greg. He took it on himself to decide simply being in a long-term relationship wouldn't be enough to convince Mr Bamford.'

I shake my head slowly, then sigh, waving my hand in a gesture of dismissal. 'It's fine. Whatever works for this deal. A heads-up would have been nice, that's all.'

'Absolutely. What happened?'

'Mrs Bamford asked me where my ring was. I told her you were too cheap to buy me one.' At his sceptical look, I tell him what really happened.

'Do you think I should get you a ring?'

'No point doing that now.' Besides, if I ever do wear an engagement ring on my finger, highly unlikely though that is, I think I'd want the sentiment behind it to be real. 'But on the subject of things it would be nice to have a heads-up on, is there anything you want to tell me about Aiden and Marie?'

Rav shakes his head. 'There's nothing to say.'

'That's not the impression I got from Aiden.'

'What did he tell you?' Rav turns his head – I presume to see where Aiden is.

I give Rav the gist of our conversation.

'It isn't a big deal,' Rav insists. 'Marie and I had a brief thing. It didn't mean anything, and it's been over for years.'

'Aiden made it sound like it was a serious relationship.'

He grimaces. 'What is Aiden playing at? Marie and I were together for about six months. I made it clear from the outset there wasn't going to be marriage in our future. Unfortunately, I think she took the relationship more seriously than I did and thought we were headed towards marriage. Which is why I ended things.'

'You ended things?' I check. 'So she didn't leave you for Aiden.'

Rav grimaces. 'I admit I may not have been as open in how I ended it with her. I didn't exactly ghost her, but over time I started to pull back and eventually we called it quits. Aiden was always interested in Marie, trying to persuade her that he was the better man. It probably did seem like she left me for him, but we were over anyway as far as I was concerned.'

I stare into Rav's face trying to see whether he's being sincere or whether he was hurt when Marie left him. But his expression is inscrutable.

'Why is Aiden trying to put a wedge between us if he thinks he's seduced Marie away from you?'

Rav sighs. 'Aiden and I have known each other since university. I always ranked higher than him in exams and he's always been … jealous, I guess. But rather than limiting our rivalry to studies or business, he's made it a personal mission too, even when it comes to relationships. I don't know why he feels the need to be in competition with me.'

Having grown up with everything I did being compared to Rav, I can understand what it's like to have a nemesis you can never live up to. I could almost feel sympathy for Aiden. But what kind of man tries to cause friction between an engaged couple? If Rav and I had been in a real relationship, the consequences could have been so much worse.

'Don't you think this would have been helpful information to share with me, since you knew she'd be at these events?' I ask.

'I didn't want to risk you calling off our arrangement.'

I furrow my brow, not understanding his logic. 'Why would knowing about Aiden and your ex make me change my mind?'

'Because it could be uncomfortable for you to get embroiled in Aiden's jealousy. Marie's mentioned, on the rare occasions I've seen her, that he's insecure about her feelings for him.'

'Even though they're married.'

'Yes,' he says curtly.

Since Marie feels close enough to Rav to disclose how Aiden feels, a small part of me wonders whether there is something to Aiden's concerns. 'So I'm here as your first line of defence?'

'That's one way of putting it.'

'So this thing about Mr Bamford preferring to sell to a family person is a load of crap?'

'No, it's true. But my history with Aiden and Marie was an added incentive. And another reason Greg added the engagement embellishment. I'm sorry. You have every right to be angry.'

'I'm not angry.' I shake my head emphatically. 'I'm not. But if we want this arrangement to work, we need to be as honest with each other as possible. No secrets. There's no need to hide anything. We should be the only people we're not lying to.' I pause. 'Ironic, huh?'

'Maybe. But I agree. No secrets. I promise I'm not hiding anything else.'

Chapter 10

The following evening, I'm in Bath, meeting up with my three friends – Lucia, Eden and Sophie – for dinner at Lucia's home. One of the things I love about my project-based consultancy work is the freedom it gives me when I'm between projects. I can travel around the country or the world, packing up and moving on to the next place whenever I want. But I always make sure any time I'm in England, I catch up with as many of my good friends as I can fit in. And with these three in particular.

I was with them when I got the news about my dad being in hospital. They refused to let me travel to Sutton Coldfield on the train alone, so Eden took time off work to drive me up then offered to stay with me at the hospital. They checked in with me daily and sent care packages for the family.

At my last catch-up with them, one made a throwaway comment that the best way to get my parents to stop worrying about my single status would be to tell them I had a boyfriend. I couldn't stop running the idea over in my mind until the next time my parents suggested helping me find a match, I finally blurted out I had a boyfriend.

Naturally, I've told the three of them all about Rav and my scheme and, as much as I try to keep the conversation about all our lives, they're only interested in how everything is going with my so-called love life. I've already given them the gist of the events so far but the main thing playing on my mind is my cousin's wedding, which is in a couple of days. And I'm still not sure it's a good idea for Rav to come.

'It's a ridiculous amount of pressure to put on him,' I moan. 'On any relationship. Can you imagine?'

'Maybe it won't be that bad,' Lucia says.

'What are you talking about? Of course, it will be. It's impossible to remain optimistic when I'm literally going to an event where both wedding and marriage are synonymous with settling down.'

'I've never seen you worried like this,' Eden says. 'It's a small wedding, isn't it?'

'Exactly. Very few people. Lots of scrutiny and, you know, wedding vibes in the air.'

'But didn't you say your cousin is marrying a white girl?' Sophie asks.

'Yes.'

'So half the guests won't be from your culture,' Sophie continues. 'There won't be the same pressure as if it was four hundred Indian people.'

'True. There will be fewer people. But that means there will be concentrated attention on us. Me in particular because I'll be one of the only single people there.'

'Well, you won't be single,' Sophie points out.

'Which will make it worse,' Lucia says.

'Sure, as soon as you're at a wedding, everyone thinks they have a right to question your relationship status. When you're single, you get asked when you're going to find someone or whether you want to meet their nephew, or their godchild, or their butcher's best friend's plumber,' Eden says.

'And when you're part of a couple, you're always going to get asked when it's your turn,' Lucia adds.

Eden's Ethiopian-British, Sophie's white British and Lucia's Italian. Their family dynamics are as different from mine as it's possible to get, but it sounds like when it comes to weddings and marriage, some things are universal.

'So you agree, it's a bad idea for Rav to come with me.'

'I don't think you can get out of it now,' Lucia says.

'He could always have an emergency business meeting,' Sophie suggests.

'That's a possibility,' I agree. 'We don't have to give too many details. Rav can simply call my dad and say he got the dates mixed up and has a prior engagement.'

'Although, Annika, your dad might be disappointed he can't come.'

I grimace. What would Dad think if Rav didn't go to this family wedding? Will telling Dad Rav is busy be an acceptable excuse, or will he read something into it that isn't there? He'll think we've argued and start worrying that I'm not on my way to settling down any time soon.

I throw my hands in the air. 'This is a ridiculous situation. Why did I think blurting out to my parents I had a boyfriend was a good idea in the first place?'

'You only have yourself to blame. You wouldn't listen to us when we tried to talk you out of the lie,' Sophie says wryly.

'Of course, I didn't. Why would I take relationship advice from you three?'

'Hey, I'm very happily married, thank you very much,' Eden protests.

'Yeah. But you've been loved up for so long you don't remember what it's like to be single,' Lucia replies.

'Well, you're not single either,' Eden retorts. 'How long have you and Bill been together?'

I say nothing while my friends continue to discuss me and my scheme as if I'm not here. The four of us met in Malawi. Lucia and Eden were working on the same environmental project as I was, although Eden was with a different organisation. Sophie had been working in the same area on an infrastructure project. That had been six years ago. None of them go into the field anymore – Eden stopped after she got married, whereas Lucia and Sophie ended their posts before they met their current partners and haven't travelled for work since they settled down.

Although they all seem happy with their choices, I can't help feeling they've had to make big sacrifices for love.

'Can we talk about something other than my situation now?' I beg. Much as I appreciate hearing their thoughts and getting different perspectives on the matter, I don't want our time together to be all about my life.

'Not yet. This is the most exciting thing that's happened in years,' Eden says. 'I need to live vicariously through you. Putting aside all the intrigue behind your pretence, what's Rav like? Obviously, he's gorgeous based on that picture you sent us. But do you like him?'

'It isn't really important whether I like him.'

'But surely it's easier to pretend to be a couple if you like and fancy each other,' Lucia says.

'Fancy him! I wouldn't go that far.'

'So you're not attracted to him? Honestly? I don't believe you,' Eden says.

'He's attractive,' I admit. 'Handsome. But that's not the same thing as attraction. Which is good because I'm not looking for that kind of thing at the moment.'

'So you don't feel anything when he touches you?' Lucia asks.

'No, that's fine. We've been practising and it seems to be going well,' I reply without thinking.

'Practising?' All three exclaim in unison.

I groan at the realisation I let the truth slip. I hoped to keep our practice sessions a secret because the idea of having to work on being affectionate with a man is still too embarrassing to voice out loud. I now explain the need for PDAs in front of the Bamfords, although we haven't kissed on the mouth yet. I expect we're both hoping the pecks on the cheek will be more than enough.

'This whole scheme feels so odd to me,' Lucia says. 'I still can't believe your parents have changed so much from when we first met. You used to tell us all the time that your family would never expect you to have an arranged marriage, and then suddenly they're offering to find you a match.'

I nod in full agreement. 'To be fair, they accepted Nish's and Shakti's partners without hesitation. So I don't think they're expecting me to have an arranged marriage per se – they're offering to make introductions as one option for me to consider. I guess I should think myself lucky that I have alternatives to making a love match if I need them.' I shake my head. 'What is surprising, though, is how much more they care about me being on my own these days. Oh, I know they've always made comments about being settled but generally they always acted as if they were fine with me being single for the rest of my life, as long as I was happy. Either my dad's illness has made it a much bigger issue for them, or they've been lying to me about how they really feel.'

'We've met your parents,' Eden says, putting her hand on my arm. 'I don't think they would ever lie to you deliberately. But, in my opinion, they always hoped you would want to settle down one day. And the likelihood is that your father's illness did bring that out into the open.'

'Parental expectations,' Lucia says with a huge eyeroll, and we all huff in agreement.

'The part of the scheme I find odd is this business thing of Rav's. Why is it so important for Rav to be a family man?' Sophie says.

I furrow my brow. 'I thought I'd told you it's because it shows Rav is able to make a commitment; that he would look after the company employees as if they're his own family,' I reply even though I still don't fully understand it myself.

'I sort of understand it,' Lucia tells us. 'My parents' business is family-run and they'd always prefer to keep it in the family. Luckily, my brothers are happy to take up the reins.'

'I guess it's the same for the Bamfords, since the company's been in their family for generations,' I say. 'Now that I've met them, I can see how important it is for them to sell their business to the right person, to someone who also shares their values.'

'And doesn't the current owner have any direct family he can leave it to?' Sophie asks.

'That's the real tragedy,' I reply with a frown. 'They had two sons but they lost them in a car accident a couple of years ago. And their sons' wives and children. All at the same time.'

We're all silent for a moment, thinking about the tragic circumstances that have led Rav and I to make this arrangement.

'I hope Mr Bamford finds the right person to buy his company,' Eden says.

'Me too,' I reply. 'Although I also hope that person is Rav.'

'Yes,' Sophie says, 'but, if you want to be more certain, it sounds like you need to amp up the kissing practice.'

And with that, we're back to joking about PDAs and my alleged attraction to Rav.

Chapter 11

After the success of the cocktail evening the previous week and the time I introduced Rav to my family, I'm no longer worried about having to convince people we're a couple. Everyone appears to have bought our act. But that doesn't mean I don't still think Rav attending my cousin's wedding is an incredibly bad idea.

Wedding season never usually bothers me. In fact, I love going to my friends' weddings whenever I'm in the country. I've even happily been a bridesmaid at least nine times. But this year, something has me feeling on edge.

Is it simply because there's pressure now to make my parents believe I'm ready to settle down? I've had no problem going against expectations in the past; my parents may have been concerned or, on occasion, tried to persuade me to change my mind, but once they saw how happy and fulfilled I was regardless of whether it was career, relationships or any aspect of my life, they would always support me. Or so I thought. Maybe since my father's illness, their concerns about my current lifestyle are greater. Or maybe Eden was right – the concerns were always there and they're just more open about it now.

Weddings automatically make people think about romance and forever after. It's almost inevitable that any unmarried couple will be asked when it will be their turn up the aisle in the same way a single person will be asked why they aren't in a relationship. I'm used to that. I expect it.

But this time, my relatives will be the ones asking the questions and, with Rav on my arm, I'm going to be under even greater scrutiny. Even my cousin, who grew up in a town one hundred miles away, has heard of Rav. He's like the poster child for perfection in the wider South Asian community, not just our area.

Luckily, it was only close family and friends of the bride and groom at the registry office wedding service, so Rav didn't need to attend. But now I'm at the reception venue waiting for Rav to join me before we walk down the receiving line.

I'm one hundred per cent certain as soon as we are seated at our table, we're going to be of almost as much interest as the bride and groom, to my relatives at least. Finally getting to see me in a committed, serious relationship.

But I'll deal with it if or when it happens. Right now, I want to celebrate the love of my cousin and his new wife. They look so happy and completely besotted as they stand together greeting their guests.

I'm not entirely sure if I'm just imagining it but people seem to be giving me sympathetic looks. Since Rav isn't here yet, they probably think I've been stood up. That's even worse than Rav being my date to the wedding.

My parents walk up to me, Mum clearly supporting my dad.

'Is everything all right with Rav, Niki?' Mum asks. 'I thought he would be here by now. We should go in soon – we can't hold up them up any longer.'

I glance at my phone, which has been permanently glued to my hands since I arrived at the venue. Still nothing from Rav.

I'm about to call him again, but then I notice my dad's smile widen and hear a flurry behind me.

'I'm so sorry I'm late,' Rav says, putting his hand on my

shoulder. I turn, probably the happiest I've ever been to see him – especially after witnessing my dad's reaction to him. 'Traffic was a nightmare.'

He leans forward to press a kiss to my cheek. I try not to act surprised by the gesture but I pull away, a little embarrassed of the blatant, affectionate gesture in front of my parents. But when I look, they're already heading towards the receiving line.

Rav holds out a hand to me. 'Ready for battle?' he asks, with a grin.

I clasp his hand. 'Loins girded. Let's do this!'

The day passes quickly with the wedding breakfast and after-dinner speeches. Soon the tables are being moved, space is being cleared for the disco, and we're standing waiting for the bride and groom to have their first dance.

I glance around the venue, decorated in a simple ivory and green theme. It looks classy and elegant. I spot Dad sitting at one of the remaining tables, smiling happily at people who come up to him.

Usually, at a party, even where he isn't the host, Dad is the kind of person who goes from group to group, making sure everyone is comfortable and enjoying themselves. Seeing him remain seated is another stark reminder that he isn't back to full strength.

The master of ceremonies announces the arrival of my cousin and his wife, drawing my attention back to them.

As the music starts, I turn to Rav and ask, 'Do you want to dance?'

He shakes his head and raises his hands as if to ward me away. I'm not too surprised by his response. At the social events we used to attend as teenagers, he would always be sitting to the side, surrounded by his groupies, instead of being on the dance floor.

'Come on,' I say. 'You have to dance with your pretend girlfriend.'

'My pretend girlfriend should know that's not going to happen.'

'Well, okay, but don't think you're getting off this lightly. As

103

your pretend girlfriend, it's part of my job description to keep bugging you until you dance with me.'

'Good luck with that,' he replies with a smirk.

Admitting defeat, temporarily, I join my friends on the dance floor, losing myself to the rhythm. After a few fast songs, I return to Rav, who has now seated himself at a table in a back corner.

He smiles and says, 'This is different to most of the weddings I've been to before.'

'In what way?'

'It's very understated.' I bristle at the implication my cousin has put together a cheap ceremony.

'It's elegant,' Rav continues. 'I like it. In many interracial marriages I've been to where one of the couple is desi, they still take a lot of the traditions from the Indian side, I've noticed.'

'Well, Indian weddings can be very vibrant and vivid. Who wouldn't want some of that colour in their ceremony?'

'Your brother's wedding was different as well.'

'Was it?' I don't think Rav's trying to insult anyone, but I can't be sure.

'For an Indian wedding, yes. I think so.'

'What do you mean?'

'For a start, it was only one day, and the bride wasn't wearing mehndi.'

'That's true. Neither Nish nor Kaya is particularly religious, so they didn't want to make a big deal. To be honest—' I shut my mouth.

'What?' Rav asks.

'It's okay. Nothing important.' I was about to be uncharitable and tell him my parents weren't really into the one-upmanship that can sometimes be a part of our community, at least not about showing off wealth by hosting extravagant events. When it comes to boasting about their children's accomplishments, they'll shout it from the rooftops.

'Is this what you'd want your wedding to be like?' Rav asks.

104

I casually glance around the room to make sure nobody could have overheard his question – which would sound strange coming from my supposed-to-be boyfriend. Thankfully, there's nobody close enough to hear.

I shake my head. 'It's not something that will ever be relevant for me.'

'Oh, of course. Because you don't intend to get married.'

'Well, never say never. Perhaps once I've reached retirement age, I'll want to settle down with someone who's also retired and who can travel the world with me.'

He smiles. 'Sometimes I think you don't plan anything, and then other times you surprise with me with the plans you have for the long term.'

I take a sip of wine then shrug. 'It's not really a set plan as such, is it though? It's the only circumstance in which I can see myself saying "I do". What about you? When you get married in …' I scrunch my forehead, trying to remember what he said '… in three years, do you think you'll have a multi-day event?'

'That will depend on my bride. The ceremony doesn't bother me. I'm more interested in the marriage. If my future wife wants a lavish affair, she can have it.'

I nod approvingly. 'You sound like a very amenable husband.'

He raises his glass to toast me. 'I hope you find me a very amenable suitor.'

I grin. 'Absolutely.' I clink my glass against his then glance over to where my parents are standing with my cousin and his wife, who are clearly looking in our direction. I imagine Rav and I, sitting together in the shadows away from other people, are creating an intimate picture for them. There are definite smiles of approval on their faces. 'Thank you for coming. I know this wasn't in our arrangement. You have to let me know if there's something I can do in return.'

'It's fine. There'll inevitably be a few unexpected events we're invited to now we're out in the open.'

'Hopefully, none will be as dire as a family wedding.'

'No, honestly, it isn't that bad.'

'That's because nobody asks you when you're going to be the next one getting married.'

'Of course, they do. Every time I go to a wedding or any event, the aunties and uncles tell me it's time I think about settling down.'

'Really?' I say, knowing I sound incredulous. 'I just assumed that was something that happened to single women. So what do you say to them?'

'I say I agree with them.'

I lean forward. 'And?'

'That's it.'

'You're kidding?'

'No. I get approving nods and smiles and then we change the topic.'

'That's so unfair. If I said I was ready to settle down, even with you here, I bet they'd ask if I wanted to be signed up to matchmaking services or have an introduction through family friends. How come you get off so easily?' I hold my hand up. 'No, it's okay. I know the answer to that.'

We watch the dancing for a few minutes.

'Your brother and sister, and your cousin. They're all love marriages, aren't they?' Rav asks.

I turn to look at him. His expression is wistful. I can't help but feel surprised. When he told me he planned to ask his parents to help find him a bride, I just assumed he was happy for affection to come after the marriage.

'Yeah, they are,' I reply. 'Actually, my parents and both sets of grandparents also married for love. Which makes my parents' sudden offer to find me a match even more bizarre.'

'You mean they expected you would have a love marriage?'

I shrug. 'I guess. I assumed they knew and accepted that I didn't want to get married at all. My dad's health scare has turned everything on its head, which is why we're both here,' I say, raising my hands in a comically exaggerated gesture, aiming for levity. This conversation is suddenly getting more serious than I want it to.

A loud, cheery pop song begins to play, so I excuse myself to join Nish and Kaya on the dance floor. There's no point asking Rav to dance when I already know he'll turn me down.

And I need to put some distance between us. Our arrangement doesn't include sharing personal confidences, and besides trying to act as though we're in love, there's no need for us to get to know each other any better than we already do.

After a couple of disco numbers, the slow songs start to play – I would love to dance but I need a partner. I look over at Rav, who's talking to one of my cousins, hoping he'll take pity on me. He catches my eye, but he shakes his head when I indicate the dance floor.

I expel a breath. I could ask someone else but I'm already anticipating the questions and concerns it could raise. With no choice but to sit this song out, I go over to my dad's table to check on him instead.

Mum is sitting a few tables away, chatting to her friends. Dad hasn't been without company either, with a stream of people coming up to speak to him all evening, so he doesn't need his daughter by his side. But he is the ultimate raconteur and I love hearing his stories, especially ones of the people attending the wedding.

While we're talking, I notice, from the corner of my eye, Rav coming towards our table, but before he can reach us, he's accosted by one of my aunties. I don't go to rescue him – a little, petty payback for not dancing with me.

'Your mum and I are happy that you and Rav are a couple,' Dad says.

'You approve of him then.'

'Of course. We couldn't ask for a better suitor for you.' Dad puts his hand up as if to stop me interrupting him. 'I know that it's probably still too soon to talk about marriage but you've been together a year and you've managed to make your relationship last while you've been away on two projects. Your mother and I are relieved that you've got over this idea that you can't have a relationship or marriage because of your work. We have to admit it did worry us.'

His smile is as strong and sunny as it's always been. I can only offer him a weak one in return. I don't know how to respond to him. I hate deceiving my family but if my arrangement with Rav gives my dad this much pleasure, I find it hard to regret my choice.

We talk a little more until I hear the opening bars of one of my favourite numbers, a slow song. I start to rise then fall back to my seat. There are only couples on the floor and I don't want to draw attention to the fact I'm alone.

'Go on, Annika,' Dad says. 'You love this song. I'll be all right here.'

'It's okay, Dad. I have no one to dance with, unless …' I gesture to the dance floor.

'Oh, not me, Niki. Sorry. But you go.'

I shake my head, trying not to look too disappointed, when suddenly Rav's hand appears in front of me. I don't know why he's changed his mind but I'm not letting the opportunity pass. I take his hand and we go to the dance floor. He puts his arms around my waist and gathers me to him. I guess it makes sense to be this close if we're pretending to be in love. I put my arms around his neck and nestle my head on his chest.

It's strangely comfortable dancing with Rav. My head rests perfectly just below his shoulder. I can breathe in his cologne – it's woodsy and citrusy but there's an underlying note I can't identify, subtle and intoxicating. My eyes widen and my breath catches when I realise the scent is Rav. For a few moments, I am swept away by the romance of the song and his warm, comforting body.

'You know, there's something I've thought of that you can do to return the favour as part of our arrangement,' he says, the word 'arrangement' bringing me back to reality, like a bucket of cold water.

'What's that?' I ask.

'You're going to hate it.'

'I am? Why?'

'Because it's wedding adjacent.'

'What is it?'

'I'm a groomsman at one of my best friend's weddings. As part of the reception, there will be a dance routine.'

'A routine? That sounds amazing.'

'Yeah, it's not my kind of thing, but all the groomsmen are doing it. I can't say no.'

'And you want me to help practise your steps with you?'

'Something like that. The bridal party live in Dubai, so we have to rehearse without them. I've only had one lesson so far, and I was able to have one of the dance instructors as my stand-in partner. But now you're here, maybe you could ...' He tails off.

'You want me to be your stand-in.'

'Yes.'

'What kind of routine?'

'It's a Bollywood-style dance number. I know it's a lot to ask but I—'

'I'm in.'

Chapter 12

The following Friday, I'm standing on one side of a large dance studio, bopping my head to the beat. I've seen videos of extravagant sangeets in films and wedding videos but I've never had the chance to learn any of the moves before.

There are eight other couples in the room. Rav is standing in the centre, talking to a group of men. He grins when he notices me – I don't know whether it's happiness to see me or because I'm bouncing up and down on the heels of my feet as I'm barely able to contain my excitement for the lesson to begin. He walks over to me with a man who looks surprisingly similar.

'Annika, this is Kesh,' Rav introduces his friend. 'He's the groom and the person to blame for us being here today.'

I shake hands with Kesh. 'Oh, lovely to meet you. Congratulations on your wedding.'

'Thank you. It's lovely to meet you too. I've heard a lot about you. Sorry, Rav dragged you into this, but I'm glad he doesn't have an excuse not to turn up.'

'Of course, I'd be here, mate. I wouldn't let you down,' Rav says, clasping Kesh's shoulder. 'Although getting married and deciding on a sangeet as a reason for us to meet up is a little drastic. You could have simply invited me for a drink.'

'What with your busy schedule?' Kesh replies. 'I've already tried that.'

'It's good of Esha to go along with your plan. Only reason I can think of for her saying yes to marrying you.'

I give Rav a curious look. I don't think I've heard that teasing quality in his voice before. I listen, fascinated, as the two of them talk as if they haven't spoken in years rather than the days I know it has likely been. Of course, Rav's relationship with Greg is also easy-going, but there's always an invisible line of respect they need to maintain as business partners. It's nothing like the banter between Rav and Kesh. There's such a strong bond between them – I can understand why Kesh asked Rav to be a part of his groom's party.

I have many friends, but I don't think I'm as close to any of them as Rav is to Kesh. Although I've never missed having a 'best friend', I do wonder what it's like to have someone special like that.

'Talking of punching above your weight,' Kesh says as he turns to include me, making me realise I haven't been following their conversation for the last couple of minutes. 'I can't believe my upright friend is pretending to have a girlfriend. And that anyone would believe this troll could attract someone like you. How in the world did Rav manage to persuade you to be part of his scheme?'

'Believe me, he's the one doing me the favour,' I reply. Rav has already told me Kesh is aware of our arrangement but no one else knows.

Kesh shakes his head. 'It's hilarious. But at least it gives us a chance to meet. I've heard so much about you.'

Curious, I'm about to ask what Rav has said when a clap from the front of the room draws everyone's attention to the instructor. Kesh clasps Rav's shoulder. 'Speak to you later,' he says before going to the front.

I listen as Kesh goes through the events at the sangeet, which will take place the evening before the wedding ceremony. It will start with the bridal party performing a routine aimed at teasing the groomsmen, who will then perform a dance number where they pretend to flirt with the women. Finally, the two parties will dance together, which is where I come as the stand-in for the missing member of the bridal party. I would love to be at the sangeet but that's not likely to happen, so helping Rav with his dance moves is the next best thing.

The instructor outlines some simple moves for the men to try. Rav stares intently and I see him mouth the instructions as he tries to perform the steps. It's like watching wood try to dance. When the instructor calls a break while she takes a small group to the side to work on some moves, I go over to Rav. He has his eyes closed but I know he's trying to work through the steps.

'You need to get out of your head and enjoy the music,' I say to him.

He frowns. 'I don't like dancing.'

'But you do like Kesh.'

'I am trying.'

'Let's practise together,' I offer. 'We can go through the steps here.'

'Here?' He looks around at the others in the room.

'Nobody's going to be watching us,' I reassure him. 'They're all going to be working on their steps too. Come on, we can walk through the moves. We don't need to worry about tempo yet.'

Rav doesn't look eager but he nods in agreement.

We practise some of the routine. I'm happy to ignore any mistakes in an effort to get to the end at least, but instead, we have to stop and start again every time Rav makes a mistake. I can hear him voice his frustration under his breath.

'Come on, Rav. Don't overthink this. It doesn't have to be perfect. No one expects that.'

'I don't want to look like a fool.'

'You won't. Trust me. You'll get it. You can't expect to get everything right from the beginning.'

Rav looks like he disagrees. I shake my head, realising Rav is a

112

perfectionist and the reason he doesn't dance is because he doesn't excel at it. I completely understand not wanting to do things you're no good at, but there can also be a lot of joy in just trying.

'It's supposed to be fun, Rav,' I say, standing opposite him and grabbing hold of his hands. 'Come on, you're moving like there's a pole up your butt. You need to loosen up.' I move his arms in a wave motion. He narrows his eyes; his arms remain heavy and unresponsive.

I expel an irritated breath and drop his hands. 'Copy me,' I order him as I start moving my head from side to side. They'd already done a warm-up at the beginning of the class but Rav seems to have frozen right back up again.

With obvious reluctance, Rav follows my actions as I rotate my head, then shake my hands to loosen my wrists. He even copies me when I extend my arms to the sides and do the worm motion.

'Excellent,' I say, beaming at him. 'Now the whole body.'

I shimmy and wriggle. Rav stands still.

'Shimmy,' I instruct. 'Or wiggle your whole body. Loose limbs.' Although my initial aim was to get Rav to relax, I have to admit I'm having fun seeing whether I can get him to mirror me. 'Let's wiggle, wiggle, wiggle. Wobble, wobble, wobble.'

I notice Rav glance around the room and follow his gaze. Some other people have stopped what they're doing to watch me.

I laugh. 'Come on,' I call over to them. 'Wiggle with me.'

A couple joins me, then a few more. After a while, a few of us are laughing together, calling out dance moves and demonstrating made-up steps. Rav isn't one of them. I pout, disappointed, but I can't force him to relax, so I give up and allow myself to have fun chatting with the other people there.

Because Rav isn't the only groomsman whose dance partner is abroad, I and a couple of the other girls volunteer to rotate between the men to give all of them a chance to practise with a partner.

Occasionally, when I'm dancing with the other men, enjoying

their company, I catch a glimpse of Rav standing at the side, glaring at my partner. I almost stumble at the brooding intensity in his gaze. He's doing a great job of feigning jealousy but I worry slightly that he's taking Greg's suggestion that we always pretend to be a couple when we're together a little too far.

Perhaps I'm enthralled in the banter and flirtation we're acting out through the choreographed steps, or maybe secretly, I love the idea of somebody getting jealous over me, but the next time Rav and I are paired together, the moment he pulls me against him, heat flares and engulfs my entire body.

It's unexpected. I've danced with Rav before, only a few days ago, and my body didn't react this way then.

Whatever the reason, I have to ignore this flash of attraction. It's entirely inappropriate for our situation. And if Rav suspects anything, he could call off our pact. I don't want that to happen – we're in too deep. My parents are convinced by our act, so much so they're suggesting other events for us to attend, and I've not seen my dad look so happy when talking about my future with Rav since he fell ill.

I'll just have to keep my reactions under control.

We're now practising the final group dance. The last steps involve Rav twirling his partner outwards, then as he brings her back in, he dips her. At this point, Rav is supposed to lean in for a kiss but his partner's hand will come up and cover his mouth at the last minute, in old-Bollywood-film style.

The first time we practised the move, I was somewhat over-eager with my gesture and ended up slapping Rav in the mouth. It was incredibly mortifying, even though Rav took it in good humour. All he said was he hoped his real partner didn't pack such a powerful punch. But there was a slight wariness when we were instructed to try that part of the routine again.

The next few attempts are much better but we're still slightly off with the beats and none of the group is in sync with each other. Kudos to the instructors for maintaining a positive outlook because I can't imagine how some of these people, who clearly have two left feet, will master the dance routine in a month.

I'm probably not one to talk, though. I love dancing, moving to the beats and following where the rhythm takes me, but this evening has shown that I'm not so good at following the steps I'm meant to. I'm determined to take this last practice of the evening seriously.

I mentally count the steps as I go into the turn. Rav's arm supports my weight as I bend backwards for the dip. Rav's face moves towards me. Something in his eyes makes my breath catch. I'm momentarily unable to move. I don't bring my hand up in time and Rav's lips make contact with mine.

His expression is as shocked as mine must be, but probably not for the same reasons.

Although it was the most fleeting contact, heat flames across my face and it isn't caused by any embarrassment but by the desire that pulsed through me and the impulse to deepen the kiss.

But any kind of physical attraction will only complicate what is a convenient arrangement – I can't risk everything falling apart now. As I see it, I have two options. And the best and safest option is to ignore my feelings completely.

'I'm sorry,' I say, 'the timing of this part of the routine is so tricky.'

'Nothing to apologise for. It was an accident. And if I'm being honest, I preferred that to the slap in the mouth.'

I snort. 'Well, I'd hope so. I don't think my kisses are that bad.'

He shrugs. 'Perhaps we should redo it just to make sure.'

My jaw drops. Does he mean the kiss or the move? Before I can ask what he meant, Kesh comes over to us.

'Hey, Annika. Thanks for helping out today.'

'I had a great time. This was lots of fun. It's going to be a great routine.'

'Thanks. You know, my bride's family is organising a plane to

115

Dubai. There are some seats available if you're free then. Why don't you join us?'

I blink a couple of times. 'Pardon?'

'Didn't Rav tell you my future wife lives in Dubai?'

'Yes, he mentioned that. But I couldn't impose.'

'Nonsense. As one of my groomsmen, Rav gets a plus-one. But I'd love for you to come as my guest anyway,' Kesh says. I can't interpret the look that passes between him and Rav.

'Are you sure it won't be a problem?' I ask, hardly daring to believe I'll be able to watch the sangeet, not to mention attend a traditional wedding service.

'It's all good, Annika. I'll let Esha's family know. Let me have your passport details soon so I can sort out the ticket. And of course, you're invited to my side's evening wedding reception, which is in August. But that's in Kent so it shouldn't be hard for you to travel. Excuse me,' he says, putting a hand on my shoulder, 'I need to say goodbye to the others. See you at the next practice.'

Rav turns to me with a wry expression. 'I'm sorry, these things seem to escalate, don't they?'

'It's fine.' I gather my belongings and we head towards the door.

'Do you fancy going somewhere for a quick drink or getting something to eat?' Rav asks.

'To be honest, I feel a bit hot and sweaty. I'd rather go back home and eat there.' I widen my eyes when I realise what I just said. 'I meant your place.' During my chat with Kesh, I'd done my best to put the accidental kiss and Rav's cryptic comment out of my mind, but the thoughts come back as fast as the blood rushing to my cheeks.

Rav grins. 'It's your home whenever you're in London.'

'Thanks but I'm not going to impose on you when we don't have an event.'

'It's no trouble. I have a spare room. And I'm not at home that much anyway. It's better than couch surfing. And wouldn't

116

your family think it was odd if they heard you were sleeping on a couch instead of staying with me?'

I chew on my bottom lip. I'm getting used to Rav's thoughtful generosity and what he says makes sense, but I already feel as if the boundaries of our pact are becoming blurred. I'll need to tread carefully.

Instead, I say, 'It's starting to rain. Shall we get a taxi back to yours then?'

Once back at Rav's flat, I take a quick shower while he gets the table ready for dinner.

The aroma of Mexican spices greets me when I walk into the living room. Rav has sensibly ordered our meal while we were in the taxi and it arrived while I was getting dressed.

'I feel like I've both discovered and hurt muscles I've never used before,' I say, stretching out my arms and trying to ease out the twinge in my back. 'It's so frenetic.'

'You looked like you were having fun, though.'

'Oh definitely. I always wanted to take Bollywood dance lessons but never looked into it.'

'Just Bollywood? Not classical Indian dance then?'

'Classical looks so intricate. I'd love to learn something like Kathakali but I don't think I'd have the discipline.'

'You think classical is harder than Bollywood?'

'I don't know for sure but it looks more disciplined. It must take years to become proficient at Kathakali or any other types, whereas Bollywood looks like something you can learn for a dance recital at a wedding.' I raise my eyebrows as I make my point.

As we eat, we talk more about the routines and I offer to work with Rav on the groomsmen group dance. I would love to see the final performance after the hard work we'll be putting in.

'I hope Kesh didn't put you on the spot when he invited me as your plus-one. I'm not expecting to go,' I say.

'I'd love you to, but it's not part of our arrangement, so please don't feel you have to come.'

'To be honest, I would love to go. I've never been to a real big Indian wedding before.'

'You haven't? How's that?'

I shrug. 'I guess I've never been invited to one. Most weddings I go to are like Nish's or Rohit's. One-day events at most.'

'Then you must come. You're missing out if you aren't a guest at a true Rajasthani kind of wedding extravaganza.'

'Are you sure?'

'Yes. It would help me a lot, to be frank. Single man alone at a wedding – you know how that goes. And this one will be full of single Indian ladies.'

'Not every unmarried woman is after you.'

'No, but their parents are.'

I laugh. It's the truth but he sounds hacked off. 'It must be so tough being such a paragon of virtue.'

'The last thing I am is a paragon.'

'Seriously. You must know that all the parents in Sutton Coldfield compared their kids to you and your accomplishments.'

'I guessed as much from how I was treated at the social events.'

'What do you mean?'

'Not many people my age wanted to take the time to get to know *me*.'

I turn to face him. I'd never thought about how Rav must have felt as the yardstick people were measured against. From what I remember of those parties, Rav was always surrounded by a group of people, with girls fawning over him.

'But you had loads of friends,' I say. 'You were always with people.'

He raises his eyebrows as if surprised I would notice that, then shrugs. 'Nobody I felt particularly close to. When I tried chatting with them, either they told me about what they were up to, but not in the way you do when you're engaging in casual conversation, it was more like they were telling me they were better than me, or they didn't give me the time of day.'

'That sucks.'

He gives me a pointed look, and I feel like I'm missing part of our conversation.

'What?' I ask.

'You happened to be one of those people too.'

My mouth falls open as I widen my eyes. I cannot remember him ever trying to talk to me, and I tell him that.

'Loads of times, but one in particular I remember I came to talk to you, I must have been around sixteen. I said hello, and you deliberately turned your back on me.'

'Why?'

'I don't know why you turned your back on me.'

I bite my lip. I'd actually wanted to know why he came over to talk to me in the first place. We weren't friends at the time, so what was the occasion? But it feels a bit graceless to clarify this misunderstanding when the matter is clearly a sensitive one for him. 'That sounds very rude of me, and I'm sorry. I don't remember doing that. But I will admit it's possible I ignored you. Especially if it was around the time of one of your many amazing accomplishments our parents used to boast about.'

He bends his head in embarrassment.

Grinning, I say, 'Go on, tell me what you'd done.'

'I'd just found out I got a full scholarship to my sixth form.'

I burst out laughing. 'Well, that would make sense. It does ring a bell. Nish was disappointed because he didn't get the scholarship. And, now I remember my parents saying I had to start revising for the entrance exam straight away. So on top of my classes and homework, I had to look forward to additional studying. Long story short, Rav Gohil was not someone I wanted to be around.'

'Hopefully, that's changed now.' He winks and leans towards me.

'Well, of course. Now we have this arrangement.'

I watch the humour and happiness fade from his face until it resembles a solemn mask.

'Of course, that's all it is,' he says in a clipped manner before excusing himself.

I stare at him as he leaves the room. What have I said wrong this time?

Chapter 13

A week before the gala weekend, we're meeting at Greg's flat. He's not explicitly told us it's another relationship test, but I can't help feeling like I'm about to get a performance appraisal outlining areas for improvement.

At least things haven't been awkward between me and Rav, which I'd been concerned about since the dance practice. I admit I glanced at him several times during the tube journey here, but there was no frisson of excitement, no tingling feeling even when he caught me staring. The desire I'd experienced while we were dancing must have been a heat-of-the-moment thing. Nothing to truly worry about. Which is a relief. Things are going well with our pact. I don't want anything to ruin it. Particularly not my unpredictable libido.

Greg greets us and leads us to his lounge, where Tinu is waiting. I indicate for her to come over to me while I hang up my coat.

'What are you doing here?' I ask her.

'Greg invited me. Give a second opinion.'

I nod but I can't help that flash of concern again when I see Tinu send Greg a shy but flirtatious smile. I'll have to arrange a time to chat with her properly, to find out what's happening. I thought she was one hundred per cent invested in finding a potential husband – she was taking the singles events and online dating seriously. If she wants a bit of fun before she settles down, I'm not going to interfere as long as she knows what she's getting into.

'Annika.' Greg's voice interrupts my thoughts. 'What can I get you to drink?'

'It depends. What are you making for dinner?' I ask. Both Greg and Rav laugh at my question.

'I hope you weren't expecting a homemade meal,' Greg says.

'Greg doesn't cook,' Rav adds. 'When I said Greg invited us round for dinner, I meant a takeaway or delivery. Perhaps, at the most, something ready-made we can put in the oven. What is it tonight, Greg?'

It's only at that moment I realise there aren't any discernible food smells. The place smells like citrusy furniture polish. Greg holds up several leaflets.

'These are the ones that came through the door, but we can look online if they don't take your fancy.'

'Do you never cook from scratch?' Tinu asks, scrunching her nose.

'Never needed to,' Greg replies with a shrug. And I can't help feeling pleased with the less than impressed expression on Tinu's face.

'Does Rav cook?' Tinu turns to me.

'Ask him.' How weird for her to be filtering questions through me when she can ask directly.

Greg makes the sound of a buzzer. 'Fail. As a couple, you'd be expected to know the answer to that question, Annika.'

'Oh, sorry,' I reply, rolling my eyes. 'I didn't realise the test has already started.'

'We've said you've always got to be acting when you're in public.'

'Fine. Yes, Rav can cook. But since you can't, Greg, shall we order dinner first? Then perhaps I can choose what I'm going to drink.'

As we decide on our food, I notice Tinu and Greg are definitely flirting with each other. I send her several *be careful* looks but she's either ignoring them, or my looks aren't as easy to interpret as I hope, because she's now finding every little excuse to touch Greg. Seriously, Rav and I missed a trick not observing them when we were practising our affection. At the rate they're going, I wouldn't be surprised if Tinu and Greg excuse themselves and disappear into a bedroom.

'How are you feeling about the weekend?' I ask Greg, hoping to interrupt them.

'Fine, although I wish I was able to stay the whole weekend. I'm worried I'll miss something important on Sunday morning.'

'I'm sure you won't,' Rav says, and I get the impression this isn't the first time he's tried to reassure Greg.

'Why won't you be there on Sunday?' Tinu asks.

Greg flashes her a charming smile. 'It's my grandmother's ninetieth birthday. The whole family is meeting for brunch so I'm driving to my parents' after dinner on Saturday night.'

'That's so sweet,' Tinu says. She gives him an adoring smile.

'My grandmother's great. I would love to introduce you one day. I think you'd like her.'

Tinu simpers, but I think Greg was offering more out of pure flirtatiousness than because he has any intention of following through.

'It can't be helped,' I say, more determined than ever to have that chat with Tinu sooner rather than later.

'I know,' Greg replies with a shrug. 'It's difficult being in this kind of situation. Buying Bamfords would be such a vital part of our business growth.' I notice Rav give a quick shake of his head and Greg stops talking.

I narrow my eyes and stare at Rav. What doesn't he want Greg to tell us? Despite how well we've been getting on so far, I'm more aware than ever that we're still playing our parts.

So I guess asking Rav questions about his business plans isn't part of our deal. Part of me gets that. I don't need to know the finer details of his business in order for us to carry out this charade. But, as his girlfriend, wouldn't I need to know more than the vague details he's shared so far?

I huff with annoyance. It's not like me to second-guess myself, even though these circumstances are unique. Am I holding back for no reason? Wouldn't I ask any person more about their work, something they were passionate about, particularly if how I act could have an impact on it? And is the reason I'm not asking Rav to explain because I'm worried about crossing some arbitrary line I've created?

My phone rings. I check the number – a work colleague. I ask Greg if there's somewhere I can take the call in private and he points me to a door that leads to his bedroom.

Earlier in the week, one of the companies I usually consult for contacted me about a problem that had arisen. They wanted me to fly out to help. Because the garden party is coming up, I didn't want to risk going in case I wouldn't be back in time, so I told them I wouldn't be able to go on site but offered to help remotely. Over the last few days, that's what I've been doing – either from my family home or using Rav's home office.

I'm enjoying the troubleshooting aspect of the work – it's a different direction for me and an interesting challenge. I'll probably be helping them out remotely for another week. I wouldn't mind doing some more work like this in the future; I could quite easily be tempted to continue it once things with Dad are better – if only travel was part of the job too. I couldn't be home-based permanently. I have too much wanderlust in me to give it up.

When I return to the others, I see the pizza has arrived. Greg and Tinu have already started eating but Rav waits for me.

'Oh, this smells so good.' I grab a slice and touch it against Rav's slice in a cheers gesture.

'Everything okay with work?' Rav asks. I nod since I've just taken a huge bite. But after the way he's been excluding me from his business problems, I wouldn't be in the mood to share with him even if my mouth wasn't full.

'How are *you* feeling about this weekend?' Greg asks me.

I chew quickly, tilting my head from side to side as I try to empty my mouth. 'I still can't decide whether it will be fun or incredibly intense,' I reply.

'It's an unusual situation, that's for sure,' Rav says, glancing at me. 'I don't like all this uncertainty. It's out of my control.'

That doesn't surprise me. I've already learnt that Rav likes to have everything organised and scheduled in advance. Control is so important to him. In fact, I'm surprised that each time something unexpected crops up to do with our scheme, he agrees without hesitation. I thought he would take time to think through everything first before coming up with a plan that minimised all possible risks.

'I still don't understand why Mr Bamford wouldn't want to take the deal that offers him the most amount of money,' Tinu says.

'It's a private company. The family owns all the shares so they can decide what's of most value to them,' Greg explains.

'It's still bizarre that they've made attendance at their garden party an important part of their decision-making process,' Tinu replies with a shrug. 'Do the employees know that potential buyers will be there?'

Rav and Greg exchange glances. They both look concerned. Rav grimaces. 'I don't know what they've been told. They must know Mr Bamford's retiring but I don't know if they're aware of what's currently happening with the company.'

'They must be worried about their jobs,' I remark.

Greg presses his lips together. 'That's going to be one of the problems with our bid proposal.'

'What do you mean?' I ask.

Rav shakes his head. 'It doesn't matter.'

I tut. 'I'd rather not go into this situation blind. Anything you can share about the business has got to be helpful, don't you think? Wouldn't they expect me to know some of this stuff?'

Rav and Greg exchange glances again. This time Rav doesn't need to shake his head for me to know the answer is still no.

I give up. I don't know how I can persuade him to share what the problem is with me, but I'm not going to waste time worrying about it right now. I guess I just have to take my cues from Rav. A random memory pops into my head of our first dinner and Rav mentioning his suitable bride would be someone whom he could discuss work with. I hope when that time comes he'll be able to open up to her.

Greg claps to get my attention. 'I think the most important aspect of this weekend is making sure you two look like a real couple.'

Tinu rubs her hands together. 'Well, you've already made a great start with Annika's family.'

'And there were no major problems at the cocktail evening. But this weekend will be a different kettle of fish,' Greg says.

I now definitely feel like I'm going to be graded. It's like we're right back at the beginning again in many ways. I'm not sure what we're supposed to be practising today. Like Tinu and Greg said, the last couple of events we've been to have been fine, more than fine, really.

'What more do you think we need to do?' I ask.

'We, I mean you, need to work harder on the physical affection,' Tinu says.

I close my eyes. I should have seen that coming.

'Don't you think we've practised that enough?' Rav says. 'I thought we did a great job at the cocktail evening.'

'I disagree,' says Greg. 'This event is specifically for Mr Bamford and his wife. They are going to be observing us carefully. You don't need to make out in front of them,' he continues, rolling his eyes, 'but I'm sure they'll expect to see you kiss when you think no one's looking.' Greg uses air quote when he says *think*. 'It's only natural for a couple in love to want to, and it will prove to them you love your partner and you're a family man at heart.'

Tinu is nodding in vigorous agreement.

I narrow my eyes. 'So are you saying that you think we need to find a moment where we know Mr and Mrs Bamford are watching us but we have to pretend we don't think they're watching us and then we kiss as if we don't know they're watching us.'

'Exactly,' says Greg.

Rav and I laugh.

'He's serious,' says Tinu.

'Come on,' Greg says, 'you have to take this seriously. Our future depends on this.'

'Greg!' Rav's voice is sharp. 'Don't be overly dramatic,' he adds but I can tell he wasn't happy with what Greg let slip, which means there's some truth to it. The future of their business rests on buying out the company.

I have been so caught up in my need for a pretend suitor I haven't spent enough time thinking about the importance of our arrangement for Rav. I just assumed it was part of his plans for world domination. From what Greg is saying, though, there is a lot more at stake than simply adding some wealth to their portfolio.

I don't know why Rav doesn't want me to know all the details, but I have to respect that for now. So far, Rav has played his part to perfection for me. I'm not going to offer him anything less.

I expel a long breath. 'Okay, let's try again.'

'Do you want Tinu and I to demonstrate what we mean?' Greg asks, putting his arm around Tinu's waist and drawing her closer to him.

'I don't think I've ever wanted to see anything less,' I reply, making a gagging motion.

'Fine,' Tinu says, putting her hand up in defeat. 'But what about pet names for each other.'

Rav and I exchange glances. I don't think either of us are the type to use pet names.

'What about *babe*?' Rav asks me with a cheeky grin.

'Sure, and I'll call you *diddums*.'

'No pet names then,' Tinu says with a sigh. 'How about ring-tones? You should have a specific ringtone for each other.'

'No problem,' I reply, pulling out my phone and configuring Rav's contact.

'I think I have the perfect one for you,' Rav says, pulling out his phone too.

When we've finished, Greg says, 'Okay, Rav. Call Annika.'

'The Imperial March' plays. I look around at the others' stony expressions. Apparently, only I think it's hilarious.

'You're not taking this seriously!' Greg says.

'Fine, I'll change it,' I reply. 'Let's see what Rav's chosen first though.' I call his number.

The melody from a beautiful Bollywood love song begins to play.

I lock eyes with Rav, shaken that he's picked this song for me. His expression almost echoes the lyrics – looking at me like he adores me; like I'm his whole world.

'Excellent, that's exactly what we want from you,' Greg says.

Flustered, I tear my gaze away. Was it really just pretend?

Chapter 14

On Saturday, Rav and I drive into the courtyard of the country club where the Bamfords are hosting their annual company get-together. It's a grand, imposing venue – a former 'gentleman's' home, according to its website.

The events will start with an outdoor picnic and barbecue for families; then we'll be able to check into our rooms for a quick outfit change before the gala in the evening. Only the Bamfords and the potential buyers are staying overnight, so on Sunday, there's going to be a lavish brunch followed by a brief business meeting while the other other-halves and I can treat ourselves to a spa session if we feel so inclined.

We leave our bags in the car and walk straight through the reception foyer to the gardens at the back.

I let out a low whistle. The whole place looks like a scene straight out of *Alice in Wonderland*, but elegant and tasteful, not surreal. There are low tables to one side with food suitable for children. Near those tables are a large bouncy castle and other children's games, including a large draughts board and skipping ropes. To the other side are some wooden lanes for nine-pin bowling. Beyond those, there are croquet hooks in the ground and in the distance are four posts around a square, possibly for a game of rounders.

Mr and Mrs Bamford are standing on the patio surrounded by people I don't recognise but who I presume work for the Bamford business.

'Do you want to go over to speak to them?' I ask.

Rav shakes his head. 'This event is a chance for Mr Bamford to thank his employees. I don't want to get in the way of that. We can find another way to let them know we're here.'

I tilt my head, a little surprised by his answer. 'Okay, do you want to get a drink then find somewhere to sit or we can wander round and see what else they have?'

'Let's wander round. You ... we should enjoy our time this weekend. Don't think of it as a business event.'

'That's a bit difficult to do considering we're here to make a good impression.'

'I'm here to make a good impression. They're not going to be judging you.'

'Of course, they're going to be judging me too. We're a team.'

Rav blinks rapidly then smiles warmly at me.

'What?' I ask, puzzled by his reaction.

'Nothing. Let's go.'

We wander around together looking over the available food and drink, but Rav tells me he wants to check out the make-it-yourself ice cream sundae station. I try to point out that it's meant for the children but he pretends not to hear. Preferring a drink of the alcoholic variety, I head to the table serving pink gin cocktails.

When I glance over at the sundae bar, I find Rav standing behind it while serving a queue of children. He sees me and pulls out his phone. A few seconds later, I receive a text message with the words *Help me*.

I chuckle then go over. He tells me some of the children were under strict instructions by their parents not to make their way to the bar until an adult was around to supervise, so when they saw Rav at the table, they rushed over. Despite his message, Rav seems to be in his element. He makes sure to check with each of the child's parents if it's okay for them to have a sundae. I don't think it's something I would ever have thought to do. Rav's going to make a great father one day. I'm pleased it's part of his life's plan.

Someone from the hotel staff comes over eventually, allowing Rav to leave; otherwise, I'm sure he'd have stayed at the station all day entertaining the children.

While Rav and I are playing a quick game of Connect 4, the Bamfords come over to say hello and to thank us for stepping in with the ice creams.

'We're expecting a children's entertainment company to arrive any minute now,' Mr Bamford explains.

'I hope they come soon,' Mrs Bamford says, looking around at all her guests. 'I want the children to have fun, not feel like they need to be on their best behaviour, and for the adults to enjoy themselves too without having to worry about their kids.'

'Well, I'm sure Annika could come up with some games for them. She was always good at keeping us all entertained while we had to attend the grown-up parties when we were younger,' Rav says.

My head jerks up, my eyes widen, but the Bamfords are smiling in my direction, so I try not to betray how startled I am by Rav's comment.

'It was a long time ago,' I explain, 'and I was practically a child myself, so it was easy to let my imagination run wild.'

'She's being modest, as always,' Rav says, draping his arm around my waist. He then tells them about some of the games I instigated in the past.

I can't believe Rav remembers the details and, after the Bamfords move on, I say that to him.

'Oh, come on,' Rav says, 'you were famous for it. Everyone who came to those events was desperate to join, not wanting to miss out on all the fun.'

'I can't believe you remember something that happened twenty years ago.' I shake my head. 'I was just trying to keep me and

131

Shakti entertained during those interminable evenings but other kids ended up joining us too.' I pause. 'You never did, though.'

'I would have if I thought I was welcome. Once I tried asking but I never got a reply so I assumed I couldn't.'

I gasp. He makes me sound like I was really rude to him when we were younger. 'I don't remember that. I would never have intentionally ignored you.' Anyone could join our games, they never had to ask. 'How old were we?'

'I don't know, maybe eleven or twelve.'

'I'm afraid to ask if it was just the one time?'

'I tried again a few times, but eventually I gave up.'

'I'm so sorry. I was probably too caught up in trying to organise everything and think of the games.'

He waves his hand, brushing away my apology. 'We were kids.'

I head into the hotel to use the bathroom to gather my thoughts. I honestly don't remember any occasions when Rav asked to join our games. I'm mortified if I did ignore him. Even if he has been my lifelong nemesis, I wouldn't deliberately be rude to him. Would I?

As I leave the bathroom, I see Rav standing in the corner with someone. I wasn't expecting him to come inside too. I'm about to walk over to him when I realise he's with Marie. She has one hand on Rav's shoulder and the other is smoothing out his tie. Rav leans forward as if he's about to press a kiss close to Marie's mouth.

Something swirls in the pit of my stomach. What is happening? I hear a sharp intake of breath behind me and I turn to see Aiden looking in Rav and Marie's direction. I turn back to see Rav take Marie's hand off his shoulder and squeeze it. I don't know if they heard Aiden too but Rav leaves without looking around. Marie watches after him so they don't see us.

'I guess now you know. I'm sorry you had to see that,' Aiden says, his expression impassive.

'See what?' I try to keep my tone light and unconcerned. I still don't understand what I just saw and what it means, but there is no way I'm giving Aiden Watson the satisfaction of knowing I feel wrong-footed.

'Rav and Marie together.'

'It's fine. I know they dated.'

'Do you think it's in the past for Rav? He wants my wife and he always has.'

For a moment, I'm stunned and hurt. Rav shouldn't be acting that way with someone else, and definitely not with a married woman. Not when he's supposed to be with me.

But I don't have a right to those feelings. My relationship with Rav is a business arrangement. I've let our time together cause the edges of our agreement to blend so much I'm not sure what my true feelings are anymore.

Whatever the reasons for my initial reaction, I don't have time to delve into it right now. I need to respond to Aiden. I carefully school my expression.

'I'm not sure I appreciate what you're implying here but Rav has no interest in your wife. He's with me now, and he would never do something like that.'

'Rav has always wanted what I have. And he can't get over the fact Marie is with me. Just because you're engaged to him now, you shouldn't be too sure he isn't still after my wife.'

'But I can be sure. Because I know Rav.' And it isn't a lie. I do know intrinsically that Rav wouldn't try to interfere in someone else's marriage. 'Look, I don't know what game you think this is, but I'm not playing. Why are you doing this?'

Aiden doesn't reply. He gives me a look of pure, sneering distaste then walks over to Marie. She beams at him as he approaches, but the happiness fades as Aiden speaks to her. I can't hear what he's saying because it isn't above a whisper but as Marie puts her hand on his arm in a placating manner, Aiden shrugs it off roughly, then stalks away.

I try to find somewhere to go, but there's only lavatories behind me. I watch as Marie crumples, tears falling.

133

My first instinct is to panic and run away. I'm not the best at dealing with unhappy emotions. But I can't leave a sobbing woman on her own. I walk over to her, fumbling in my bag for a tissue packet and handing one to Marie.

'I'm sorry. I'm so sorry,' Marie says.

I pat her on the shoulder, torn between desperately hoping someone else will come along to rescue me and not wanting anyone to see Marie's tears. I grab Marie's hand and pull her into the bathroom I'd exited only minutes before. One of the upsides of being in a luxury venue is that the bathroom has a small dressing area with an armchair and vanity unit.

'I'm sorry,' Marie repeats. 'It must be the hormones.'

'Hormones?' It takes me a moment to twig that Marie probably isn't talking about a bad case of PMS. 'You're pregnant.'

Marie cries harder than before. 'It's the worst time. Aiden is so busy trying to win all these accounts I barely see him anymore. We were going to wait. But it just happened and I've wanted a baby for so long. My career's in a good place. It's the perfect time for me.'

I'm at a loss at how to react appropriately. I don't have the right words to comfort Marie. But my gut instinct says Marie doesn't want words. She wants to talk.

'Then I saw you and Rav and how happy he is. How relaxed. Even today, while Aiden is finding every opportunity to speak to Mr Bamford to impress him, Rav is spending his time with you. The way he looks at you as if you're the only person in the world. He never looked at me that way. And Aiden doesn't anymore.'

'I'm sure that's not …'

'Aiden is just so jealous. He's always competing against Rav. In business. In his personal life. And I'm caught up in it. He won't believe that there's nothing between Rav and me. I don't even want there to be. But it hurt a little when I heard the two of you were engaged.' Marie gives me an apologetic look. 'Rav always told me he wasn't looking for a long-term relationship because he isn't planning to marry until he's thirty-five. Then you came along, and even though he's not thirty-five yet, he's ready to settle. It brought his rejection back to the surface. It was just me he didn't want to marry. What was wrong with me?'

I open my mouth, ready to reassure Marie. But what can I say without admitting the engagement isn't real? I can't risk Rav's business simply to make Marie feel better.

'Sometimes, I think I was rebounding from my break-up with Rav when I met Aiden. The speed we did things, getting married within six months of meeting, was exactly what I needed.' She gives me a tremulous smile. 'Aiden was so different when we first started dating. He bent over backwards to get me anything I wanted. He was so romantic – whisking me away to Paris or Rome for the weekend. I really believed he cherished me. And I needed that, after the way things ended with Rav. But now this pregnancy is making me reassess everything.'

Marie pauses to take in a couple of deep, shuddering breaths. 'Thank you, Annika. I don't know why I've been telling you all this.' I have no idea why Marie has confessed everything to me either. It isn't even as if alcohol had loosened her tongue. I guess Marie has been keeping things bottled up inside, and I just happened to be around when she was ready to spill. 'You're easy to talk to.'

'A lot is going on for you right now. Can I get you anything? Should I find Aiden?'

'Oh no. Please don't bother him. He's already annoyed with me after seeing me talk to Rav. I sometimes think he'd have left me if it wasn't for this business deal.'

I tut. 'It sounds like you and Aiden need to sit down and talk things through. Force him to make time for you. I'm sure things aren't as bad as you say. But if things don't work out the way you hope, you're a strong, capable woman and you'll get through this.'

Marie bursts into tears again. 'You don't know how much I needed to hear that,' she says between sobs.

This is becoming surreal. Why have my words been so impactful? I'm great at cheering my friends up if they've had a bad day and I'm great at offering an ear if they want to vent, but I've always known I'm not their first choice when it comes to deep emotional issues – I presume because my live-for-the-moment, always-look-on-the-bright-side approach isn't always empathetic enough.

I wait until Marie is calmer, then help her fix her make-up to cover up any signs that she's been crying. We walk to the garden together but go our separate ways once we reach the patio.

As soon as I'm alone, I expel a long breath.

'There you are,' Rav says, putting his arm around my waist and pressing a kiss on my temple. 'I was beginning to think you'd abandoned us. Is everything okay?'

'Absolutely fine,' I say. I debate whether I should tell Rav about Marie but decide that there is nothing to be served by telling him. I don't want him to use Marie's situation to gain an advantage in his business dealings. Not that I think Rav would. But he could share the information with Greg, and I have no doubt Greg would use it somehow. 'Where's Mr Bamford?'

'He's joined the softball game.'

I look over to where an informal field had been set up. Greg is already fielding while Aiden and Mr Bamford are standing around waiting to bat. When it's Aiden's turn to bat, he concentrates before striking the ball with full force, sending it straight to the outfield. There's a lot of pent-up emotion behind that strike. After Aiden has run round the posts, he saunters over to Mr Bamford. Even from this distance, I can tell he's boasting about his performance.

'Aren't you going to join?' I ask Rav.

'I'm going over now. But I wanted to make sure you knew where I was first. To check you wouldn't miss me while I'm gone.' Rav winks.

I grin. The attentive boyfriend is starting to feel more like a natural role for Rav.

'Mrs Bamford has been looking for you,' he adds. 'She wants to introduce you to some people.'

'Introduce me?' I ask in surprise.

'That's what she said.'

'I guess I'll go look for her then.'

Rav glances at his watch. 'Shall we meet in reception around four p.m.? I'll bring our luggage, then we'll check into our rooms.'

'Sure. See you then.' Rav presses a kiss to my cheek. It's a careless gesture. One he's done many times since our practice dates. But this time, my nerve endings flare at the touch of his lips, sending sparks through me. My eyes widen as I watch him walk away.

This is unexpected. What does my reaction mean?

I hear Mrs Bamford calling my name, beckoning me over. She's standing with two other women and they are all holding croquet mallets.

'Annika, we were about to play croquet and thought perhaps you could join us. Tracy, here,' Mrs Bamford says, indicating a blonde woman in her early forties, 'her son is about to start his final year of high school and has been thinking about taking a gap year. I told her about your work. Do you mind answering some questions while we play?'

'I'd be happy to.' One of the ladies passes me a mallet and the four of us walk over to where the croquet hoops have been set out.

As we play, I tell the others about my job and the kind of volunteer work available on my projects. I love chatting about what I do and speaking in schools about the opportunities available used to be one of my favourite roles when I was an employee of the company I now consult for on a freelance basis.

Unfortunately, since I've moved to a consultancy position, working on projects for a number of companies, I no longer get to speak to students. I didn't realise how much I missed that until speaking to Tracy.

'I love working for Bamfords,' the other lady, Gail, says with a small smile at Mrs Bamford, 'but I wish I had the chance to travel more.'

I nod. Exactly what I never want to say.

'I'm happy staying right here,' Tracy says. 'Your job sounds fascinating, but I couldn't spend so much time away in a different country. I'd miss England too much. It must be difficult for you and your partner with you being out of the country for such long periods at a time.'

'We make it work.'

'How do you manage when you're on one of your projects?' Tracy asks.

'Technology helps. But Rav's busy with his work so we find the months fly by. And then, when I am in the country, we make the most of our time together.'

'What about when you have children?' Gail asks.

'Come now,' Mrs Bamford interrupts, 'this isn't an interrogation. I'm sure Annika and Rav will sort these things out. Marriage is about compromise after all.'

I give her a tight smile. I'm grateful for the intervention but I'm also so tired of hearing that compromise is necessary for a relationship. It always seems to me that people call it compromise, whereas, in actuality, it involves sacrifice on one or both parts. I get that there has to be give and take in a relationship but I can't help feeling that compromise often ends up with neither party getting a result they're genuinely happy with.

I glance over to the softball area. The game must have finished or be on a break, but Rav, Greg, Mr Bamford, Aiden and others are still standing around deep in conversation.

Although he isn't as tall as Greg or Aiden, there is still something imposing about Rav. Even from a distance, Rav must have felt my stare. He smiles and lifts his hand in a brief wave. I feel a strange pull in my chest.

'Oh, to be young and in love,' Mrs Bamford says with a knowing look. 'You two can't keep your eyes off each other.'

I smile at her words, but as I continue to watch Rav speak with the people around him, I can sense a tension in how he's standing. The smile on his face is strained, quite different from the genuine smile he gave me moments before.

I excuse myself, then walk over to him. I wouldn't usually interrupt a conversation, especially one where business might be discussed, but I feel compelled to support Rav. I put my arm around his waist as I ask the group how their match went. Rav relaxes as he puts his arm around me and presses a kiss to the top of my head.

'It was a good game,' Rav replies. 'Aiden's team won, but it was close.'

'We were discussing business,' Aiden says abruptly. His implication that I'm not welcome is obvious.

'Actually,' Greg says, 'we were beginning to talk about sustainable development. You know about that, don't you, Annika?'

'On a global level,' I reply with a nod.

The other people introduce themselves and ask questions about sustainable development goals. I'm actually in my element, but I try not to monopolise the conversation, often glancing at Rav to make sure my presence isn't annoying him. He looks as proud as any real fiancé would when their partner is being impressive.

By the time the chat starts to dwindle it's around four p.m. Rav and I hold hands as we walk over to the reception. Our joined hands feel natural, comfortable, as if we've been walking this way for years.

'Checking in, please. Rav Gohil and Annika Nath,' he says to the receptionist.

The receptionist goes through some formalities with us and then produces a key.

'Here we go, Mr Gohil,' she says. 'Room 18 for you and Ms Nath.'

Rav stiffens. 'Pardon.'

'Room 18. It's on the third floor. There are lifts at the back of the hall and to the left.'

'I think there must be some misunderstanding,' Rav says, 'we were expecting two rooms.'

'I'm sorry. Mr Bamford only booked one room for you both.'

Chapter 15

'I'm sorry. I never even considered Bamford would assume we'd be sharing a room,' Rav says.

We're both standing in our hotel room, our eyes riveted to the queen bed, taking up most of the space.

'Don't worry,' I say. 'It's a natural assumption to make.'

'I gave reception my number so they'll let me know if a room becomes available straight away.'

'Rav, it's fine.' I rest a hand on his arm. 'I don't think this is some part of your diabolical plot to get me into bed.' Although I probably wouldn't complain if it is.

The thought surprises me but I'm okay with it. Rav is an attractive man and, in any other situation, I wouldn't have a problem sleeping with him. But because it would hugely blur our arrangement, sex with Rav is off the table.

'Perhaps I can stay with Greg at his family's and come back in time for brunch tomorrow.'

I roll my eyes. 'How is that going to make us look if you'd rather go with your business partner than share a room with me?' I have no idea why Rav is making such a big deal. 'I don't mind sharing the bed. It's big enough, but I'd be happy to sleep on the couch if you prefer. It looks pretty comfortable to me. And remember, on some of my old projects, I've slept on camp beds in makeshift tents. The couch is definitely a step up from that.'

I watch as he visibly relaxes. 'If anyone has to take the sofa, it'll be me. But you're right, that is a huge bed. I think we can safely stick to our sides if we share.'

'Perfect. Nothing to worry about, apart from the rest of the plan for the evening.'

The gala consists of a formal dinner followed by dancing. I don't think it's likely the music will be the latest club hits but at the same time, I doubt we're going to be waltzing at the Assembly.

'I was thinking about having a quick nap before the gala begins but …'

'No, that's fine,' Rav says. 'You should rest. I'll go back downstairs. I'm sure there are people still around – it'll be a good opportunity to get to know some more people. I also want to catch up with Greg, so I'll leave you to it.' He glances at his watch. 'The gala starts at six. I'll be back around five-thirty to get ready if that's okay with you.'

'That's fine with me but are you sure you'll only need half an hour to get into your tux?' He gives me a pointed look. I throw my hands up. 'Okay, okay, I guess if you don't need to paint your face on, it doesn't take that long to get ready. I'll see you in a bit.'

Rav walks over to me and takes both my hands in his. 'Thank you for being so great about everything.'

I grin. 'I'm having fun. I would never get the chance to do this in my everyday life. So thank you.'

He chuckles. 'For what?'

'For offering to be my fake boyfriend and coming up with this arrangement.'

'It's working out well, isn't it?'

'We wouldn't expect anything else from one of your plans, would we? I bet they always work out the way you want them to.' My smile falters at his intense expression and I struggle to take in air.

'I hope so.' He bends forward and presses a kiss to my cheek, squeezing my hands. 'Have a good rest.'

Something intense flares through me. Something I recognise but don't want to name. Once Rav has left, I lie in bed, trying to nap but rest doesn't come while the images of Rav from the past couple of days flit through my mind. I have never denied that Rav is a good-looking man. Incredibly handsome, to be frank. But it has always been an objective acknowledgement, like appreciating a fine sculpture.

Now it's more. The appreciation has become attraction. An intense physical attraction I can't deny.

And surely Rav must be feeling it too, from the looks he's giving me.

Or am I seeing something that isn't there? Have the lines between what is real and what is fiction become so blurred?

Finally, giving up on any attempt to take a power nap, I decide to get ready for the gala.

Despite Rav's insistence that he would pay for any clothes I need for any of his business events, I didn't want to waste his money on clothes I'd only wear once. Last week, I messaged some friends asking whether anyone had a formal dress I could borrow and, much to my shock, I was inundated with offers. I never realised my friends had so many occasions to wear such glamorous outfits. One friend had the perfect outfit, so two days ago, I jumped in my dad's car and drove for three hours for an impromptu catch-up.

It was all so last-minute but that's what I love – the freedom to be spontaneous. It's not something I could ever picture for Rav. Knowing him, he'd panic if everything wasn't mapped out.

Despite my growing attraction to him, we are still quite different people. But that's a good thing. Knowing that Rav and I would be completely incompatible if we were a real couple is helpful to keep my focus on our scheme. Even indulging in a physical relationship won't change that.

I pause as I lay the dress across the bed.

I'm not looking for a long-term relationship with its consequent demands and sacrifices. If the past has taught me anything, it's that the perfect relationship doesn't exist for me. That's one of the main reasons if I ever do decide to indulge in a fling, I keep things on a superficial, physical-only level. But in the past, it has been difficult to make sure my partner and I are on the same page about the impossibility of any future together.

That won't be a problem with Rav. We have an arrangement with a specific end date – September, when I go abroad for my next project.

I stare at the bed, imagining us sharing it later that night. If I'm correct and Rav also feels an attraction, will we be able to resist seeing it through to its inevitable conclusion?

Would it be wise if we do? Unless I'm sure of the answer to that question, I'm definitely sleeping on the couch this evening to avoid any temptation.

I'm sitting in front of the dressing table in a hotel robe, putting the final touches to my make-up when Rav knocks on the door. I call out for him to enter.

He looks in my direction then quickly averts his eyes, but I notice a muscle pulse in his jaw. My lips twitch. So I didn't imagine the attraction after all.

'I'm going to have a quick wash,' he says. 'I'll get changed in the bathroom.'

I nod then finish applying my mascara. When I'm satisfied with my make-up, I rise and walk over to the bed, holding the dress up.

Shall I pretend I need help doing the zip up?

I shake my head. I'm being ridiculous. This isn't some seduction routine. And even if it is, minutes before the gala event is due to begin would be the worst time to start anything.

But being alone in the room with Rav isn't a good idea right now. I'm too impulsive and I don't want to risk ruining our arrangement by leaping before I look properly. I need some distance to get a better perspective on what I want.

I finish getting dressed without any need for assistance, then style my hair. Grabbing my clutch purse, I go to knock on the bathroom door.

'Rav, I'm going to the bar. I'll meet you there.'

I can't make out the muffled sounds behind the door, but I can text him when I get downstairs if he didn't hear me.

Once I'm downstairs, I take a glass of bubbly from a waiter then enter the bar where we're gathering before dinner. I spot a few people I've met during the garden party and try to decide who to join when I'm beckoned by a group consisting of some of Bamfords' middle management. The conversation is focused on the personal rather than work, but it gives me a good impression of the company's dynamic and their tight-knit values. I make a mental note to tell Rav my observations.

For a brief moment, I recall Rav telling me one of his criteria for his future wife was someone who shared his values about business so that he could talk to them about it. At the time, I didn't think I was the kind of person who would ever fit in with the kind of corporate world Rav resides in, but this day has shown me I might have been too quick to assume. Our values aren't so different.

Not that I care about Rav's criteria. I'm still not the right person to be his wife. And I don't want to be anyone's wife. I don't know why the thought even occurred to me. But I have got to know Rav better and come to understand that his role as my nemesis was completely created by me. And much to my surprise, Rav is someone I actually quite like.

But as a friend. That's all. Nothing else has changed. One of the ladies I'm talking with gives a low whistle, making me turn round to look at who has entered. My mouth goes dry and I have difficulty swallowing when I see Rav looking like a suave, sophisticated South Asian James Bond.

'Now those men know how to wear a tux,' the lady comments, drawing my attention to the fact that Greg is standing next to Rav. With his height, Greg wouldn't normally be someone a person would miss. But despite Rav's shorter stature, there is something more compelling and commanding about his presence.

'Let me introduce you,' I say, waving Rav and Greg over.

As Rav comes up to me, he wraps an arm around my waist. I quickly glance over at Mr and Mrs Bamford, who are, as I expected, looking in our direction.

Rav leans close to whisper in my ear, 'You look absolutely beautiful.'

The simple words, quietly stated, mean more to me than any lavish compliments he makes out loud.

I swallow, feeling the heat from his fingers spread deep into my soul.

'Wow, Annika, who would have thought you'd scrub up so well,' Greg says, completely breaking the moment.

'I'd say thank you,' I reply, 'if it wasn't for the implication I don't normally look good.'

'Of course, you look great all the time,' Greg says, 'if I'm even allowed to say that in front of your fiancé. But who are these lovely ladies with you?'

I roll my eyes as Greg goes into flirtatious mode.

As Greg tries to charm the ladies, I exchange glances with Rav. He has a small smile playing on his lips. It relaxes his face completely, evoking a surprising tenderness in me. It is the small things that change my perception of Rav from an objectively handsome man to someone I'm now attracted to.

I glance away quickly, clenching the table's rim in front of me. I can deal with a physical attraction, but the way my heart melts in Rav's presence is a concern.

I mentally shake my head. Of course, I'm going to feel something towards Rav. He has saved me by offering to be my fake suitor and has gone out of his way to reassure my parents that there's no need to worry and I will be happy. He's also giving me the chance to experience a luxurious lifestyle with this gala and our upcoming trip to Dubai. I will always be grateful to him.

I try turning my attention back to the conversation but my thoughts are interrupted by Rav once more. Despite acknowledging that I'm attracted to Rav, and wanting to act on it, I still think it's the best decision to ignore my feelings. The safest option for us all.

A person from the hotel stands in the doorway to the bar and shouts, 'Ladies and gentlemen, please could you make your way into the banquet hall where dinner will shortly be served.'

The banquet hall is filled with round tables for eight people. Each table has a large floral centrepiece in either a brick or wooden base. Rav explains to me that they're a nod to the Bamfords' business. Even the colour scheme of purple is from the company's logo.

Rav, Greg and I are led to a table where Marie and Aiden are already seated. I give Marie a quick smile but barely get a glance of acknowledgement in return. I don't know whether Marie feels awkward about her earlier confession or whether she doesn't want to seem too friendly towards me in front of her husband. It doesn't matter. This evening, I'm more interested in the other people standing round the table. There is a man in his early fifties next to a similarly aged woman who is probably his wife – they must be Trevor and Frances Bishop, Rav's other main rivals. They're talking to a middle-aged woman who's on her own.

As we take our chairs, I realise all the people interested in buying Bamfords will be sharing the same table this evening. A bold move on the part of Mr Bamford but awkward for everyone else. Mr and Mrs Bamford have, sensibly in my opinion, seated themselves at a table some distance away from us. Whoever arranged the seating has also organised it so nobody sits next to their business or romantic partner. Unfortunately, that means I'm seated between Aiden Watson and Trevor Bishop. Trevor holds out his hand, introducing himself. After a brief greeting, he turns his attention to Marie who is on his other side.

I take the opportunity to look around the room. None of the other guests, probably all employees, look like they're searching for a specific table. They just take any empty seat. I frown. Is our table the only one that has assigned seating? I'd rather meet and chat with some more of the people who work for Bamfords than eat with my fiancé's main competitors.

Rav's main competitors, I hastily correct myself. Then I get annoyed that I've corrected myself. We've agreed that thinking of ourselves as a real couple will help us with our pretence. I shouldn't be changing that now, simply because I want to sleep with Rav.

Sex never used to be a complicated decision. I either sleep with someone or I don't. If I can separate the issue of sex from our pretend relationship, it shouldn't be an issue with Rav either.

The waiting staff come to our table with our first course, bringing a useful reminder that the direction of my thoughts isn't suitable for the occasion. I concentrate on eating my starter consisting of prawns with sorrel, cucumber and rye bread.

Thank goodness the food's excellent – it's going to be a long meal.

After the first course is cleared, Rav comes over and crouches in the gap next to me. From his concerned expression, I can tell he noticed I was being ignored by the people on either side of me during the meal.

My face tingles as he runs his fingers down the side of my cheek while he whispers his apologies. I'm getting used to this feeling of breathlessness when he's near me, but I try to tell myself I don't like it. I shouldn't.

After we exchange a few words, Rav stands and turns to Trevor. 'I know it's considered bad etiquette to change the seating plan, but I don't get to spend much time with Annika. Would you mind very much if we swap places?'

'I think that would be fine,' Trevor replies. 'I could do with speaking to Helene anyway.' Helene being his colleague, not his wife.

I sense Aiden stiffen when he hears the conversation. 'Hey, Rav, if you're swapping anyway, why don't you sit here? That way, I can sit next to my wife.'

When Aiden catches my eye, he pointedly raises his eyebrows. I get the impression he wants to make sure I noticed Rav was asking to sit next to Marie. At that moment, I work out exactly what Aiden's up to. If Rav knows, then it stands to reason Aiden will also know that Mr Bamford is looking to sell his company to a family man. Aiden's rivalry with Rav is so strong he's prepared to eliminate Rav from the competition by trying to break up his relationship with me.

Unfortunately for Aiden, he has no chance of succeeding. I almost pity him – but if I was in love with Rav, Aiden's attempts to sow jealousy and doubt could have had serious consequences so my pity is fleeting. Is Aiden's insecurity about Rav's former relationship with Marie so intense he'll go to any lengths to win?

In the end, all the men change their seats, taking their glasses and napkins with them but leaving their cutlery. The changes draw attention to our table, and I notice Marie and Frances trying to hide their faces. It also draws the attention of the Bamfords. I hope Rav's offer to change seats to ease my discomfort isn't going to cause a problem with them since, for some reason, they gave us assigned seating.

Sitting on a table with married couples, I pay special attention to all their interactions. Perhaps it's because they've been married several years, but I don't detect any particular tenderness between them.

On the other hand, Rav is doing an amazing job at pretending he's my besotted fiancé. Being particularly concerned that I have enough to eat and drink, covering my hand with his when it's in full view on the table, accidentally rubbing his arm against mine.

After dinner, the music for the evening is instrumental jazz. I fully expect Rav not to offer to dance with me, even though I know now he has serious moves. Once Mr and Mrs Bamford are on the dance floor, the others from our table join them. Rav surprises me by standing up and holding his hand out to me.

We sway in harmony to the sounds of the saxophone. Rav's gaze holds mine as he rests his hand in the curve of my back. Then he presses the lightest kisses against my crown before he leans his head against mine and I forget how to breathe.

I don't want to admit I'm a bundle of taut nerves every time Rav is close to me. I'm not so sure it is because of the awkward situation we're in. Because of our scheme, we are forced to be in close proximity to each other. And we're trying so hard to convince people we're in love, that there is the possibility we could start to believe the act ourselves. To feel an attraction grow between us.

But there isn't anything more than that. There can't be. Just because I fancy Rav, doesn't mean I can act on it – not without risking our current arrangement becoming messy.

It doesn't matter what I tell myself; as the evening progresses, I feel myself enveloped tighter within a sensual web. I don't know whether I'm the one weaving it or Rav is, or we're completely in sync in this as we have been in many things.

I stare into his eyes, fully knowing how this night will end as soon as we're together in our hotel room. Rav is looking over at Mr Bamford. Like me, he must be waiting for the right moment to retire for the evening. No one wants to go to bed before Mr Bamford does because they don't want to miss the opportunity for a conversation or give someone else the chance to catch him alone.

But our impatience is growing and when Mr Bamford signals for another drink, I know he won't be leaving any time soon.

'It's getting late,' Rav says. 'Perhaps we should turn in.'

I nod and we leave the dance floor to return to our table. A man in hotel uniform is standing there.

'Mr Gohil. We've been trying to contact you but there was no answer on your phone. I have excellent news. We've had a last-minute cancellation. A room has opened up. If you follow me, I can check you in and get your luggage transferred.'

Rav gives me a look I can't interpret. Is he relieved? Or is he as disappointed as I am?

Chapter 16

The following Saturday, Rav and I are at my parents' house getting ready for our family party, which is being hosted by my aunt who lives in Derby. That morning, we drove up together since I was in London for Friday evening's final dance practice before Kesh's wedding. After the practice, Kesh invited us out for drinks with the rest of the group. I would have liked to go but Rav refused, explaining he had a lot of work to do. Strange to think the next time I see some of the others will be on the plane to Dubai in five days.

While Rav is upstairs doing some work, I'm helping Mum prepare some snacks in the kitchen. Rav's been grumpy and standoffish since he met me at the train station on Thursday. He barely said a word to me on the drive here – I'm getting a little tired and fed up with his behaviour, particularly since he's also acting that way in front of my parents.

I'm not surprised when my mum asks, 'Is everything okay with Rav? You haven't had a fight have you?'

'No.'

'He isn't upset that we've given him the guest room, is he? Was he expecting to share with you? Dad and I weren't sure what you wanted to do. You can share if you prefer. We don't mind.'

I widen my eyes. Rav and I hadn't even talked about our sleeping arrangements – we both assumed we would be in different rooms – it's the last thing I expected my parents to worry about.

'No, that's fine,' I say quickly. I can't imagine anything more uncomfortable right now than having to share a room with Rav under my parents' roof.

'I know. Why don't I pack these snacks for you and the two of you can go to Sutton Park for some fresh air?'

'Don't you need my help to prepare for the party?'

'I've managed on my own before.'

I automatically bristle at the implication I haven't been around as much to help out at family parties but before I say anything, I catch the concern on Mum's face. If she's worried about us, Dad will be worried too and I'm not going to let anything, least of all Rav, cause any more untoward stress for Dad.

'A walk in the park sounds exactly what we need, Mum. I'll tell Rav.' I give her what I hope is a reassuring smile, then go upstairs.

I don't give Rav any choice in coming for a walk. He continues to be stiff and uncommunicative on our way to the park. He's almost back to the old Rav – the person I imagined him to be when we first came up with this scheme – rather than the person I know now. Or at least the person I thought I knew.

Do I truly know him that well? We're both just putting on an act – not only in front of other people – but perhaps with each other too.

At first, I wonder whether he's behaving this way because of what almost happened between us last weekend.

But we're not talking about that. Neither of us have brought it up since. And it's been a week. We're pretending it didn't happen. I don't have a problem with that. Mainly because it will complicate our arrangement if we put a physical … sexual element to it.

On the night of the gala, after Rav went to check in to his room, I didn't linger downstairs and texted Rav that I was retiring for the evening. We were heading into unknown territory, and I wanted to approach it with a clear head rather than give in to my body's commands. Which was being more vocal in letting me know what it wanted.

And it's one thing thinking about sleeping with Rav when we're dancing close to each other getting lost in the moment, and a completely different proposition in the cold, harsh light of the morning.

It didn't seem to be an issue the morning after the gala, almost as if it never happened. We had breakfast with some other couples and then left. The drive back to Rav's flat was surprisingly not awkward. We talked about the weekend, concentrating on the Watsons and Bishops rather than ourselves. Rav believes he is in with a good chance of getting the deal and is convinced Mrs Bamford absolutely loved me. I have to admit I do get on well with Mrs Bamford – she's like an Indian aunty to me. So if she has any influence on her husband, as we suspect she does, Rav's belief may be justified.

During the car journey, as we spoke about anything but what happened between us after the gala, I couldn't tell whether Rav was avoiding the topic altogether or whether it didn't mean anything and wasn't even on his mind.

It's now hard to reconcile the suave, charming, sexy man I almost went to bed with, with this taciturn person walking next to me in the park.

'You know you can talk to me about your work,' I offer. 'Let me know what's worrying you.'

'It's nothing. It's fine. I shouldn't bother you with it.' He reaches out for my hand and gives it a quick press.

'Maybe I won't be able to offer you advice or solutions but I'm a good listener,' I reply. 'Have you heard something from the Bamfords? Didn't the weekend go as well as you thought?'

'That's part of the problem. Neither Greg nor I know what Bamford is looking for from these events. We know he's from the old school of business – someone who prefers to transact with someone he can trust. And he believes that people in committed relationships are more trustworthy. But beyond that?' Rav shrugs.

'From speaking to Mrs Bamford, it sounds like they were hoping to sell to another family-run company. But as that's not the case, if I had to hazard a guess, I would say the garden party and gala were a chance for them to see who interacted with the employees and is prepared to care for them as if they were their own family.'

Rav purses his lips. 'That's an interesting observation. I'm not sure how any of us fared under those criteria then. It's hard to judge these things in a short span of time.'

'Well, at least you engaged with the people there. From what I saw, Trevor Bishop only spoke to Mr Bamford and the senior team. You spoke to lots of different groups. More importantly, it looked like you fit right in with the people, happy to listen and chat away.'

'*You* did, you mean. I just followed your lead.'

'Then we must make a good team!'

He inclines his head. 'That's true. But, if you're right about what they're looking for, it's all thanks to you that I engaged with them.'

I shrug. 'I like meeting people. I enjoyed myself.'

'You did?' He raises his eyebrows. 'All of it?'

I quickly turn to stare at a nearby bush, realising I'm heading in the dangerous direction of bringing up what happened the night of the gala. To change the subject, I say, 'Can I ask why this is so important to you? What happens if you don't get the deal? Isn't there another company you can buy?'

'Not easily.' He sighs, then tilts his head towards a nearby patch of grass where we lay down a blanket. Once we're seated, he looks at me again, probably weighing up what he wants to tell me. 'It won't be the end of the world if we don't get this deal. But it would be a big step forward for our business strategy. If we don't get it, it will take much longer, maybe even years longer, to reach our goal for growing the business. And there are so many people relying on us. I would hate to let them down.'

'You mean investors?'

'Yes, some. We aren't financed by a big venture capitalist company. We have personal investors who believe in us and what we're doing. But more than that, we have employees who believe in us too. Some even gave up secure jobs to take a chance on the company.' He pulls his knees to his chest, then rests his head on them. 'I'm not sure whether we'll be able to keep all of them on if we don't get this deal now. And if any of our investors want to withdraw their funds, which they can do at any time, it becomes harder.'

Obviously, Rav's finances are none of my business, but having heard about his large city bonuses for many years, I admit I'm a little shocked to hear this.

'I've invested a lot in this company; so has Greg. We've both got savings set aside for retirement, which we can invest if we need it. We just need to make sure we've planned for every eventuality. And not knowing precisely what Mr Bamford is expecting to see in the deal memo creates more uncertainty for everyone. It's not your standard business acquisition, that's for sure.'

It sounds a lot like Greg is right and their future business depends on this deal.

'Why didn't you tell me this before?' I ask.

'I didn't want you to feel under pressure knowing how important this could be.'

I put my hand on his arm. 'I wish you had told me. I could have tried to find out more at the garden party. Perhaps I can help now. Do you want me to contact Mrs Bamford? She suggested we meet up in London for lunch and shopping one day?'

'I couldn't ask you to do that. That's not part of our arrangement.' He leans back on his elbows and raises his face to the sun.

I kneel and gently grip his chin, turning his face so I can look him directly in the eyes. 'Our arrangement is for me to pretend to be your long-term partner. Wouldn't that include taking someone up on their invitation? Anyway, I like Mrs Bamford. I'm happy to arrange to meet her – I wasn't sure whether it would have been appropriate.'

'You're going above and beyond,' he says. My skin burns where he presses his lips on my forehead.

'I'm not,' I reply shakily, putting distance between us. 'But thank you for telling me what's been on your mind. I'll help any way I can.'

sI stare after him as he folds the blanket. After the weekend, I could no longer deny the chemistry between us, even if we seem to be ignoring it. But now, after hearing him open up to me about his work, it feels like we've crossed that emotional bridge too. We're growing closer and with each day, he feels more and more like my friend. I've always shared my worries about my family with him. I think I convinced myself it was because Rav needed to know the details to play the fake-suitor role properly. And I tend to be an over-sharer generally. But that's usually with inconsequential things.

With Rav, I've found myself opening up in a deeper, more meaningful way than I have with anyone for a long time.

I've missed having that someone in my life, to share these things with too.

But what does it mean? I can't be developing deeper feelings for Rav, can I? Once that thought has entered my mind, it won't leave and I find it hard to concentrate, even as I'm going through the motions of helping my family finalise our contributions to the party back at the house.

* * *

By the time we leave for the party a few hours later, Rav is much more relaxed. He offers to drive my parents – although I suspect it's because he likes being in control. They readily agree because the alternative is me driving us, and, as I heard Mum mutter, they'd rather make it to the party in one piece.

The drive to my aunty's house takes about forty-five minutes. I'm so relieved Rav's earlier sullenness has disappeared because I wasn't looking forward to a tense atmosphere in the car. Instead, Rav and my parents talk about topical issues and engage in general chitchat. No questions about our relationship or our future plans. In fact, they speak to Rav as they speak to Kaya and Tony – as an accepted member of the family.

And the guilt makes my stomach churn.

Once we're at my aunty's place, Rav is swept away by the relatives who have been anxiously waiting to meet him. We have to answer pretty much the same questions as when Rav met my family as my boyfriend that first time – on this occasion, we get through without a hitch.

'Your mum tells me you're going to Dubai this week for a wedding,' one of my aunties says to me in Bengali.

'That's right. Rav's best friend's wedding,' I reply in English. My aunty and I have always communicated this way but it's also an easy way to remind my aunty that not everyone in the room understands her, since I know Rav speaks Hindi rather than Bengali.

'When will it be your turn to get married?' she asks. I immediately regret her picking up on my message and speaking in English.

'Aunty,' I say in an admonishing tone, 'don't say that in front of him. We don't want to scare him away.'

Rav looks over at us. 'It would take a lot more than that to scare me away.' I catch my breath at the tenderness in his smile and the warmth of his expression.

It's not real. It's an act for the family. It's not real.

'It's a shame you're going away the week we'll be in London,' Mum says, coming up to us with a plate of pakoras. 'I would have liked to see your flat, Rav.'

'I didn't know you were going to London,' I say to Mum. Why is this the first time I'm hearing of it?

158

'Yes, Dad and I thought we'd treat ourselves to a trip to the West End. We'll go up early, do some shopping, then stay overnight at a hotel.'

I glance at Dad. He's sitting at a table with some of his oldest friends. He looks like he's enjoying himself but like before, he's not up and about – instead people are going over to chat. He's not back to his old self yet.

I want to ask if Mum honestly thinks Dad is up to a trip to London but I know it will spoil the mood. I can wait to ask her when we're alone.

But if they are planning to be in London, I would prefer to be with them so I can make sure my dad's okay and not getting too tired. 'Can't you go another week, sometime when I'm around?' I ask.

'I would love it if you came to my place,' Rav adds, which wasn't my intention. We've already agreed to enough family and business events, so I would have thought he'd want to limit the situations we'd have to carry out this pretence.

'A friend had a ticket she wasn't using,' Mum explains. 'We thought it was a shame to pass up the chance to see a play. Your dad and I don't go out very often.'

My parents have never seen a play – not while I've been alive anyway. I can't help but think there is something more behind this visit to London. I really hope it's not some part of a bucket list they're trying to complete before they die.

'You're welcome to stay at my home while we're in Dubai,' Rav says. 'I can leave my key with the concierge.'

'That's kind of you, Rav,' Mum replies. 'We've already booked a hotel. It's part of the experience, isn't it?' She puts her hand on his head before moving to the next group.

I watch her, still completely unconvinced my parents decided on a whim to go to the theatre. Why are they keeping secrets from us? I look over to Nish and Shakti. Do they know what's happening?

Rav comes to stand next to me and gives my hand a gentle squeeze. 'Is everything all right?' he asks.

I blink to centre myself. 'Everything's fine.'

'You're looking pensive. What's on your mind?'

I shrug. 'Just thinking about my parents' impromptu trip this week. They could have waited until we're back and around.'

'Would you prefer to cancel Dubai?'

I look at him in surprise. Wouldn't he mind if I didn't go to his friend's wedding? 'No. I'm looking forward to it. If there's something more to my parents' trip, it doesn't look like they're going to tell me, so there doesn't seem much point staying home.'

Rav turns me to him and lifts my face so he can look into my eyes.

'You know your parents, so I'm not going to try telling you there's nothing to worry about. I'm sure your parents have a good reason for whatever they're doing and will tell you everything when it's time for you to know. You can always tell me how you're feeling – share any concerns with me.'

Tears come to my eyes at his words. Rav knows exactly what I need to hear. He's more supportive than any real boyfriend of mine has ever been.

It's not real. This will end soon. He's just pretending.

I need the reminder more than ever.

Chapter 17

A week later, Rav and I are finally in Dubai at the hotel we're staying at for Kesh's wedding.

The wedding celebrations for the majority of the guests will begin with the sangeet the following evening. But this evening there's a small reception for any of the wedding guests staying at the hotel. Although we took a morning flight, we didn't get into Dubai until the early evening – all we have time to do is check in and settle into our rooms beforehand. Rav and I have separate rooms, of course. Rav's staying in a suite for the groomsmen. I'll be sharing a room with one of the other wedding guests.

The room we have is huge, with two queen-sized beds. We even have views over the ocean and of the Burj Al Arab. I thought the country club rooms were opulent but this is definitely, by far, the most luxurious place I've ever stayed at.

I'm hanging up my outfits for the various wedding events when there's a knock at the door. I open it to find a young woman, probably in her early twenties. She tells me she's my roommate, but she didn't want to use her key in case I was otherwise occupied.

I laugh. 'No, Rav's upstairs with the other groomsmen. How do you know the bride and groom?'

'My boyfriend is the bride's cousin. His real cousin. Their parents are sisters. I'm Kelly, by the way,' she says, holding out her hand.

'Annika,' I say, shaking her hand.

'Is that your legal name or your daknam?'

My lips quirk, amused that Kelly knows about a daknam.

'It's my real name. I never had a daknam. My parents call me Niki, but that's part of my real name. Does your boyfriend have a daknam then?'

'Yes. It's Chotu. His legal name is Jeetraj, but I think his daknam is so cute I use it instead. I'm so excited about this wedding,' she continues as she begins to unpack. 'It's my first one. I've bought so many new outfits, and I've been researching what everything means. I find your culture so fascinating.'

'That's nice,' I reply somewhat weakly.

After a few seconds of unpacking, Kelly tilts her head. 'Did I hear you say Rav? Is your boyfriend's name, Rav?'

'That's right.'

'No way! Not Rav Gohil?'

'Yes, do you know him?'

'I know of him. Chotu has mentioned him. He hasn't met Rav but he's heard so much about him, of all his accomplishments. He really admires Rav. Looks up to him. He's dying to meet him while we're at the wedding. Chotu wants to go into investment finance as well.'

'How has he heard of Rav?'

'From Kesh, or from his cousin Esha I should say. Kesh is proud of Rav.'

I know Rav is well known within our local community – he's often the topic of many conversations among family and friends – but it still surprises me how word gets around. Though by now, when it comes to Rav, I shouldn't feel too surprised anymore.

'What's Rav like?' Kelly asks, sitting at the foot of her bed.

'Like any other man. Pulls on trousers, et cetera.'

162

She waves my comment away. 'Come on. You must be so happy. I bet you feel like the luckiest woman in the world bagging Rav.'

My smile falters. I want to tell her that *bagging* Rav isn't what makes me lucky. I want to make it clear I don't need a man or anyone else to make me happy. That Rav isn't some prize to be won. But I don't. Because I know she doesn't mean anything by it. And she doesn't need to know where I stand when it comes to relationships.

Instead, I offer to introduce her boyfriend to Rav later at the reception – she jumps at the opportunity, texting her boyfriend immediately. I wait for her to freshen up before we head down.

The sun has completely set when I walk out onto the large balcony bar where I agreed to meet Rav. Beyond a couple of texts checking if I was okay and settling into my room with no issues, I haven't heard from him since we checked in. I expect groomsmen's duties will keep him busy for the next couple of days.

Rav is already there, standing with some friends next to the railing. He's wearing a light, cotton kurta that moulds tightly to his broad shoulders. A slight breeze plays with his hair, which is not gelled back this evening. Subdued lighting from the moon and lamps in the bar casts a shadow over him, emphasising his strong features. I catch my breath at the utter perfection that he is.

When he spots me across the room, his mouth widens and his eyes, his whole face, lights up as if I'm the best thing he's ever seen.

And oh, for a second, I wish the look was real.

My eyes widen at that thought. It makes no sense. I sat next to the man for almost eight hours on the plane and didn't experience this reaction. I'm probably just caught up in how romantic everything feels while being at a destination wedding.

'Oh, is that Rav?' Kelly asks when she notices the direction of my gaze.

I take her and her boyfriend, who has joined us, to introduce them to Rav. For my peace of mind and to prevent any more untoward thoughts about Rav and me, I decide it's best if we stay with groups of people.

Kesh comes over to me while Rav is still chatting with Kelly and Jeetraj. He draws me away from the others.

'While I have a chance, I wanted to say thank you for dragging Rav to the dance rehearsals,' Kesh says. 'He would have found some excuse not to come if you weren't there.'

'I'm sure that's not true,' I protest. 'Rav would never let you down.'

'Oh, I know he would have practised the dance on his own in private but having him keep joining us at the rehearsals was unexpected. It's been great spending time with him again. Lately he's been so wrapped up in work.'

'I'm glad too. And thank you again for inviting me here. It's an amazing venue.'

Kesh nods. 'You're good for Rav. He's been waiting for someone like you.'

My smile falters. 'Kesh, you know this isn't real.'

'He talks about you a lot. How pleased he is with the way things are going. How proud he is of you. Perhaps it doesn't all have to be pretend.' Kesh gives me a knowing look, then lightly touches my arm before moving to greet other guests.

I'm so confused by Kesh's words. Has Rav indicated to Kesh he wants this thing between us to be real? And what? Does he want a real relationship with me, or is he hoping we can have an affair? I don't know what to think. All I know is that I need space to process what this means. I excuse myself from the group, pleading tiredness from the long day of travel. Rav's expression makes it clear he doesn't quite believe me. He also excuses himself and puts a hand in the small of my back as we leave the reception.

'Is everything okay?' he asks. He's frowning, which makes me realise it's the first time this evening I've seen him look anything other than relaxed and peaceful. And I've caused it.

'Everything is fine,' I say, reaching up to cup the side of his face in my hand. 'I just know it's going to be a hectic couple of days, and I need to pace myself.'

He grins. 'Okay. Goodnight. Sleep well. I'll see you tomorrow.' He presses a kiss into my palm.

I swallow. *This is just pretend,* I repeat to myself. *It's part of the pretence.*

But I know something's different between us.

* * *

The next morning, I don't see Rav at breakfast. He's already busy with the other groomsmen and the bridal party, who are going through the final arrangements for the wedding festivities. After that, they'll be rehearsing their performances for the sangeet. Although I would love to watch Rav practise his moves, the bride's father has organised a minivan to take the guests who are not involved in the ceremonies on a tour of Dubai.

Despite travelling a lot, I have never been to the United Arab Emirates before, so I'm looking forward to exploring the area.

After we return to the hotel from the tour, I spend a few hours lying by the pool and relaxing in the sun before the evening's festivities begin. Part of me wishes Rav could be here too, although I'm sure it's the idea of seeing Rav in his swimming trunks that mostly appeals to me.

At least how I feel doesn't go any deeper than physical attraction – I'm not suddenly falling in love with Rav. Now that would be a cause for concern.

After a couple of hours luxuriating by the pool, I return to my hotel room to prepare for the sangeet. The room's empty. I haven't seen Kelly since we returned from the tour.

After getting dressed, I go down to the large ballroom where the sangeet will be. There is a raised platform where the musicians are already seated, playing tunes to welcome the guests. In front of the platform is a wooden area that has been set up as the dance floor or performance area. To the left and right of the dance area are several round tables – a glittering sea of silvers, reds and golds. In the middle of the room are several rugs with larges cushions strewn over them for guests to lie against.

Although the room is already beginning to fill up, I can't see anyone I recognise but I know that Rav and the other groomsmen will arrive shortly before the bride and groom and will be seated near the front so they can have easy access to the floor when the time comes for their performance.

I find my seat at one of the tables, a bit further back, and introduce myself to the others who are already there. Soon we're chatting away until a loud horn signals the arrival of the wedding parties.

The performances are wonderful – sharing a mashup of cultures. The whole room watches, claps and sings along. Some guests even stand near the table dancing to routines they recognise. There is a buffet banquet laid out at the back of the ballroom but we constantly have waitstaff coming up to our tables, offering us canapés and making sure our glasses remain full.

About two hours into the sangeet, we're watching a classical dance performance. At the end, the lead dancer walks over to the bride and coaxes her onto the dance floor. The bride invites her friends.

I move to one of the rugs nearer the front to get a better view. I know Rav's dance will be soon. The bridal party's routine is flawless. When their dance ends, the ladies tease the groomsmen mocking their dance movements, which signals it's the turn for the groom's party to take to the floor.

Rav takes his position, looking stiff and nervous. I will him to relax. He has natural rhythm, and if he can stop thinking about being perfect and just enjoy himself, I'm sure everything will be fine.

He looks over to the table where I was sitting. He frowns then looks around the room, his face relaxing when he spots me on the cushions. I beam at him and do a little shimmy giving him the thumbs-up sign. He grins and wiggles his shoulders to relax them.

I can't take my eyes off him. I knew he would be good but he dances like poetry.

At the end of their dance, several people around the room stand to applaud. I only make it as far as kneeling but my appreciation is just as loud. The ladies sashay back onto the floor, and the performance I know step for step is about to begin.

My eyes narrow as I watch the lady partnered with Rav. I remember the steps and I'm absolutely sure she doesn't have to touch him that often in the routine. And running her hand down his chest seems a little unnecessary to me. The final steps begin and Rav dips the lady on cue. This is when she's supposed to bring her hand up to cover his mouth. Instead, she grasps onto his forearm. I hold my breath waiting for Rav's lips to meet hers, but he halts seconds before.

I close my eyes in relief.

I'm not jealous about Rav dancing with another woman, am I? I can't be. I don't even want to think about what this could mean.

The next performer is a classical musical act. I feel sorry for them though, as not many of the guests are paying attention, still swarmed around Rav and the others, congratulating them. The sitar player tunes up her instrument, giving the universal sign for people to take their seats.

The sangeet will go on for another couple of hours but I don't expect to stay for all of it. If there's anything I do know about an Indian wedding, it's that I'm going to need a lot of energy if I want to last through the following day. I'm already exhausted from this evening, and I wasn't even participating in it.

Rav throws himself onto the cushion next to me. I fling my arms around him.

'You were amazing,' I say. 'I told you, you have moves.'

'I'm just relieved it's over,' he replies, returning my hug. 'Have you enjoyed yourself?'

'Of course. Were you able to?'

'Yes. But it's warm here. Do you want to go for a walk outside?' he asks, then stands up.

I really should refuse and go upstairs to sleep. Instead, I say, 'Sure' and hold out my hand for Rav to help me up.

We walk from the hotel to the private beach along a path illuminated by lamps on small posts at regular intervals. Once we leave the path, the only light guiding us is from the moon.

As we walk, we talk about the day – Rav wants to know what I've been up to and how I found the tour.

I stand at the water's edge and inhale deeply. 'Thank you for letting me come here with you.'

'I'm happy you're here and that you're having a good time.'

'Of course, why wouldn't I? I'm not difficult to please.'

He shrugs one shoulder. 'Well, I don't know.'

'What does that mean?' My voice rises in shock.

'To be honest—' He breaks off.

'What?' I ask, pumping his arm as if that will get information out of him faster.

'Well, you used to intimidate me a little?'

'What?' That was the last thing I expected Rav to say. Rav was a paragon. 'How could *I* intimidate *you*?'

'If I remember correctly, one of the last times I saw you before Nish's wedding was at a doctors' social event. You were around eighteen at the time and I wanted to talk to you but was unsure whether I should approach you.'

'Why?' I'm not sure whether I'm asking why he found me intimidating or why he wanted to talk to me. But in some ways, I'm desperate to know the answer to both.

'Watching you handle yourself around all the people asking questions about your career and future, you looked so assured. Like you had your life figured out. It was refreshing for me. You didn't care about anyone's expectations or what people thought. You wanted to do something you were passionate about and that was that.'

Funny, the impression I gave was so far from the truth, although I do admit, 'I was probably a big know-it-all at that age.'

'That's not what I mean. In the end, I did try talking to you. Do you remember?'

I narrow my eyes as I cast my mind back to the party Rav must be talking about. 'Vaguely. You said something about your degree and I thought you were really arrogant.'

'Yeah, I tried to impress you with my qualifications and it backfired completely. You didn't have the time of day for me.'

I laugh, then pause, arrested by what he just said. 'Wait a minute. Impress me. Backfired. What do you mean?'

'I told you. I wanted to get to know you. You were intriguing and you're beautiful. I've been wanting to get to know you for some time now.'

I'm reeling from what he's said. Who would have thought Rav, my childhood nemesis, was interested in *me*. I never would have guessed. 'Why didn't you try any other time?'

'I did. At Nish's wedding.'

'Wait, I was the one who came to speak to you but you practically dismissed me.'

His lips quirk. 'That's not how I remember it. We'd only started chatting when someone interrupted us. I spoke to them as briefly as I could but when I turned back to you, you'd already begun walking away to join another group.'

'That someone being your girlfriend,' I say with a pointed look. 'It would have been rude of me to have stayed when she wanted to speak privately with you.'

'I didn't have a girlfriend at that time.'

I try to clear my head. I'm sure my family mentioned his girlfriend. It was many years ago, though. 'I can't believe you remember all this.'

'You are an unforgettable woman.'

I suddenly recall Rav telling the Bamfords at the cocktail evening it was at my brother's wedding when his view of me changed. Could he possibly have been telling the truth? At the time, I presumed it was quick thinking. I'm not sure I'm ready to continue that line of thought yet so I redirect our conversation. 'Well, you managed to forget me by the time we met at the hotel last March.'

'No, I didn't.' He gives me an amused look.

'Of course, you did. You thought I was Shakti.'

'I knew who you were. I just pretended not to.'

I laugh in surprise. 'Why?'

'I don't know. It was silly. I couldn't believe it when I saw you in that hotel bar. And you spoke to me!' He places his hand on his chest as if he was star struck.

The words he's saying to me don't feel real. It sounds like he's been interested in me for a while. This is so surreal. Why didn't he say something before? I wonder how I would have reacted if he had – would I have even given him the time of the day? Probably not, I have to admit. I'd cast him in the role of nemesis for too long.

Now though, having got to know Rav better, I can see I was being so prejudiced and judgemental. Perhaps everything happens for a reason. Maybe we weren't friends when we were younger because we were destined to be in each other's lives at this exact point in time. Like fate, almost? I scoff at how fanciful I'm being.

I stare at him, watching the shadows play across his face. He is so beautiful. I run my tongue across my lips.

The humour leaves his face and he takes a step closer to me. The urge to move towards him is strong. With the moonlight, and the balmy night, combined with what he's just revealed, the whole atmosphere is beginning to feel a little too romantic for my comfort.

I step back. 'It's getting late. We should get back.'

He sighs deeply. 'Of course.'

We're silent on the way back. Does Rav's admission mean there was something more behind his proposal to act as my fake boyfriend? A thrill goes through my body at that thought. But it also scares me – I'm worried about what it signifies. For now, I decide it's best to put this conversation to the back of my mind even though there are so many questions I want to ask.

I want to spend the night with Rav, but that isn't a good idea right now when my thoughts are so confused. It's not like I haven't resisted attraction before, where I know it could never lead anywhere. I can this time too.

It's not like I have a choice.

Chapter 18

The following morning my alarm goes off at eight o'clock. After the previous night's festivities, I should have been able to sleep for a week. But once I got into bed, my mind kept running wild, replaying last night's conversation.

I hear Kelly bustling around getting ready. I'm deliciously exhausted but I reluctantly throw off my duvet cover. The baraat begins at ten so there's no time to waste.

I've chosen to wear a sari even though I'm no expert at getting them right. For my first attempt, not only do I wind the cloth around my waist too tightly for me to move easily, I also make the rookie error of draping the sari *before* I've put my heels on. My next attempt isn't much better since I completely mess up the size of the pleats making my pallu look wrong. I'm tempted to give up and wear the same anarkali suit I wore the previous evening when Kelly comes to my aid. Apparently, she's spent days watching videos on how to wear a sari correctly.

By the time we get to the driveway, at half past nine, guests are already lined up waiting for the groom's procession. The driveway is a rainbow of bright fashion with ladies dressed in various saris, lehengas, salwar kameez or anarkali suits. I fleetingly observe that none of the female guests appear to be dressed in customarily Western clothes, although plenty of the men are wearing suits.

Suddenly excitement sweeps through the crowd, and I can hear the distant drumbeats signalling the procession is starting to make its way down.

A group of the groom's family and friends are singing and dancing next to the groom, who is riding on a white horse. This is a tradition that I've heard so much about but only experienced through videos or films. But these never show the true joy, celebration and chaos of the occasion.

I spot Rav amongst the dancers – he appears relaxed and like he's enjoying himself. He needed this weekend away to rest and recharge from the stresses of his work. It looks like it's done him a world of good. Annoyingly, there are no visible signs that our late-night conversation prevented him from getting a good night's sleep.

As the procession gets nearer, Rav sees me amongst the crowd and gyrates his way over to me. He lifts my hand and encourages me to do a twirl under his arm.

As the groom approaches the outdoor mandap, Rav and the other family members take turns hugging him before joining the crowds gathered to watch the bride come out to greet her future husband. Only the sounds of a conch being blown can be heard as the bride and groom exchange flower garlands. Then the crowd erupts with cheers.

The ceremony is conducted in Sanskrit but because there are guests attending from around the world, the assistant priest gives a brief description at each stage, which is an unexpected delight for me since I've never had the individual elements explained to me before.

I can't help feeling a pang of loss at the idea that I will never have this experience. Not so much the religious rites or a large traditional Indian multi-day event but having the person I love wait for me, the simple exchange of vows, making the commitment to spend the rest of our lives together.

I glance at Rav, standing next to me, pride and joy written on his face as he watches his friend. And briefly, I imagine him standing at the front of a room, waiting for me to walk up the aisle.

But I decided a long time ago that this couldn't be mine unless I was willing to sacrifice a big part of myself.

I always knew attending weddings would be a dangerous idea. They can often make people's thoughts move in weird directions. That's the only explanation I have for why I'm starting to think of Rav as someone more than just my co-partner in our arrangement.

It's just because we're spending so much time together pretending we're in love that it's starting to feel real. It's only proximity. I know this. I have to keep repeating it to myself like a mantra.

Sure, Rav isn't the person I thought he was. He's not as strait-laced as I expected. But our values aren't aligned. And even if we shared the same values, what kind of future would we have with me abroad for half the year?

There is no need to go there. I know relationships aren't meant for me. That's the whole point of us entering into this arrangement in the first place. I need to stop thinking about Rav and any feelings I may or may not have for him, real or otherwise. It can only lead to heartbreak.

But the attraction between us is strong; it's palpable. Is it really only because we've spent so much time together that we feel this way? I don't know if I want that to be true. I watch Rav as he's observing his friend with his new wife.

No, the attraction exists. I'm certain of it. Perhaps it would never have developed without our fake arrangement. But that doesn't stop it from being any less real.

The only question now is what I should do about it.

At the end of the day, Rav wants the same kind of wedding and marriage as his friend. He wants a family. He's made plans for this. Our arrangement isn't going to change that. Not even if we give in to this attraction between us.

But the sound of a shehnai draws my attention back to the couple who are now taking the seven turns around the fire in the middle of the mandap, I realise it isn't the time or place to be thinking about this.

After the ceremony, the guests move to the banquet hall while photos are taken outside. As we walk to our table, Rav stops me and turns me towards him.

'I never got a chance to tell you how beautiful you look today.'

I feel the heat rise in my cheeks. I'm used to Rav complimenting me, but usually, they're part of our deception. This time I know he truly means it.

'You look quite dashing yourself,' I reply. He's wearing a deep blue raw silk sherwani with gold motifs on the collars and the cuffs. The aristocratic look heightens his masculinity.

The temptation to fling myself into his arms and see where the passion takes us is strong, but the occasion stops me from acting on my impulses.

The thing is, I reflect after we've finished eating our lavish meal and are being forced to listen to too many, too long wedding speeches, attraction and passion should be instinctive. It shouldn't need the amount of introspection I've been doing. If the two of us had met in different circumstances, I'm sure we'd already be indulging in a no-strings affair.

After the meal, there is an hour break before the evening disco. I return to my room to change out of my sari into trousers and a kurta, which will be more comfortable for dancing. Nothing about my clothes says *I'm here to seduce you* – I'm not sure whether that's a good or bad thing.

Only twenty-four hours ago, I'd convinced myself sleeping with Rav would be a monumentally bad idea. Now I've done a complete one-eighty. It's as if I'm too weak to resist Rav's pull. But then again, it's also possible Rav could be having second thoughts and already regretting our flirtation.

Here are the things I know:

1) Rav and I are attracted to each other.
2) Neither of us is looking for a relationship at this stage in our lives.
3) I would like to have sex with Rav.
4) Sex doesn't have to be complicated.
5) Our arrangement makes things complicated.
6) Both will be over in a month anyway.
7) I'm sure I can keep the sex and our arrangement separate.
8) There's only one way to find out if Rav can.
9) Dubai is definitely not the right place to find out.
10) With this list making – Rav is rubbing off on me more than he should.

I chuckle at that last one. If Rav was trying to make this decision, he wouldn't make a simple list. I can imagine him creating a spreadsheet balancing all the pros against the cons, which he would then sort into categories with weighted variables. Only a few weeks ago, that version of Rav would have irritated me. Now it's endearing.

There wouldn't be any point in me making a pro and con list, though – I'd load it heavily in favour of the pros of having sex with Rav.

After the break, I go downstairs to the ballroom where the disco has started. Rav is at the bar talking to someone I don't recognise. Not wanting to disturb him, I see some of the people I've spoken to previously sitting at one of the tables and go over to join them.

By the time Rav comes over, there are no available seats. He stands behind my chair, resting his hands on my shoulder.

'Would you like me to get you something to drink?' he whispers. My stomach clenches at the warmth of his breath.

'I'm good with water,' I reply, indicating the bottles already on the table.

Once the bride and groom have had their first dance, others join. I stick to dancing as part of a group. I already know my body likes dancing up close and personal with Rav a little too much.

And the one thing I am certain of is that *nothing* can happen while we're in Dubai.

After an hour, I take my seat again, using a napkin for a fan. This time when Rav suggests we take a walk along the beach, I refuse. I don't want to risk getting swept up in romance – when or if we have an affair, it needs to begin with a clear head.

I suggest instead that we wander through the hotel – there are still many of its facilities and grounds I haven't had a chance to see yet. As we walk, we chat about the wedding and the last event for the Bamfords. There is still no more information about what that will be, but Rav doesn't seem worried.

We stop briefly at a gift shop, which is still open. I look around, trying to find something for my nephews and nieces. I already bought souvenirs for my parents when I was at the souk. After we leave the store, Rav hands me a brown paper bag. I frown. I didn't see him buy anything. Inside the bag is a toy camel. As I lift it out, I must have pressed something because the camel begins to emit a loud Arabian refrain. I hastily stuff it back in the bag. We both burst out laughing, completely dispelling the sexual charge between us.

Ultimately we make our way to some gardens. The scent of the blooms is heady. At some point during our tour, Rav took hold of my hand and as we pass under a trellis, he gives my hand a gentle tug, turning me towards him.

Every nerve in my body comes alive as he runs his finger along the side of my face from my forehead down. He cups my chin and rubs the pad of his thumbs over my lips. Gradually he lifts my chin upwards.

Lost in the moment, I'm about to step towards him when I hear something that makes me aware of our surroundings.

'Isn't kissing like this illegal here?' I whisper.

'It's private property. I don't think anyone will object.'

Don't start anything in Dubai, I remind myself. I force myself to step away. 'It's getting late. We have an early flight tomorrow.'

Rav looks at me intently, then blinks. 'I'll see you to your room.'

I nod. Nothing untoward can come from him escorting me – I'm sharing with Kelly after all.

Outside my room, he waits while I insert my key card. I push open the door and turn to wish him goodnight.

'Goodnight,' he whispers but his gaze is focused on my lips. I immediately look at his.

Eff it. I reach up and drag his head towards me. He gathers me close to his chest. Finally, finally, I'm pressing my mouth to his. The realest of real kisses.

Chapter 19

On Sunday, we get to Rav's flat by mid-afternoon. The flight back to London earlier that morning was uneventful. Like most of the guests, Rav and I used the time to catch up on some much-needed sleep. Neither of us brings up the kiss.

As I watched Rav doze on the plane, I couldn't help wondering what would have happened if the toy camel's music hadn't suddenly started playing, hadn't made me jump. If I hadn't got spooked after hearing the voices of hotel guests down the corridor and rushed into my room. If we'd carried our passion through to its natural conclusion.

Once we're back in Rav's flat, I put my suitcase in my room, then freshen up. I head to the kitchen to find Rav making coffee.

'Are you needing to work this afternoon?' I ask.

'I may have to do an hour or so.'

'Perhaps I should leave you to it then. I'm sure I can stay at a friend's place or see if I can get a last-minute train ticket home.'

'There's no need to do that. It's been an exhausting weekend. Why don't you take it easy today? My work isn't urgent. I can leave it until later. We could have something light to eat, or we can go out for some food.'

'Are you kidding? They gave us so much to eat on the plane. I'm not going to want to eat anything for hours.'

'Why don't you stay anyway then? It's probably a good time to firm up what we're doing for the rest of our arrangement.'

'Okay. I guess there's nothing to rush home for. I'll just check in with my parents. But you should go and do some work for an hour. You know I'm happy to sit on the balcony and read.'

The expression he gives me is inscrutable but he doesn't answer, just nods, then raises his coffee mug in a cheers gesture before going to his home office.

I have a good conversation with my parents telling them about the weekend. They haven't been to a wedding with a sangeet or groom's procession before either so they're interested in all the details. Even over the phone, Dad's voice sounds stronger. Perhaps I was wrong worrying the trip to London would be too much for him. It sounds like it's done him a world of good.

After finishing our call, I go out on the balcony and settle on the lounger. The balmy weather and muted sounds from the streets below act as a lullaby.

A while later, Rav shakes my shoulder to wake me.

'Sorry,' I say, stretching, 'I must have drifted off. I hope I wasn't snoring.'

'Only the gentlest hum.'

I laugh. 'Well, you're lucky you weren't the one sharing a room with me this weekend. I've been told my snoring is much louder than a hum.'

'Lucky?' he repeats, quirking an eyebrow. 'That isn't the word I would use.'

My mouth goes dry. Suddenly the noise from outside fades away.

'So you would have liked us to share a room?' I ask, looking him squarely in the eye. I've been dancing around this matter far too much and need to cut to the chase.

'Don't you know the answer to that?' he asks.

I snort. Apparently, Rav prefers to be cryptic. 'When we kiss in front of people now, particularly this weekend, it doesn't always feel fake to me,' I begin.

'It doesn't always feel fake to me either.'

'So you admit – there's an attraction between us. Chemistry. Or whatever the word people use these days. I don't think it's something that can be forced, even in a pretend relationship.'

'I agree. The question is, have you thought that maybe we could try exploring it?' A strange note enters his voice – seductive, persuasive.

'Exploring in what way?'

'In my opinion, the sensible approach would be to discuss it openly. Air out our concerns or possible issues.'

I laugh at the juxtaposition between his tone and what he's actually saying. 'Issues?' I ask. 'What kind of issues?'

'There's a risk, isn't there, that we could be confusing our arrangement by changing it to a ...' He breaks off.

'A sexual one?'

'Precisely.'

I want to laugh but I don't because it will offend Rav. I'm not surprised he wants us to have a logical discussion about having sex.

'Well, as I see it,' I begin, 'we wouldn't be changing our arrangement because we'll still be in our pretend relationship as far as my family and the Bamfords are concerned. The only slight difference is that we would be adding a separate, sexual element between the two of us.'

'Like an addendum?' He chuckles but then gets serious quickly. 'And you don't see a problem with that?'

'No. I'm attracted to you. I would like us to make love. But that doesn't change anything fundamentally.'

'So as far as you're concerned, everything, including any sexual relationship, ends when our arrangement ends.' He sounds irritated but I can't understand why.

'Precisely,' I reply, deliberating copying the word Rav used. 'I think the fact we're having this discussion rather than simply acting on our instincts shows that a relationship between us would never work in the real world.'

He tilts his head in surprise. 'Do you believe that?'

'Of course, don't you? Fundamentally nothing's changed. We want different things in life. You still have a life plan that involves getting married and having children.'

'And you want to stay footloose and fancy-free. We're too different then?'

'For a relationship in every sense of the word, absolutely. But now we know where we stand, and that works perfectly for us. We know that nobody's going to develop deeper emotional ...' I cast around for the right word '... feelings. Neither of us is going to get hurt. And we don't have to keep pretending we don't have this amazing chemistry. How many people can say that at the start of an affair?'

'You sound very sure.'

I shrug. 'No-strings sex isn't a big deal for me.' It has never been because that's the most I've been able to offer to previous partners. 'But you sound less convinced. You think about it. If you don't like the idea, we can stay as we are. What's the phrase? "No harm, no foul".'

Rav nods slowly. 'You're right. We don't want to be hasty about this.' He glances at his watch. 'I still have a couple more things to do. I'll be finished by dinner. Do you want to order a takeaway and then perhaps we can watch a film or TV show while we eat?'

'Why don't I make us something light and simple. We've eaten a lot of delicious but very rich food this weekend. Would you mind?'

'Of course, I don't mind,' he says.

'Great. I think I'll pop to the shops before they close.' I stand up. As I walk past him to go inside, I can't help running my hand casually along his arm.

I'm not going to force him into doing anything he doesn't want

182

to, but I'm not above flirting with Rav or trying to seduce him now we both clearly want to have sex with each other.

The visit to the shops gives me ample time to consider my conversation with Rav. I don't like the fact I'm second-guessing myself because of his cautious outlook. I'm not surprised by his attitude but I am surprised at myself – by the backwards and forwards nature of my thoughts.

Sex doesn't have to be a big thing. The only time it has ever been a problem for me in the past is when I start to suspect my lover isn't on the same page as me and is looking for some commitment I'm not prepared to give.

Having a sexual relationship with Rav won't affect the basis of our arrangement. I still don't want a long-term relationship and Rav still isn't planning to get married for another few years. Nothing will change in that respect. And I am always careful to make sure feelings don't develop. I can't imagine that being a concern for Rav, so I'm not sure why he's hesitating.

We talk about the plan for the rest of the summer during dinner. In only four weeks, it will be the Bamfords' At Home and my family's end-of-summer get-together. After that, our arrangement will end. It's strange to think this will all be over in a month.

I wonder for a brief moment if I will ever see Rav after that. We don't run in the same circles – it was a complete coincidence that we met all those months ago at the hotel. Or will we keep in touch? I'm attracted to him, yes. His offer to help me with my deception was kind, even though I'm helping him in return. But are our outlooks on life too disparate for us to maintain a friendship?

I try not to define the tight sensation in my chest at the thought of never seeing Rav again.

'You seem miles away,' Rav says, interrupting my thoughts.

'Just thinking about how fast this summer's flying by.'

'It's been an eventful one.'

'I bet you sometimes regret bumping into me at that hotel.'

'Never.' He traps my gaze with his.

What does he mean by that? Is he flirting with me?

It can only mean he's thinking about our earlier conversation on the balcony. He hasn't mentioned it since I returned from the shops. Naturally, we didn't bring it up while we were eating – even I know it isn't a polite topic for conversation over dinner.

Rav suggests I move to the seating area while he clears away the dinner, insisting on doing it alone since I cooked. I carry my glass of wine over to the sofa. If anything happens between us this evening, sharing the couch would be a good start. If Rav chooses to sit in the armchair instead, it's a sign that intimacy isn't on the agenda. For this evening, at least.

I remain standing, casting my eye over the dimly lit living area with the cushions and the wine. It almost feels too staged. As if I'm trying to seduce him. If something happens between Rav and me. When it happens, I want it to be because we can't resist each other – the way it felt before in Dubai when we had to stop ourselves from making love right then and there.

I start scrolling on my phone. We need to get out of the house, and out of our heads. I look for some place where we simply enjoy each other's company. I find a comedy night at a nearby pub. That sounds the right kind of relaxed, non-charged atmosphere we need right now.

Within half an hour, we're seated at a small table listening to comedians try out new material. We invited Tinu and Greg along but both declined. My hope was that being in public in an environment listening to funny people would ease some of the tension I was feeling during dinner, but the dark cellar and the chairs pressed close together out of necessity are creating an intimate atmosphere.

As we listen to the acts, Rav's laugh reverberates through my whole body, tightening my lower stomach and causing me to clench my knees together.

This is a mistake. Handsome, sherwani-wearing Rav is irresistible but this relaxed Rav is the sexiest thing I've seen.

He drinks some of his pint, resting his hand on the table after putting the glass back down. Unable to resist, I cover his hand with mine.

Rav gives me a sideways glance and even in the low light, I can see the smile on his face, which has nothing to do with the comedian on stage. He moves his hand only to turn it so our palms face before he interlaces our fingers. I am vaguely aware of the audience laughing around us, but all of my focus is on his touch, his look. On Rav.

We lean towards each other in an almost synchronised move, and our lips meet.

We break apart as the audience breaks into applause for the finishing act.

I lean towards him again but Rav pulls away at the last minute.

'Let's get out of here,' he whispers against my ear.

Chapter 20

A week later, I moan in protest as sunlight fills the room. Rav places a mug of tea on the bedside table next to me then bends over to kiss my forehead.

'Morning, sunshine,' he says. 'It's almost ten. We'll need to leave in an hour if we want to get to my parents' by lunchtime.'

I pull myself into a sitting position and reach for the mug. 'Are you sure it's a good idea?'

Rav shakes his head. 'Not when you look like that – very tousled and sexy,' he says, taking the mug from me and putting it on the table before he leans over and kisses me fully. 'I think leaving this bed is an unbelievably bad idea.' He pulls the duvet away before covering me with his body.

As always, desire immediately flares between us. After our first night together, I had to force myself to return to Sutton Coldfield that Monday, otherwise, I would have been tempted to stay in bed all that week just waiting for Rav to come home from work for a repeat performance.

As we make love for the fifth time since I came back to London the previous evening, I'm beginning to think going home was a major error in judgement.

Having sex with Rav has been a revelation. If I'd known what kind of passion lurked beneath his reserved exterior, I would have jumped into bed with him weeks ago.

And, as with everything else in his life, he's definitely an Overachiever.

A lot later, I voice my protest when Rav finally moves away. 'We really do have to go. My parents are expecting us,' he says.

'Well, that's as good as a cold shower.' I drink some more of my now lukewarm tea. 'Aren't you worried we might be taking things too far with getting your parents involved? Perhaps we should tell them the truth about our deception.'

Rav's gaze moves from my face down my body and back up. He gives me a quick kiss. 'I think you're too distracting at the moment. Why don't you get ready? We'll talk more in the kitchen.'

I have a quick shower, then get dressed into a simple knee-length sundress. I wonder whether it's proper or whether I should be wearing a salwar or sari. I grimace. Since I don't have those with me, it's not an option. And I don't know why I care so much about what I'm wearing. But I remember Shakti's words when Rav was coming over to meet my parents for the first time in his role as my fake suitor – there are certain expectations.

I do want Rav's parents to think well of me. Because it reflects well on my family. That's the only reason. It's not as if I'm meeting my prospective in-laws. Even if I'm nervous as if that's exactly what I'm about to do. Which is ridiculous.

'Do you want to eat something quickly before we leave?' Rav asks once I join him in the living area. 'We've booked a place for lunch so we probably shouldn't have too much.'

My stomach churns but it's not from hunger. I put my hand up. 'I don't think I could eat anything right now.'

'Are you okay?' Rav asks, concern on his face as he walks over to me and lifts my chin so he can inspect me.

'I'm a bit nervous. It's silly, I know.' I attempt to give him a reassuring smile.

'I don't want to force you to go if it's going to make you uncomfortable. Meeting my parents isn't in our pact.'

'In a way, it is because it's part of my lie, isn't it,' I acknowledge. 'We can't convince my parents we're in a serious relationship if we hide it from your family. But I never wanted you to have to lie to them because of me.'

'In a way, we're not pretending.'

'What do you mean?'

'We have a physical relationship and haven't been seeing anyone else, so I'd say we are an exclusive couple,' Rav points out. 'The only thing we're not telling them is how long we think this relationship will last. And they don't need to know that detail.'

'That's a good point.' I laugh. 'It's funny how having all those practice dates were practically us dating in real life, but without the stress and expectation. It has been the best of both worlds, hasn't it?'

Rav nods. 'Yes. We have someone to talk to, share thoughts with, and now we've taken things one step further.' I swear he's about to waggle his eyebrows suggestively. 'I mean—'

'I know what you mean.' I give him a playful swat. 'But the best part is that we know there's no future. No unreasonable expectations mean that neither of us will get hurt or have our heart broken.'

'Exactly. Come on,' he says, giving me a light tap on the bum. 'Let's go and get this over with. I love my parents but there are better ways I can imagine spending my weekend.'

* * *

An hour and a half later, we're entering Rav's parents' home.

The four of us are standing in the hallway. It's all a bit awkward. I'm not expecting a hug or an air kiss but I don't know whether they expect me to pranam. I'm holding a plant and a box of chocolates so that's not possible,

188

'Thank you for inviting me,' I say finally. 'I brought these for you.' I hand over my gifts.

'Thank you, Annika. That's very thoughtful of you,' his mother says, although it looks to me like she's critical of my offering. 'Come through to the lounge.'

My mum still has an accent when she speaks English, as do many of our family friends who also grew up in India before emigrating to England as adults. Somehow I've got this idea that all Indian mothers around the same age as my mum speak with an accent. I laugh inwardly even as I acknowledge my own stereotypical assumptions. Rav's mother speaks with received pronunciation and I remember Dad telling us Rav's parents were born in England.

Rav's father speaks to him in Hindi. There are enough similarities to Bengali and coupled with the small amounts of Hindi I've learnt from Bollywood films, that I get the gist of what he said.

'Do excuse us speaking Hindi,' Rav's mother says. 'We prefer to speak Hindi, although we can speak Marwari. Do your family speak Hindi or Bengali when you're at home?'

I shake my head. 'English.'

'I thought both of your parents are Bengali.'

'They are.'

'So it's just in front of the children they speak in English.'

I shake my head again. 'No, they speak to each other in English as well. We always have.'

'How do you communicate with your family when you visit them in India?'

I give a polite smile. 'We understand Bengali and speak enough of it to be understood. I don't remember it being a problem, although I haven't been to India since I was a teenager.'

'What? I thought your parents grew up in India. Why don't they visit?' Rav's mum says.

'Oh, my parents do,' I confirm. 'They try to go every two or three years like we did when we were younger, but I haven't been able to join them much since I took my GCSEs. The last time we went, we did a tour around the country so I have seen a lot of it. Unfortunately, I just haven't been able to fit in a visit recently.'

'And your brother and sister don't go either?' Rav's dad asks.

'Nishal and Shakti both went after they got married. They had small receptions for family over there. But I wasn't able to make it because of work commitments.'

Both of Rav's parents look like they've sucked lemons. I suspect I have failed to meet some invisible yardstick of Indian-ness. It's not the first time my family has been considered not 'desi' enough for the community.

My parents have a wide circle of friends but they are probably more on the periphery of the Indian community in our area, whereas Rav's parents have been a strong, possibly integral part of it. My parents never made a big issue of the importance of being desi or from the South Asian diaspora. Growing up, I never felt the need to question my identity. To me, I was simply British born to Indian parents. I knew I would never be thought of as British – there would always be a coda after my nationality. In the same way, I know if I go to India, I would be thought of as an outsider there too. I've always been comfortable straddling both worlds while knowing I would never fit in either one.

We go out to a nearby bistro pub for lunch. I'm subjected to an interrogation similar to the one that Rav faced when he met my family.

Rav's father sounds genuinely interested in my work. He tells me he wanted to travel when he was younger but went straight into medicine instead. I can tell Rav's mother is less than impressed with the kind of work I do.

I forgot how much his mother intimidates me. She always has. But I recognise that severe, disapproving expression from community events. I don't think I've ever seen her without it. Even at the social events, when she's talking to a group of people, she had the same look. At least I know it's not just me that's bringing it out of her.

She would make a formidable mother-in-law. What a relief she won't be mine.

'When do you think you will stop taking jobs abroad?' Rav's mum asks.

'I have no intention of stopping any time soon. As long as there's work available, I'll go where I'm needed,' I reply.

'What about when you have children?' she says. 'You'll have to stop travelling then.'

'Ma!' Rav says, a hint of anger in his tone. 'Don't put the cart before the horse. The relationship is still very new. We haven't even thought about marriage or children.'

'Well you should. Annika, you can't wait that long. You're already thirty. It's not long until you'll be considered a geriatric mother.'

I choke on my chicken. Rav hands me some water, then rubs my back until my coughing fit subsides.

'You'll have to excuse my mother,' he says. 'She sometimes forgets she's retired from obstetrics.'

'I didn't realise someone in their thirties is considered geriatric,' I reply.

Rav's mother purses her lips together. 'I don't want to be too old to play with my grandchildren. Rav, you need to be sensible and start thinking this through. Didn't we discuss that you would start a family within the next five years? Isn't that the plan?'

I look at Rav with curiosity. So he's already shared his plan for a wife and family in three years with his parents. This is interesting.

'Plans change,' Rav replies in a clipped tone.

I clear my throat to cover my laugh. I appreciate him lying to support me – if there's one thing I know, Rav doesn't change his plans. From the narrowing of Rav's mother's eyes, it's clear she shares the same sentiment.

Still, it's fun that he's pretending that I'm the one capable of making him change his goals.

I turn towards Rav. 'Perhaps that's something we do need to talk about. We still have a few years based on your original timetable. I can't think of a good reason for us to accelerate the timetable. Can you?'

Rav snorts. He squeezes my knee as a friendly warning I shouldn't take this too far.

'You know that Rav was going to ask us to find a match for him,' his father asks, beaming at me.

'I do,' I say, beaming back at him.

'You've saved us a lot of trouble,' Rav's dad says.

'We'll see,' Rav's mother replies.

I give Rav a cheeky smile. If I were really a prospective bride, Rav's mum would have demolished me by now. I pity his potential future matches. Although if his mother is helping him find a wife, she'll weed people like me out in the first batch.

Rav turns the conversation round to less controversial topics. Luckily, nobody brings up my ticking biological clock and general unsuitableness for matrimony with Rav for the rest of our visit.

But that doesn't stop us from leaving as soon as we can after lunch. I think it may be the first time I've come away empty-handed from an Indian aunty.

On the way home, Rav apologises for his mum's comments, but I understand where she's coming from. She only wants the best for her son. We want the same thing. It's just a shame, in the long run, the best for Rav can't be me.

Chapter 21

I love my life, and never more so than three days later when I'm eating risotto on a terrace in Siena while overlooking the countryside. My friend, Sigge, whom I've been trying to arrange a video chat with since I got back to England, texted me unexpectedly and invited me to stay with him for a few days, telling me he had something exciting to share. I'm doing some more troubleshooting work for one of my clients, but I can do it from Italy as easily as I can from England so there was nothing to stop me. Last-minute flights were available, and by Tuesday lunchtime, I was in Italy.

With my dad's illness, it's been a few years since I've travelled outside England apart from for work and the unexpected trip to Dubai recently. Being able to visit my friend effectively on a whim is exactly what I need – to remind myself why I chose the lifestyle I have.

The only slight hesitation was Dad's health. Dad and Mum have been convincing me that everything is fine – without their reassurance I probably wouldn't have flown out, particularly since I've only recently been to Dubai and I'm spending lots of time with Rav – not that my parents have any problem with me being with Rav.

I'm not completely convinced everything is as good as they make out because they never gave me much detail about their trip to London and I can't help feeling they're hiding something. In the end, Dad convinced me to go with the one thing he knew I couldn't argue with – that it would make him happy. He also implied, with a big wink, that he wanted more alone time with Mum, which I'm trying to burn from my memory. But it is small things like that which help me believe things are starting to get back to normal with my dad.

Sigge has taken some time off work so he can show me around the city. I originally met him five years ago when we worked on the same project in Africa – the one and only time we worked together. When the project finished, Sigge went on to start his own company but since he's pretty much a digital nomad, he can work anywhere, so he hasn't settled in one country – a little bit like me. We keep in touch because we share a love of sailing, and we've met up over the years ever since we got our international sailing licences.

'So tell me about this exciting opportunity you couldn't wait to tell me about,' I begin after we've eaten and are enjoying the rest of our bottle of wine.

'It actually involves us both,' Sigge says.

'An opportunity for the both of us?' He nods. 'Are we going to sail somewhere?' I ask. It's been a while since we had a chance to take a boat out and I'm already giddy with anticipation.

'Kind of.' Sigge tells me all the details of a yacht being chartered to sail in the Indian Ocean. 'It's a chance of a lifetime. But the only downside is we'll have to leave soon. You'll have to be ready to fly out next Monday.' He's already been accepted as a crew member and, when a last-minute vacancy came up, he gave them my name.

I've never sailed in the Indian Ocean before, although I've dreamed of visiting the Maldives or Mauritius. The sailing expedition isn't a luxurious trip for some wealthy person, though – it's a small party around some lesser-known islands. This experience is everything I've always wanted to do, a life goal of mine, which I'd even shared with Rav when we were exchanging emails before agreeing to our arrangement.

Based on the dates Sigge gives me, I would only need to crew for around ten days, which means I would be back in time for the Bamfords' At Home and our family's end-of-summer party. The only downside is I'll have to miss Kesh's evening wedding reception but I can't see it will be a problem.

It sounds perfect. I shouldn't be hesitating to say yes. So why am I?

'Come on,' Sigge says. 'You can't be thinking of turning this down?'

I shrug.

'Is it because of Rav?'

I shake my head uncertainly. 'We made a deal about what events we'd need to attend,' I say because, of course, I've told Sigge about my arrangement with Rav.

'By the sounds of it, this wedding of Kesh's isn't part of your deal – rather it's an added bonus that Rav benefits from.'

'But I went to the wedding in Dubai.' I hold my hands up. 'No, you're right. I never committed to going.' But for some reason, I have this urge to speak to Rav about it first – although I'm sure he will understand and won't mind me missing Kesh's reception. He wouldn't stand in the way of this opportunity.

I tell Sigge I'll let him know as soon as I can once I return to England.

'So it is because of Rav you're hesitating to say yes, because of your feelings for him.'

'You know we're only pretending to be in a relationship!' I say with slight alarm.

'It's more than that,' Sigge says, patting my arm. 'I can tell from the way you speak about him.'

'Okay,' I admit, 'we're now having a kind-of fake couple with benefits arrangement. But we both know it will end when I leave for my next job.'

'No.' Sigge shakes his head emphatically. 'The Annika I know would never think of possibly giving up a sailing trip for a man.'

'I'm not saying no. I just need to some time to think about it. Honestly, our relationship is purely no-strings attached without any deeper feelings getting in the way. I mean, I do like Rav. He's a good person. And, of course, I'm attracted to him. But …' My voice peters off as Sigge says nothing but looks at me intently in a caring but clearly 'doesn't believe a word I'm saying' kind of way.

I have never been one of those people who constantly has to be with their partner. But Rav and I have a very short time left together – it's only a month until our arrangement ends and I will be leaving Rav for good. I can't deny I only accepted this trip to Siena because it's during the week and Rav is working. Going on the sailing trip would mean ten days away from Rav. I almost don't want to give up the remaining time we have left.

And the thought worries me. I'm *not* that person.

Now, I'm determined to take up the offer. But I should still let Rav know first.

* * *

When I return to England on Thursday, I go straight from the airport to Rav's flat. I've been buzzing with excitement, knowing that I get to see him soon. It feels like it's been a long time.

But I've put everything back into perspective – it's still only a fake relationship. Good sex as an added benefit doesn't change anything. We have one month and two agreed events, the Bamfords' At Home and my family party, left. There is no reason to turn down the sailing trip.

It's only five p.m. when I arrive at Rav's flat. I'm not expecting him back for another couple of hours. I take my bag into his room where I've been sleeping since we returned from Dubai. I decide to cook us some dinner, a dish that is easy to make but that can be left in the oven if we somehow become distracted.

I hear the front door open at around seven-thirty so I walk into the hall. Rav grins and strides towards me. He reaches out and lifts me into his arms, bringing my lips to his. I hold tightly to his shoulders and wrap my legs around his waist, my lips not for a moment leaving his mouth, not even to take a breath, as he scrambles to open his bedroom door. Moments later, I'm falling backwards onto the foot of the bed, bringing Rav down on top of me.

As I anticipated, it's a while before we get to eat.

Over dinner, conversation turns to Rav's work. He seems a lot more relaxed discussing his ideas and concerns with me now. Although I love that he opens up to me this way, a small part of me worries that maybe we're potentially blurring the lines, going beyond the casual relationship we both agreed to. I consider bringing it up for a moment, but then I feel foolish. Rav knows nothing has changed fundamentally. I still don't ever want marriage and the whole white picket fence thing and he still plans on finding his match in three years. It's only arrogance on my part to even think there's something to worry about.

It's much later in the evening before I get the chance to tell Rav about the sailing holiday.

I expect him to be excited for me but instead, he straightens, looking stern. 'You mean you'll be leaving soon and be gone for two weeks?'

'Closer to ten days. I'll be back before the summer bank holiday weekend.'

'So you're not going to be here for Kesh's wedding reception?'

'No. At least you don't need me there. You probably won't even get to spend much time with me. It's a shame, as I wanted to go, but it can't be helped,' I say with a casual shrug.

'Can't be helped?' he repeats with a quirk of his eyebrow. 'My parents are expecting to see you there.'

'Sorry. I'm sure they'll understand. You told me it isn't a formal function. You said there'd be dancing and a buffet so I don't think one person not turning up will make that big a difference,' I say.

'But you promised that you'd be there. You made a commitment.'

I don't answer, taken aback by Rav's insistence that I attend. I never considered it to be an official engagement. Kesh invited me but he made it sound as if the event was something informal. It's not like it's a sit-down, plates-per-head event. I assumed it was the kind of Indian free-for-all reception where anyone who knows the groom or his family is invited and if they turn up, they turn up. If they don't, they'd hardly be missed among the five hundred or so guests there.

'I'll be here for the At Home. Don't worry, I'm keeping my end of our deal,' I try to reassure him, even though I know Rav would not need to worry.

'That's all it is to you still? Part of our arrangement?'

We're currently sitting on the floor covered by a throw blanket, leaning against the couch, where we ended up after making love for the third time that evening. I reach around me for my underwear and T-shirt. 'You know it's more than that,' I say as I get dressed.

'Forgive me for thinking you're not acting as if it is.'

I huff. 'Why are you making such a big deal of this? You brought up our arrangement. Your friend's wedding was never part of that. I've been given this once-in-a-lifetime opportunity and you want me to turn it down for dancing and curry.'

Rav also pulls on his clothes, every action showing how annoyed he is.

'The thing is, Annika, it isn't once in a lifetime for you, is it? You can travel at a whim any time you want. If you want to go sailing, you can. You have a licence. Other opportunities will come up.'

'Not like this one.'

'Perhaps not. But what's so unique about this one that you

break a commitment you made to Kesh. And to me. I have to say, I think you're being selfish.'

'Selfish! I'm selfish?' Unbelievable. I'm getting tired of being told I'm selfish just because I want to live my life on my own terms.

I don't understand why Rav is reacting as if I'm the problem. It's almost like he doesn't understand the opportunity I've been given. And that nonsense he said about it not being once in a lifetime. What is that supposed to mean? I tidy up the throw and the pillows while I gather my thoughts.

Rav stands with arms akimbo, not helping or even offering to. After a few moments of silence, he sighs deeply. 'I still have a lot of work to do. I'm probably going to be busy tomorrow and this weekend so I understand if you'd prefer to go home and spend time with your parents before you leave on your trip. If I don't see you before you go, I hope you have a lovely time.'

He leaves the room without even looking at me. I resist the urge to throw the pillow I'm holding at his receding back, although I do chuck it onto the couch with a little more force than strictly necessary.

Rav's behaviour makes no sense. He knows how important it is to me to have the freedom to choose what I want to do and when I want to do it. I thought he understood me. I thought he was different. I guess I was wrong.

* * *

After our argument, Rav didn't come out of his office for the rest of that evening so I slept in the guest room. He had already left by the time I woke up the next morning. I decided to come home. It's been three days, and I haven't heard from him.

I still don't understand why Rav's so angry. I didn't really commit to going to the wedding reception with him – we didn't make any definite plans and that's usually something Rav likes to do well in advance.

199

I mull over our conversation all the time. Perhaps it wasn't anger so much as disappointment. His parents were expecting to see me. I am letting him down in front of them, showing my travel was more important than supporting my boyfriend. They already made it clear they thought my travel would get in the way of our future.

'Is everything okay, Niki?' Mum asks as I help her make dinner.

'Everything's fine, Mum,' I reply. 'Just thinking about this trip. Whether I should go.'

I've told my parents about the sailing trip and even mentioned the conflict with Kesh's reception, although I haven't mentioned my argument with Rav. Their only advice was to do what I think is best.

But I'm not sure what that is.

This is exactly why I avoid real relationships. I shouldn't be expected to make that choice between a partner and the lifestyle I lead.

Nish, Kaya and their children are coming over later to go over details for the party. Although the event is timed for my nephew's birthday, because it's the August bank holiday weekend, it's always been our yearly excuse for a final large get-together before the weather changes.

'Do you think Dad will be up to having loads of people for a party?'

'Yes, Niki. By the time of the party, I'm sure he'll be fine.' Something about the way she phrases her answer makes me think there's something she's not telling me. 'Is Rav still coming to the party?'

'As far as I know,' I answer truthfully. I presume Rav will still need me to pretend to be his girlfriend at the Bamfords' At Home and, as part of our arrangement, he'll come to my family party, which will be the last event. They're on the same weekend so we wouldn't do one without the other. But I don't know if he's still too angry to want to attend both.

With my parents being so tight-lipped, Nish's visit will give me the perfect chance to check if he thinks Dad is well enough for our summer party. And since I'm sure my parents will have already informed him of my trip, I debate whether I should ask his advice too. He does know Rav relatively well from when they were at school together, even if they were never close friends. He might be able to provide some useful insight into why Rav reacted the way he did. But on second thought, I dismiss this idea as, knowing Nish, he'll likely side with Rav just to spite me.

As I finish making dinner, I weigh up the opinions of the people I have already asked – Tinu, Eden, Lucia, Sophie and others. All of them agree with my parents – I should do what I think is best.

But the more I think about it, the more I realise the advice I was given was deliberately vague – and so unlike my parents. With my visits to Dubai and Siena, they were the first to be incredibly positive and encouraging, unafraid of speaking their minds and pushing me to go. If they really believed that this sailing opportunity was the best thing for me, they'd be wholeheartedly supportive of my decision. Which makes me think that maybe I was too quick to judge, that I should have tried to listen, to understand Rav's side of things.

I decide I should go to the reception after all. Rav's right, I can't let him down in front of his parents. Not when we're a team and equally committed to this arrangement. I call Sigge and tell him I can't join. Sigge only laughs and tells me he knew my answer before I'd picked up the phone and he's already organised a replacement.

I also try calling Rav to let him know I'll be at the wedding reception. He doesn't pick up so I leave a message.

When I share the news with my parents, they both look relieved. But before I have a chance to find out why, Nish and his family arrive, removing any chance of me continuing this conversation with them.

After we've eaten and discussed party plans, Kaya and the

children leave while Nish hangs around at Dad's request – I can only presume Dad wants to talk about something medical-related in private. But then the doorbell rings and I open it to see Shakti standing there. She mentions Mum phoned her a couple of hours ago to ask her to pop round.

Once we're all seated in the living room, Mum takes hold of Dad's hand – something I haven't seen her do since we were in the hospital room.

'We have something to tell you,' Dad begins.

A freeze passes over me and something claws at the pit of my stomach.

Everything I suspected is right. Dad's recovery hasn't been going as well as they'd hoped. He's been seeing a specialist about other options – their trip to London 'to watch a play' was a lie they told to cover up the fact Dad was meeting with a consultant to discuss a possible operation. They've been able to schedule an operation for the week before the bank holiday. It's not going to be open heart surgery this time. All being well, Dad reassures us he'll be back to his old self before we know it, but they want us to know that all surgery comes with risks, so they're getting their affairs in order over the next few days.

Nish asks a barrage of medical questions, while Shakti wants to know what she can do to help. I should say something, contribute as part of the family.

But all I can think of is how Mum and Dad didn't say anything to me when I told them about the sailing trip. They would have let me leave even though it meant I wouldn't be here for the operation.

I realise the timing of their announcement conveniently coincides with my earlier decision. If I'd agreed to go on the sailing trip would they have even told me about the operation at all? I can't help wondering whether it's because they really believe I'm so selfish I would put a once-in-a-lifetime sailing trip above my dad.

Because right now I am being selfish. I'm thinking about *me* and how *I* feel when my dad is the priority. But I want to focus on anything other than my dad's upcoming operation and how we might still lose him. I want to cry and for my parents to comfort me, like they used to when I was younger, but I can't because it's my parents who need my support.

I wish someone was here to tell me everything'll be okay; that my dad will get through this.

I wish Rav was here.

Chapter 22

The following weekend I'm beginning to regret my decision to come to this blasted wedding reception. Rav never did call me back, though he texted to let me know what time he'd meet me at the venue. Clearly, he doesn't want me to meet him at his place beforehand. I don't need to be here. Instead, I could have been back home helping Mum prepare for Dad's operation, but she encouraged me to come – to clear the air at least. Although, I can't help feeling her insistence might also be an excuse to get me out of the house for a few days, a break from my constant worrying and fussing over Dad.

Now I'm at the reception and Rav's nowhere to be seen. Granted, there are probably over two hundred guests here, but my body always instinctively knows when Rav is near. I'm about to introduce myself to some random guests when a few of the people from the Dubai wedding come over to say hello. Naturally, they ask where Rav is and are understandably surprised to hear we've come separately.

Thank goodness this event wasn't part of our arrangement or we would have failed miserably.

I've been there almost half an hour before Rav and his parents show up. I roll my eyes. If I'd known he was using 'Indian time', I wouldn't have rushed to be punctual.

Rav's father greets me warmly but Rav is as frosty as his mother. I pretend not to notice but I'm not spending my evening with people who clearly don't want me here. I give them ten minutes to see if anything changes but there's no sign of easing tension, so I excuse myself to join my new friends on the dance floor.

Occasionally I glance over at Rav, standing at the side, glaring at me. Even with his stern and cold expression, or maybe because of it, I still feel that pull towards him, making me want to throw myself into his arms and wrap myself tight around him. Part of me is tempted to apologise just so we can have sex again.

It's not just sex though. I've missed him. I've wanted to talk to him; to confide in him about my family's situation and how I feel about it. My mouth tightens as I remind myself that Rav isn't there for me in that way, and I shouldn't expect him to be.

Yet again, I'm thankful this isn't a real relationship. Things become more complicated when feelings are involved. This way, we can walk away without anyone getting hurt. But Rav is acting as if even the possibility of going away on a sailing trip was a major betrayal for him. One of the first things I told him during our email exchange was that I've always wanted to go on a working sailing holiday. Okay, it isn't my dream research trip but it's still an opportunity of a lifetime. I really thought Rav, of all people, would understand that. It's something we do have in common – we're not afraid to chase our goals in both work and life.

He needs to stop being so stubborn or this arrangement between us isn't going to work for much longer. And, as I understood things, the evening at the Bamfords' house could be the deciding factor on who buys the company. If Rav is the business mastermind people claim he is, you'd think he'd have the sense to make sure I'm on his side right before such a major event.

I'm so annoyed with him.

But I recognise what I'm really angry about is life and how unfair it can be. I'm angry with myself for wallowing in self-pity when I should be thinking of Dad. And all I've wanted, since I heard the news, is for Rav to hold me and reassure me that things will be okay, to stop me from feeling so scared about what might happen.

As the night draws on, I eat, drink, dance and laugh as if I haven't a care in the world. Rav and I are forced into each other's company because it could start to look odd to the other guests if we're avoiding one another when we're supposed to be in love. But it doesn't stop him from being stiff and guarded in my presence.

Rav's father must have noticed his son's behaviour because he comes over to me while I'm taking a hydration break from the dance floor. After exchanging a few observations about the wedding reception, he turns to me and says, 'I hope my son hasn't upset you?'

My eyes widen. 'No, not at all.' The last thing I want is for Rav's parents to be concerned about our relationship and to think we're having issues.

'Rav's ma worries about him. He's been stressed about work lately. He thinks he has to carry the world on his shoulders. He's so stern and serious all the time when he should be relaxing and enjoying life. You know, we were a little surprised when we heard the two of you were dating.'

I wait for him to explain further but he only smiles. I've never heard Bobby Gohil speak as much as he's doing now.

'When you came to visit us, we could see straight away that Rav was different around you. Happy. Back to his old self.' He pauses, waiting for me to contribute … *something*.

'Okay,' is all I have to offer.

'Whatever disagreement you have. I know you can sort it out. Rav needs someone like you.' He places a hand on the top of my head as if giving me his blessing, then walks away.

I glance in Rav's direction and meet his gaze head-on. I give him a tentative smile but he frowns and then goes back to talking to the people around him.

It's getting late and I need to think about where I'm spending the night now. When this plan was originally discussed, it was a given I'd be heading back to Rav's place. But with the way things are between us, I've ruled out that option. I glance at the time. If I leave soon, I can probably get to a friend's house before they go to bed or find a hotel. If the worst comes to the worst, I can sleep at the railway station and take the first train home in the morning – even as the thought occurs, I roll my eyes at my flair for the dramatic.

Someone from the groom's party comes up to me. The groom and bridal parties have been asked to perform their dance from the sangeet and they're going to a separate room to have a quick rehearsal.

I'm not really sure what this has to do with me until he says that his dance partner couldn't come over from Dubai for the reception so Kesh suggested I dance with Rav and Rav's partner can take the other lady's place.

Although it sounds convoluted and would make more sense to me if I simply step in as this man's partner, I'm not going to make a fuss, particularly not when Kesh came up with the idea.

When I enter the room we're rehearsing in, Rav comes over to me. I smile at him. He nods in return – there's no pleasure to see me or affection in his expression. We walk towards the others and take our place as the intro to the song begins to play.

This is awful. We're both awkward and stiff in our movements, our timing off and throwing off the whole routine.

'Come on, Rav,' Kesh calls out. 'You can do better than this.'

'Perhaps you both need to loosen up first, try some wiggling and wobbling,' someone else calls out, replicating the shimmies we did at that first dance rehearsal.

Everyone else who was at that rehearsal copies him and soon there's more of us wobbling and wiggling. Kesh comes to stand next to Rav to try to get him to join in and soon enough they end up laughing as they start shaking some moves.

By the time we're on the dance floor, ready to perform in front of the guests, Rav is at ease in my company once more, seeming relaxed and even laughing at some of my jokes, as if everything is fine between us. Being back in his arms, if only for the duration of the dance, feels like the most natural thing in the world. I missed this connection, his touch, so much.

After the dance, we stand around chatting with the others – Rav's arm around my shoulder and mine around his waist. When he casually presses his lips against the top of my head, I hope everything will be okay.

'I missed you,' I say in a low voice. He stiffens and I grimace, knowing I've ruined the moment. 'We need to talk.'

He nods. 'Not here. We can talk tomorrow. I presume you'll be staying over at my place as planned.'

'If that's still okay with you.'

'Of course. We can probably leave in half an hour. There's somebody over there I need to speak to.'

I don't watch where's he going – I know he's making an excuse to get away. Instead I carry on chatting until it's time to leave.

The next morning, I wake up in the guest room to the smell of coffee. Beyond handing me a mug, Rav barely acknowledges my presence. We need to clear the air if we're going to continue our arrangement. And at the moment, that's a big *IF*.

I sit down on the dining table, trying to find ways to initiate the talk. But whenever I start to bring it up, Rav manages to change the topic or not respond by distracting himself with cooking breakfast. He gives no indication he's interested in talking things out.

I go to the guest room to grab my travel bag then head back into the living room. Rav is now seated at the dining table, reading the Sunday papers. I'm not wasting my time hanging round until he *is* willing to discuss things when I can get back home early and help Mum. There are only two days until Dad's operation and I want to make sure my parents have nothing to worry about, that everything's being taken care of. If Rav wants to talk, he can call me. And maybe, just maybe, I'll pick up.

'I'm going to head off now,' I say.

Rav looks up. 'All right. Do you have the final details for your party?'

This only confirms what I now know – he doesn't care things still aren't right between us, only interested in making sure we successfully tick off another one of our predetermined events. Hurt, I speak impulsively. 'You know what, I think it's fine. It's mostly a kid's birthday party anyway. You don't have to come.'

'What do you mean? It's part of our arrangement.'

'The whole point of this arrangement is to convince my parents we're a couple happily in love. And it's been great so far but if you're going to act like this, they will see right through our deception.' I raise my hand when he opens his mouth. 'Don't worry, I'll be at the Bamfords' if you still want me there. Although frankly, I don't know if it would work in your favour.'

I can't imagine how my parents will react if Rav doesn't turn up at the party. But with any luck, Mum and Dad will be too busy entertaining the other guests to feel too disappointed. And I hope Dad's operation is successful and he'll be back to his old self once more, so I won't have to worry about causing my parents any additional stress and they'll stop fixating on my lack of a stable relationship.

Rav bends his head. After a few minutes, he looks up at me. 'You're right. I've been acting like a cad.'

I can't help snorting at his old-fashioned description. But there's a deeper issue at stake. 'I don't really know what you want from me, Rav. This arrangement was supposed to help us both. But the way you've been acting about my sailing trip, it's worse than having a real boyfriend.'

Rav's lips become a thin line. 'I've already apologised for my behaviour. I believe when you make a commitment, you see it through.'

209

'So do I! That's why I don't commit to being anywhere until I'm absolutely certain. I told you that the first time we had dinner. I like to stay as flexible as I can. This sailing trip was the perfect example of why. I thought you understood.'

'Of course. But I thought we were partners. That we decided what to do together, instead of you just telling me you're going sailing for two weeks and you'd be missing Kesh's wedding reception.'

I sit down across from him and run my hands down my face. It was exactly because of this – the reason I hesitated about agreeing to the trip, wanting to discuss it with Rav first, as my partner – that, out of alarm, I did the complete opposite and simply announced my plans. But I don't want to tell Rav that because of what it could mean.

Instead, I say, 'I'm sorry, I guess I didn't see it that way. It was a mistake. Can we move on from it? I don't want to argue about this anymore, Rav.'

'Neither do I. And I guess I've been distant this morning because I know I owe you a big apology and I haven't wanted to say it.'

'You owe me an apology?' I can't hide my surprise.

'Yes. I didn't want to admit I was disappointed when you told me about your sailing trip. I've enjoyed the time we spent together and wanted to show you off to all my friends and family, for them to meet you. When you decided the reception wasn't as important as your sailing trip, I was angry so I accused you of being selfish. But I had no right to be angry. You were right – it was never part of our arrangement, so I shouldn't have pushed you to come. That's my fault and I accept that. I'm sorry.'

His self-awareness and his honesty bowl me over. I don't know what to say. I wish I'd had the courage to be more honest with him about how I'd behaved. That I'm partly to blame too, simply because I was scared and acted out based on my emotions rather than taking the time to think things through.

I ask, 'So why were you so cold to me at the reception?'

'I felt guilty.'

'Guilty?'

'That you'd sacrificed going on the trip to come to an event that wasn't even part of our agreement. I know how you feel about having the flexibility and freedom to do what you want to, particularly when it comes to travelling. I shouldn't have guilted you into turning your trip down.'

'It wasn't a sacrifice. Besides, it worked out best for me not to go in the end. My dad ...' I break off. For a few hours yesterday evening, I was able to put Dad's upcoming operation to the back of my mind and enjoy myself but this morning, the worries and fears are out in full force.

'What about your father? Is he okay?'

A small voice in my head warns me not to say anything to Rav. We're already confusing our arrangement by adding sex to the mix. Rav is not my real boyfriend. I shouldn't expect him to be my rock.

But then a different voice urges me to let Rav know what's happening, using the argument that it's part of our pretence. I'm only giving him information he needs to know so that we can continue with the arrangement. Nothing more to it. I listen to that voice.

* * *

The following evening, I'm on my own in the house. Dad's in hospital for his pre-op checks. Since he's been admitted to the same hospital Mum used to work at, as a favour for her, she's been allowed to stay with him overnight.

Both Nish and Shakti had invited me over to their homes so I wouldn't need to be alone tonight. I plan to head over to Shakti's once I've heard from Mum. With Nish being a doctor, I was tempted to stay with him solely to pester him

211

with questions about the procedure – but neither of us needs that stress right now.

I'm channel-surfing when the doorbell rings. We don't usually have visitors so late in the evening but friends have heard about Dad's operation and we've had a steady stream of people bringing meals around. I presume it's another casserole.

But it's not. It's Rav.

'Can I come in?' he asks after I've stood there for a few minutes with my mouth gaping like a fish.

'Of course.' I step aside. He brushes a kiss against the top of my head as he passes me, then puts the overnight bag he's carrying by the stairs.

'What are you doing here?' I ask.

'Your dad's having an operation tomorrow. Where else would I be?'

I swallow, unable to believe he's really here. 'What about work?'

'I can work from here if I need to, but Greg can keep an eye on things. I went into the office today to sort things out – otherwise, I would have stayed here with you when I drove you back yesterday.'

Words fail.

'Any chance of getting something to eat?' he asks. 'I drove straight after work and didn't stop.'

I laugh. 'We have food.' I take him to the kitchen where I warm up one of the dishes a neighbour brought round.

While he eats, we talk about inconsequential things. I'm sure he's trying to take my mind off things.

'Thank you for coming,' I say after he's finished eating and we are tidying up the kitchen. 'I didn't expect it.'

'Well you should have.'

I want to ask if he's only come down because he thinks it's what my family would expect my boyfriend to do or whether there's something more. Something deeper.

Instead, I walk over to where Rav is leaning back against one of the counters and put my hand up around his neck, pulling his head towards me and reaching my mouth up towards his. Maybe I'm the one blurring the lines now, but I want to kiss him. I want him to hold me.

For real.

Chapter 23

The week goes by in a blur. Dad's operation is a complete success. Rav was there when we heard the news, holding me tight when tears of relief overwhelmed me. Rav stayed until Dad left the hospital on Wednesday night. I don't know how I would have coped without him by my side. It's been a huge comfort having someone I can lean on.

Everything about Rav is so wonderful. I can't believe it has to end very soon. It's the final weekend of our arrangement. The day for the Bamfords' At Home has finally arrived.

We still don't know what is in store for us this evening. Rav has already handed in his proposal, so there's nothing left to do on the actual business side. Although he's not showing anything externally, I can tell he's worried we're entering unknown territory – somewhere he's not in control.

We arrive at the Bamfords' promptly at six p.m. As we stand outside, waiting for our ring to be answered, I reach out to give Rav's hand a reassuring squeeze. He grabs on to my hand when I try to let go.

The house is big, but it's not a mansion – it's very much a family home. It fits well with Rav's comment that the Bamfords aren't extravagant when it comes to themselves, although they push the boat out to treat the company employees. Although when a maid opens the door, I wonder whether I got it wrong and the Bamfords do enjoy some luxuries. We follow her through to a sitting room but it could be a library since it has wall-to-wall bookcases. I can imagine curling up on one of the large armchairs engrossed in a book – though Rav's balcony will always be my favourite reading nook.

Trevor and Frances Bishop are already there but nobody else seems to be. I try to make polite chitchat but my efforts are in vain. If it didn't mean leaving Rav on his own with them, I would probably go to look for Mrs Bamford.

I haven't seen Mrs Bamford since we went shopping a couple of weeks ago. When the day started, I felt guilty that I was meeting her to further Rav's case. Within a few hours, I was instead feeling guilty over having such a good time I'd neglected to bring up Rav at all. It didn't feel like the right thing to do even though I knew she was meeting separately with Marie and Frances. I only hope I didn't do Rav a disservice.

When I told Rav I failed to bring him up in front of Mrs Bamford, he told me not to worry. Although he'd originally proposed our arrangement, asking me to help convince Rupert Bamford he's a man who takes his commitments seriously, deep down, I know Rav would prefer the company to be sold to him because he's the best person to take it forward.

And that's one of the reasons I … I admire him so much.

The maid returns to show the Bishops and us to our rooms. After the other couple enter their room, Rav and I are taken up another flight of stairs and led to a room in the loft. Neither of us reacts in the slightest that we'll be sharing a bed. It's funny to think about how much has changed in just a few short weeks.

And in a few hours, it will all be over. We have the Bamfords tonight. Then my brother's party tomorrow. And then we're done.

There's a strange ache in my heart that I'm trying to ignore.

Rav presses a kiss to my forehead. 'Ready?' he asks. I nod. 'Brace yourself. We should be prepared for anything.'

By the time we get back down to the library everyone has arrived, including the Bamfords, all couples apart from Greg and Helene.

I join Mrs Bamford who's standing next to Marie. Marie compliments her on her house.

'She's right. You've got a gorgeous place, Aunty B,' I say, when she hands me a glass of champagne. Somehow by the end of our shopping date, I got in the habit of calling her Aunty B, which she loved, and in turn she calls me Niki. The only person other than my parents to do so. I also think of Mr Bamford as Mr B in my head, although I'd never call him that in person.

'Thank you, Niki,' she replies.

'Have you lived here long?' Marie asks.

'Since the boys were young. It's been a lovely family home for us. I've loved living here.'

I notice she uses the past tense. Are they planning to move?

Before I can ask her, Marie starts discussing home decor, a topic I have nothing to contribute to so I move away. Greg comes over to me. He gives me a strange look – as if he wants to say something but is unsure. I've never seen Greg act this way since I met him.

'Everything okay, Greg?' I ask.

'I was wondering,' Greg begins, 'how your friend Tinu is doing? Have you heard from her recently?'

'Yes,' I reply with a frown. 'I spoke to her a couple of days ago. Why?'

'She hasn't replied to my messages.'

I narrow my eyes. 'What did you do, Greg?' If he's hurt her in any way …

'Nothing! I promise. We went out a couple of times. I thought we had a good time. But she's ghosted me. Did I do something wrong?'

216

I'm surprised by Greg's questions, and his plaintive expression. I always thought he was the love-them-and-leave-them type so why does he care that Tinu isn't responding? 'Do you want me to find out?' I offer.

For a brief moment he looks eager but then shakes his head. 'No, that's okay. Thank you.'

Mr B taps the side of his glass and we all gather round him in preparation for his toast. 'Thank you all for coming to our At Home. Moira and I are happy you were able to join us. Now I know you've all been wondering what we're doing here tonight. So I won't keep you in suspense any longer. Moira and I decided we would recreate a tradition we've had for years, but which we haven't been able to do for a long time now.' He pauses and looks down at his glass. Aunty B walks over and takes his hand. He pastes on a smile. 'I hope you'll indulge us this evening for our take on family games night.'

Games night! This is going to be so much fun! I glance round the room to see how everyone else has taken the news. The look in Aiden's and Trevor's eyes convinces me they're not going to be taking part for fun. They're out to win. To be fair, I'm sure Rav and Greg feel the same – they're just doing a better job of hiding it. Rav is frowning; I expect he's worried about the kinds of games we'll be playing but I can't imagine they'll be risqué or even particularly active. None of us are dressed for an obstacle course in the garden.

I rub my hands together with anticipation. This evening is probably the closest thing to the epic death match I was hoping for when Rav first told me about this event.

Mr B continues, 'I know most of you are here to discuss Bamfords. But I promised Moira there'll be no business talk this evening. Instead, I'll meet with each company individually tomorrow morning to discuss your proposals.'

That sounds reasonable to me, although I'm not sure how or if the games will contribute in any way to the final outcome. The whole business sale has been baffling and I would love to know if Mr B thinks watching potential buyers of his company play a few board games will help him decide who to sell to. Occasionally, I've suspected that the Bamfords are a bit lonely and I did wonder whether they arranged this evening to have company. But they are both such lovely people. I imagine they have loads of friends to spend time with.

The Bamfords leave to grab the equipment, while everyone else remains in the room trying to guess what type of games there will be. At one point, I hear Aiden bring up tactics with Marie. All of us have assumed we'll be playing either as couples or as company teams.

Aunty B comes back in the room asking for help to set up two easels. She tells us we're playing a drawing game and then divides us into male versus female teams.

I can't help laughing at Aiden and Greg's expressions when they hear they won't be competing against each other, but then they swiftly turn to concentrate on their joint enemy – the women.

The game begins and within a couple of rounds we are thoroughly thrashing the men. Frances Bishop is excellent at drawing cartoons and Marie is great at guessing what my squiggly lines are meant to represent.

But the main disadvantage the men have is their apparent need to blame someone for their lack of success. If nobody guesses the answer, they spend minutes after their turn with the drawer blaming the guessers and vice versa. I even see Rav and Trevor try to instil some strategy to their gameplay, but they have no hope of catching us up and I don't hesitate to taunt them accordingly.

I admit it. I'm just as competitive as the others.

After the drawing game, Mr B divides us into three teams of three, seemingly arbitrarily. Aunty B excuses herself from the game to take care of dinner and refuses all offers to help her.

I'm in a team with Aiden and Helene. Possibly the worst two I could be with.

The object of the game is to guess as many random words described by one of our team, like a variation on Articulate but without the categories. I try my best but my team is definitely at a disadvantage because we have no common references to use for our descriptions. We struggle along but Aiden's obvious frustration gets my back up, and I have to confess I stop trying just to irritate him.

Somehow Rav and Greg ended up on the same team and they race through their words. Their minds work in a scarily similar way.

After that game, Aunty B calls us in for dinner. She's cooked a roast with all the trimmings.

Dinner conversation flows freely and covers diverse topics always introduced, I notice, by one of the Bamfords. They are consummate hosts. My attempts to find out what games we'll be playing for the rest of the evening are met with knowing smiles but the Bamfords give nothing away.

Aiden asks about the meeting order for the following morning. Rav and Greg will have the first slot with Mr B because Rav and I have to leave before the others.

'It's a shame you two have to leave before lunch tomorrow,' Aunty B says, 'but I understand you have a family party to go to. Of course, you can't miss that.'

'Yes,' I say. 'I haven't been able to go these past couple of years because I've been working on a project.'

'You don't make time to come back for family events?' Helene asks me. She's placed a deliberate emphasis on *family*. I'm sure she's trying to score points with Mr B, which is odd because she's not a member of Trevor's family.

'Once I go to a site, I tend to stay there,' I reply. 'I want to minimise air travel as much as I can. The companies I work for offset the carbon footprint of air travel and I invest in research into alternative fuels but I still feel conflicted when I'm working on climate change projects – a difficult balancing act between the speed and convenience air travel affords versus the environmental cost. That's why I don't tend to come back home once I've flown over.'

'That makes a lot of sense,' Marie says.

'Environmental busybodies,' Trevor says with a grimace, 'these activists can make development difficult.'

I bite my tongue, even though the temptation to launch into a lecture is strong. Nobody else has responded to Trevor – I second-guess whether I should say something when Mr Bamford asks for someone to pass him the potatoes.

After serving himself, he says, 'Like Annika, my boys were concerned about climate change and environmental concerns.'

'I told you they would have been fascinated by your work, Niki,' Aunty B adds.

'It's something we should discuss tomorrow when we talk through your proposals,' Mr B says, making it clear that the topic is over for the evening but not forgotten.

I exchange glances with Rav and Greg. I know they included an environmental impact assessment in their proposal because Rav asked if I would review that section before he submitted it.

And it sounds like Trevor's company hasn't given the issue due consideration so I'd say things are tipping in Rav's favour. Although, of course, I don't know anything about Aiden's company's eco-credentials.

After dinner, it's charades. Aunty B divides us into two teams. This time Rav and I are on the same team, as are all the other couples. I don't expect, for a moment, the members have been chosen at random. Mr B, Marie and Aiden are also on our team.

Mr B is completely relaxed. He doesn't make much effort to guess what we're acting out during each of our turns, although he manages to throw himself into the game when he's up to act out the items on the cards. I'm more and more convinced he's using the evening as an opportunity to observe us all.

It's Greg's turn for the other team next. He acts out a

complicated song, which the others guess because of some inspired sounds-like clues.

Marie claps. 'That's excellent, Greg. So creative.'

'Thank you,' Greg says with a bow.

Aiden scowls and pulls Marie back slightly, saying, 'He's not on our team.'

I turn to her and say, 'Greg was great, wasn't he? I would never have thought to do it like that.'

Aiden mutters, 'Why don't you show the same enthusiasm when it's your go?'

I give him what I hope is my 'if looks could kill' face. I get being competitive and wanting to win, but this evening is for fun as well. I very much doubt Mr B is going to base his final business decision on who wins a game of charades.

Aunty B announces a trivia quiz will be the final game of the evening. I'm a little sad that the evening's coming to an end. Despite the situation, with the stakes high and atmosphere tense when rival companies are competing in a supposedly friendly games night, I've thoroughly enjoyed myself.

For this game, Mr B says we can get into pairs of our own choosing. I have to admit to a slight relief when Rav selects me rather than Greg.

The dynamic between the couples is interesting to observe while we play the quiz. Trevor leaves any social or entertainment questions for Frances but doesn't listen to her suggestions when it comes to politics or history – although he would have performed better if he had. Aiden is more collaborative with Marie than I expected, especially from the interactions I've witnessed of them so far. They discuss their answers and come to a consensus – their turns always taking longer than any other team's – but it's a pleasant surprise. It makes me wonder if, while they do have a lot of issues to iron out, deep down they do truly care for each other and work well as a couple. They do well on the quiz. Rav and I don't perform too badly either. We don't win but our areas of knowledge complement each other's, and where neither of us knows the answer for sure, we agree on our educated guesses. We make a perfect team.

After the quiz, the Bamfords serve brandies and a cheeseboard but Rav and I don't linger too long.

As we head up to bed, I wish it doesn't have to end. I don't know whether I mean the evening or my time with Rav.

Chapter 24

The next day, after leaving the Bamfords home, we drive straight to my parents' house, where we'll have less than an hour to get changed before we head over to Nish's for the party. Thank goodness it's a lovely day – it means we can go ahead with the planned barbecue.

Our family has always held a party on the summer bank holiday weekend. To begin with, it was a celebration of the last days before school started but over the years, as well as my nephew's birthday, it's been a celebration of the end of summer, the last chance for family and friends to get together before the weather changes and the humdrum of life restarts.

Seeing my family together, enjoying each other's company reminds me how much I've missed out on these celebrations by working abroad. Dad's health concerns have been a reminder of how important my family is to me. I may complain about how I sometimes feel as if I'm being excluded from the family – the truth is they've got used to doing things without me around. My presence is a bonus rather than essential. From now on, I'm determined to change that. Part of the reason I always want to live life to the fullest is because I never want to take life for granted. But I never want to take my family for granted either.

I hear a sound I haven't heard for a long time – the deep,

hearty laugh that is undeniably Dad's. He's joking, manning the barbecue – going from group to group, making sure everyone enjoys themselves and has enough to eat. Just like old times. So different from my cousin's wedding where he stayed at the same table for the whole evening. I finally have my daddy back.

Since Dad's operation, I don't feel as anxious about his health. The doctors have assured us that the operation was a success and Dad is expected to make a complete recovery. I'm optimistic things will remain okay. Even Mum isn't hanging over his shoulder, making sure he's not overexerting himself – she's busy playing with the young children or chatting with friends from the community.

I can leave for Suriname without worries.

It also means, eventually, I'll be able to tell my parents my relationship with Rav has ended without worrying about any negative implications for my dad's health.

Fingers crossed, when I *do* tell Mum and Dad that Rav and I have broken up, they won't suggest I start online dating or offer to help me find a match. And if they don't give up trying to get me to settle down, I'll happily go back to ignoring them.

Right now, I don't want to dwell on the end of my relationship with Rav. It'll happen soon enough.

I can't help noticing the special bond that has formed between Rav and my dad over the weeks. If Mum's to be trusted, my parents always hoped to have Rav as their son-in-law one day, but that's not unusual – I'm sure it's been the same dream for many parents in our community. But Dad will be disappointed when I tell him that Rav will no longer be part of our family. For a moment, I wonder whether Rav and I can come up with a way to end our arrangement that would allow Dad and Rav to remain in touch.

I laugh at my naivety. After we end our arrangement, there's no reason for Rav and me to stay in touch, let alone him and my father. It's probably kinder to cut all ties. I rub my hand over my chest when I feel a slight pang.

Under normal circumstances, without the need for a fake boyfriend, if Rav had approached me in that hotel all those months ago, I probably would have exchanged polite greetings and then found a way to excuse myself. I would still be thinking of him as the perfect kid who could do no wrong; still proper and aloof.

I would never have thought, in a million years, Rav would become one of my favourite people.

I always knew one of the risks entering this fake relationship was that being forced to spend time together, pretending to be in love, could confuse things – could make us believe we had developed real feelings for each other. Even though I know those feelings will disappear over time, I can't imagine not having Rav in my life.

As a friend. As more?

The mere fact I'm asking the question makes it clear it's better for us to have a clean break once I leave for my project. It'll be safer that way.

The following morning, I walk Rav to the door to say our goodbyes. He asks me if everything is all right since I haven't said much. I shrug. I've been a little distant with him, but I have to start pulling back so that we can end things – the next time I see him will be just before my flight. Our final goodbye.

'That Rav's a good boy,' Mum remarks once I return to the living room.

'Yes, he is.'

'You're still planning to go on this new job soon?'

'Yes, of course. Why wouldn't I?'

'I thought because you're with Rav now …'

'Rav doesn't ask me to give up my work.'

'Will he visit you?'

'In Suriname?' I shake my head. 'There's no point. You know visitors are restricted from coming to the worksite. I'd only be able to see him at the weekend. Besides, he's busy with work.'

Dad comes into the room carrying a tray with mugs of tea and a plate of biscuits. I immediately rush to take the tray off him.

'I could have made tea if you wanted some,' I say.

He tuts. 'I'm fine. I'm more than capable of making tea. Don't make me useless before my time.'

'Sorry, I didn't mean to overstep.'

'It's okay, Niki. But I'm fine. You can stop worrying about me.'

I mutter *ditto* under my breath.

'What was that, Niki?' Mum's sharp ears have heard me, of course.

'I said you don't have to worry about me either.'

Dad replies, 'We can't help worrying. We're your parents. It's our job.'

'But there's nothing to worry about. I love my life the way it is.'

'And that gives Dad and me great comfort and happiness. But it doesn't mean we'll stop worrying about your future.'

I take a deep breath. 'I know you may not believe me but I think about my future all the time. Financially I'm going to be fine. And when I'm ready, I'll probably buy a house and settle in one place.' Mum gives me a sceptical look. 'Okay,' I say with a grin, 'I may not settle in one place completely. I do want to have a home base one day. But while I have the chance, why can't I explore before I decide where that place will be?'

'I wish you would settle somewhere nearby like your brother and sister have done,' Mum says.

I hate that I've made her sad. The thing is, having spent the summer with my parents and family, a strong part of me believes when the time comes for me to buy my own home, I would like to live close to them. That's if I'm not living in London with … I turn my mind away from where those thoughts were leading.

'I know you don't like that I work abroad,' I say.

'We miss you when you're not here. It's only normal for parents to feel this way. We always want our children close,' Dad says.

'We're luckier than many of our friends,' Mum adds. 'Their

226

children live far away. They barely get to see them. At least Nishal and Shakti are close by.'

'Maybe we're greedy, wanting all our children to stay in the area.' Dad and Mum exchange smiles.

I expel a breath. There's a conversation I've been putting off. It's long overdue.

I bow my head. 'I'm sorry I've disappointed you.'

'What are you talking about?' Dad asks, surprise clear in his voice. 'You've never disappointed us.'

'Of course not. We're immensely proud of you,' Mum adds.

'But I haven't lived up to your expectations.'

'What expectations?' Mum asks.

'You know.'

'Actually, we don't, Annika.' Dad's tone is serious. 'We've always wanted what's best for you and your brother and sister, but it's your life to lead and we've always respected you to make your own decisions. The only thing we've ever asked of you three is to work hard at your studies so you could get a good career.'

'But you expect me to be married with a family,' I cry.

'Hope, not expect,' Mum says with a laugh, but her smile fades when she sees I'm serious.

'Then why are you so worried that I'm not married or settled down?'

'What are you on about?' Dad sounds puzzled.

'Ever since your illness, you've told me you wish I could settle down. You and Mum even offered to help me find a match!'

'Perhaps your dad's illness made us think about the future more concretely. You have so many friends, but you didn't have a special person in your life. We don't want you to be alone when we're gone.'

I flinch. I don't want to think about a time they're not around. 'Nish and Shakti told me you've been quite stressed about it for a while.'

Dad looks stern. 'Nish and Shakti had no right to say that.

227

Don't think that your love life contributed in any way to my illness for one minute.'

I want to believe him. 'But knowing I'm in a relationship with Rav has helped you feel better. I've seen the difference it's made.'

'Of course. Because Rav is a decent man. We've always liked him,' Dad says. 'But more importantly, he makes you happy. You're the happiest I've seen you in a long time. As parents, we couldn't ask for anything more than that.'

'But I'm always telling you I *am* happy, you just don't hear me.'

'We do hear you. And we know you love your work. And that makes us happy too.'

'But …' I prompt because I know there's one coming.

'But is it enough?' Mum asks. 'Will you be happy in the future if you forever turn your back on having a home, marriage or children?'

And here we are again. The point I've been making all along. 'People don't need to be in a relationship to feel happy and fulfilled.'

'Of course they don't,' my parents agree in unison, as if it's the most obvious thing in the world.

'So why is it so important to you for me be in a relationship, if you don't mind the fact I might not ever marry and settle down?'

'Because we don't want you to live with regret. And we're worried you're lying to yourself.'

My eyes widen. 'Lying to myself? About what?'

'You keep telling everyone you *can't* have a relationship because of your job. You closed yourself off to any possibility.'

'And I'm right. Having a relationship is hard work when I'm not in the country.'

'But you're managing it with Rav.'

Now would be the perfect time to admit the truth to them. That it's all been a sham. I hesitate.

I can't tell my parents the truth without discussing it with Rav first. It wouldn't be fair on him. I know he would need to think through the consequences and implications so he can prepare for any fallout. I don't want them to blame him or think less of him because he helped with my deception. I can't see any benefit to telling them. Maybe one day.

But I can pave the way for our inevitable break-up.

'We've worked so far,' I agree. 'But I haven't been out of the country for really long periods in the past year. And while our relationship was in its early stages, and we were figuring things out, the distance didn't matter so much. Soon I'll go back to my six- or nine-month projects. I don't know what will happen then. It could make having a future together difficult.'

'I know Rav; he will support you no matter what,' Mum says.

I scoff. Rav and I couldn't and shouldn't have a long-distance relationship. It wouldn't work. The thought causes a pang in my chest. My heart is telling me I should at least try. But I can't think about that now.

'He wants it very much,' Dad adds. 'It's like he told us, it works because he's busy too.'

'And when his business is more secure, and he's ready to get married and have children. Do you think he'll want a wife out of the country? One who may not have children?'

'Annika, this is why we worry. When you took your first over-seas job, you were always sure long-distance relationships would work. So optimistic. And we knew if anyone could make them work, you could. But you had a couple of bad experiences and decided that you weren't even going to try anymore. That isn't like you,' Dad says.

'We know not everyone needs a relationship to be happy or fulfilled. If it were Nishal or Shakti, we wouldn't be worried. But you do want a partner. You always have. For some reason, you don't think you can have a partner and keep doing the work you do, so you've convinced yourself you'll be happy alone.'

What they're saying is almost exactly what Rav said to me on our first practice date. He knew me then, as clearly as my parents have always known me.

And maybe they're all right. Maybe I do want someone to love. Maybe I do want to find my person. But I also want my work. I want to travel. I want freedom. I don't want to be tied down. And my parents may call it pessimistic but I know I'm being realistic when I say I can't have it all.

Chapter 25

A week later, I'm back in London to pack up my things from Rav's apartment. We'll have one last night together before we say our goodbyes. In a few days, I'll be in Suriname.

I let myself into his place. The smell coming from the kitchen makes my stomach rumble. Rav must have put a stew in the slow cooker before leaving for work that morning. I take off my shoes and then hang up my coat, ready to go through.

How quickly this place has felt like home to me. It makes leaving Rav so much harder. But I have to do it. I may love spending time with Rav, and I know how much I'm going to miss him when we've parted but I can't let my emotions get in the way of what is the rational thing to do.

Trying to make a long-distance relationship work will only prolong the agony and make it so much harder when it does end, as it inevitably will.

Before I get to the living room, I turn back and reach into my coat for my key ring.

I take a deep breath as I remove Rav's flat key from my bunch, taking it through to the kitchen with me and placing it in a pot on the counter. It's such a small act but there's a sense of finality. I have no claim to his key anymore. Our arrangement is over.

Even though it's early September, the weather is comfortable enough for me to sit outside so I make myself a cup of tea and take it through to the balcony. For once, sitting out here doesn't bring me any peace.

My mind keeps replaying what my parents said about me – about how I say I don't want to get married because I've convinced myself I can't have a family and my work but I'm not really happy being single.

I do love my job. For the most part, it fulfils me. And I'm good at it. And I've accepted that I will stay single because of it. More than accepted it. I'll be happy as long as I have my work.

But even to my ears, I sound like I'm trying to assure myself.

I'm not wrong insisting that my work isn't conducive to a relationship – not one leading to marriage and children anyway. For all Nish and Shakti accuse me of being selfish and living my life without consideration for others, I know it would be more selfish to pretend to someone that a different outcome would be possible. Particularly for someone like Rav, who has made it clear he wants marriage and a family.

I saw him with the children at my brother's party and at the Bamfords' garden party. He loves them. They are a part of the life he has planned out for himself. How selfish would I be to ask him to change that for me?

But I didn't expect it to be this hard.

Our scheme, our arrangement wasn't supposed to have complications. We discussed the risks, even laughed about the possibility of falling in love with each other.

I wonder how much of my dilemma is because I started sleeping with Rav. The sex is amazing, but I don't usually have any problems ending a relationship when it's time to leave for a project.

Starting a sexual relationship was another thing we discussed rationally and objectively. We did everything right but we're still in this situation.

I say *we*, but I don't know if Rav feels the same confusion. For all I know, he has no problem with our arrangement – the fake-dating one and the sexual one – ending after tonight.

Since coming back from Dubai, and starting the affair, whenever Rav comes back from work, he's barely made it inside the door before we're wrapped around each other, not even bothering to make it to a bed or couch.

When I hear the door open, I purposely remain in the kitchen. 'Are you hungry?' I call out to him. 'Shall we eat straight away?'

Rav gives me a small, slightly curious smile as he approaches me.

'Everything good?' he asks.

'Great. The food you made smells fantastic. Can't wait to dig in.'

'Let me wash up and I'll be right with you.' He gives me a brief kiss. It makes me want to cry. Unlike the pecks we shared while faking our relationship, this kiss was casual in the way kisses are when you're so comfortable with someone, the action has almost become second nature.

Dinner is a subdued affair. Neither of us seems to want to engage in small talk. But we're also avoiding the other potential topic of conversation – what's happening after tomorrow.

After eating and clearing away dinner, Rav hangs up a dish towel then leans back against the counter. He suggests we watch a film together. I go over and wrap my arms around him. He envelops me in his embrace, bending his head so our lips meet in a passionate kiss.

We have one final night together. I refuse to waste any more time wishing for a future that can never happen. Instead, I'm going to make the most of these last few hours with Rav.

The following morning I wake up before Rav and gently remove his arm from around my waist. I take my things and get ready in the main bathroom rather than his en suite so I don't disturb him.

I put on a pot of coffee and begin sweeping the flat for my

stuff I've let accumulate here over the weeks. There's more than I expected. There's no doubt I've made myself at home here.

It's hard to believe that for years, I thought Rav to be cold, distant and superior to everyone around him. I put him in the role of my nemesis when we were barely teenagers and it's more than likely I'd still put him in that role if we hadn't agreed to this arrangement. Whatever happens in the future, no matter how much it will hurt, I won't regret the chance to have got to know the man Rav really is.

And I can admit, to myself at least, that it will hurt to leave Rav. Today is probably the last time I will ever spend with him. I have to ignore the heaviness in my chest each time I think about it.

But trying to keep Rav in my life and maintain a friendship of some sort will be too hard. I want more than friendship, but I know that won't be possible.

I expel a sharp, irritated breath. The way I'm feeling now is exactly why I try to avoid romantic entanglements.

I continue gathering my things and stuffing them in my bag. I pick up the camel Rav bought me in Dubai. I'm tempted to leave it here to remind Rav of me and our time together. But perhaps he doesn't want any reminders. Besides, I need it with me.

The camel plays its tune as I place it in my bag, and I hear a deep chuckle behind me.

I see Rav leaning back against the kitchen counter, holding a mug of coffee. He's wearing pyjama bottoms and nothing else. No man who spends most of his days sitting behind a desk should have such a well-chiselled chest. I walk over to run my fingers over his abs up to his shoulders, lifting my face for his kiss. I hear a mug being placed on a hard surface, then his arms wrap around me, pulling me closer to him.

'Morning,' Rav says when I force myself to break away. If we'd carried on the way we were, we would have ended up making love in the kitchen.

And sex wouldn't help the situation.

'Morning,' I reply, pasting on the brightest smile I can manage. 'I'm just doing a final check for my stuff. I've done in here and the guest bedroom. All I need to do now is check your room and that's me done.'

'You're not rushing off, are you? I thought you weren't leaving until this evening.'

'There's still a lot to do at home. I thought I'd catch an early train.'

'I can drive you home,' he says.

'That's okay. I don't want you to do a four-hour round trip for no reason.'

'I don't mind.'

'No. I'd rather take the train.'

'Something wrong with my driving?' he asks, waggling his eyebrows.

Smiling, I shake my head. There's no point beating around the bush. I may as well start the conversation. 'I think it's better to say our goodbyes here than in a car in front of my parents.'

'This doesn't have to end now, you know.'

I avoid looking at him directly. Pretending to be obtuse, I ask, 'What do you mean? Do you still need a fake girlfriend for the business?'

'I don't need a fake anything.' His tone indicates he knows what I'm doing.

I take a deep breath. 'Then I don't see why we need to continue this arrangement.'

'You don't? Honestly? Not even when our relationship became real.'

'We had an agreement. I've kept to my part. Let's not go changing the parameters at the last minute.' I blink rapidly to stop any tears – I hate downplaying what we had, but I have to. For Rav's sake.

'So you don't care at all. You have no feelings for me?' He strides towards me and lifts my chin, his gaze penetrating.

'I do care about you. Of course, I do.' As much as I wish I could deny it, I'm not going to lie to him about that. 'But what does it matter how I do or don't feel? Nothing has changed. I'm not looking for a relationship. I'm not ready to settle down.'

'I'm not asking you to.'

'Not yet, maybe. But our only options are that we try continuing this relationship and inevitably learn we can't make it work long-distance, so we break up a couple of months down the line, or we end things now. Isn't it better to avoid getting more attached to each other?'

'There's a third option you haven't mentioned. We can find a way to make this work.'

I shake my head sorrowfully. 'That's not a realistic option. Believe me, I've tried.'

'You never tried with me. Maybe it will be different this time. Don't you think it's worth giving it a go?'

I want to say yes. Yes, it is worth it. But I know too well how this will end so I harden my resolve. 'You don't understand, Rav. I don't want to.'

Rav swallows, then looks away. He pinches the bridge of his nose. 'You don't want to try seeing if we could have something that could last?'

'It won't last. I already know that.'

'You don't know. You're just jumping to conclusions.'

'Because I put experience over hope. Rav, this arrangement of ours was wonderful. We both got what we needed and more. But you have to see it's futile thinking we can make it work. What is the point of even saying we're in a relationship if I'm not even going to be in the country for the rest of the year?'

'Because I can wait until you are in the country. I'm not someone who needs a woman dancing attendance on him. Three months is nothing in the general scheme of things.'

'What about the next three months I'm away, or what if the next project after that is six months?'

'I don't know,' he says, holding his palms up. 'I don't have all the answers. What I'm saying is that I'd like to try.'

He sounds so reasonable – how do I make him understand? I always thought a long-distance relationship was possible but too many failed relationships showed me I was wrong. And if Rav and I continue our relationship, nothing changes for him when we break up. Rav can go back to his original intention of asking his family to make a match. I will have been a blip in his trajectory.

I'll be the one with my heart in pieces.

All I say is, 'Rav, you have a plan. You know when you want to get married and start a family. You said you don't have time for a proper relationship. Why change that now?'

'Because things change. If there's anything you taught me, it's that I can't control everything. When we came up with our fake-relationship scheme, I didn't think it was necessary for us to like each other. But it happened anyway. I like talking with you. I enjoy spending time with you and I don't feel it's ready to be over.'

'But one day it will be over, Rav. I like my job and I don't know if I'm ever going to want marriage or children.'

He looks at me with pity. 'Sometimes I don't understand you.'

'What does that mean?'

'You live your life with such passion. You're happy-go-lucky to the point of being reckless. But then you put rules in the places where they make no sense. I like having my life in order. I like making plans. But even I know you can't plan your emotions.'

'But you can protect your emotions. You can protect yourself from getting in deeper.'

'It's too late for that. I'm already falling for you.'

The words nearly everyone longs to hear and yet they're the last thing I want Rav to say.

'I'm not going to change, Rav.' I wrap my arms around myself.

'You don't want to change.'

'I shouldn't have to change to meet someone else's expectations.'

'There's a difference between insisting you can't change or

changing to suit someone else and refusing to change, refusing to grow, to adapt.'

'You're accusing me of being—'

He holds up his hand. 'I'm not accusing you of anything. I'm telling you how I feel. I'm reaching out and asking you to meet me—'

'Halfway. You want me to compromise.'

'No. Not halfway. Start with a step. That's all I'm asking. That you take a step in my direction. I'll do the rest.'

I stare at him. Tears falling.

I want to take the risk. I want to believe that things could work out between us. I want to be that bright, optimistic person my parents remember, who thought she could have it all. I've never wanted anything more.

I lift a foot a fraction off the floor.

But it's Rav. Rav, who already has more of my heart than I've ever given to someone before. Rav, who makes me want to believe in happily ever after. And when everything comes crashing down – as it inevitably will – because it's Rav, I don't think I'll be strong enough to put myself back together.

'I can't,' I say and put down my foot. 'I'm so sorry.'

Chapter 26

It's the end of my second week in Suriname and I'm about to leave our site and head into the capital for the first time since I've been here. The project is progressing according to the schedule. Which is no surprise to anyone here. Although the work is generally interesting and challenging, I can't help the sense of déjà vu.

I've just come back to my office after resolving a dispute between a group of project leaders and the leaders of Indigenous groups. All parties managed to compromise enough to proceed with the work, meaning I can chalk it up as a successful outcome, but it's the kind of thing I deal with all the time. These incidents are only variations on a theme.

If I'm being honest, that vague feeling of discontent that I identified on my previous project in Guyana has been growing steadily for a while. I don't want to stop working abroad but I can't keep doing the same kind of projects when I've been doing them for six years now, first as an employee and then as a consultant. Maybe it's time for me to explore new opportunities. I email my client asking for a meeting to discuss the future.

Change is around the corner.

In the minibus on our way to Paramaribo, I let the conversation of my colleagues wash over me as my mind invariably goes to England. And Rav.

I'm sure friends playing amateur psychologists would tell me my feelings of discontent are because of him. But I know that's not it. Or at least not all of it.

But he is a big part of it.

I think about Rav a lot. More than I expected. With past boyfriends, it was always a case of out of sight, out of mind. With Rav, I'm discovering how much fonder my heart grows.

I want to tell him about my day. I want to hear about his day. I want to watch films together and make dinner together.

Yes, I'm unhappy about how things ended with Rav – about how much I hurt him. I convinced myself I was trying to protect him. He shouldn't have to give up his dream of the future for me.

Rav told me he's falling for me. Since he told me, I've been coming up with reasons for how it can't be true. That he doesn't know what he's feeling – that it's all in his head, that we got too carried away by our arrangement. But every time I try to convince myself, I can almost hear his voice saying I don't get to tell him how he feels. And it's true. I can't control how he feels. I can only own the way I feel.

Without Rav, I feel empty and aching. And it's worse knowing I'm solely responsible for how miserable I am.

I will always regret not being completely honest with Rav. I told him I wasn't interested in seeing if we could make things work.

I should have told him the truth. That I'm falling for him too. That the strength of my feelings frightens me. That instead of protecting him, I was trying to protect my heart from getting hurt.

I've been hurt before. When I first started working abroad, I always believed that a long-distance relationship could work if both parties put effort into it – my parents are right about that – but I never seemed to be able to make it work. I shouldn't have let two bad relationships, two relationships with the wrong people, convince me I couldn't maintain a loving one.

I don't know what the future holds. But I do know I want to give things with Rav a chance. And I need to tell him.

Once we've reached our hostel, I put my bag in my room and then immediately hunt for the nearest place with internet I could use.

In front of a computer, my hands hover over the keyboard, mentally composing an email. I draft a heartfelt message. The mouse hovers over the send button, then I press delete. This is something I want to tell Rav face to face, not have him read in an email. At the same time, I can't wait until I'm back in England so I can see him again.

I send him an email simply asking if we can arrange a time for us to speak on video chat. It's been two weeks since Rav told me he's falling in love with me. If that's true, and I really want to believe it is, then I can't believe he's going to fall out of love with me because we haven't been in contact for a couple of weeks. I know Rav isn't a fickle person. If he cares for someone, anyone – even me – his feelings would be strong, and constant, and true. I need to believe he still loves me.

But I also know I hurt him deeply. Maybe he won't be able to forgive me.

There's nothing to do now but wait for his reply. And hope.

I'm back in Paramaribo the following weekend and eagerly log into my email account. Nothing from Rav.

The gut-wrenching disappointment is proof that my feelings for Rav are real and aren't going away. But why hasn't he replied? Maybe he thinks it's better to cut his losses, draw a line under me and my issues and move on. He can always stick to his plan to look for a bride in a few years and forget about me completely.

Can I blame him if he doesn't want to talk to me?

I'm tempted to email Greg to find out whether he has any news. But I don't know how much Greg knows about us – whether he knows how real Rav and I were. Anyway, Greg is Rav's business partner. Is it appropriate to raise this with him? I can't ask Tinu because I don't know what happened between her and Greg but when I asked her why she wasn't returning Greg's calls she was very cagey. Something's happened there but I need to wait for her to tell me – not use her as a way of finding out about Rav. Maybe I could contact Kesh instead.

Or maybe I could try being patient. I'll be back in Paramaribo on Wednesday for a meeting – I can check my emails when I'm back.

* * *

The four days until I'm back in Paramaribo drag by. Thoughts of Rav consume every moment I'm not at work.

This isn't a brief affair that hasn't fully run its course yet. This is true love. For me.

On Wednesday, I'm in the foyer of one of the city's best hotels, meeting with a director from one of my client companies. The meeting goes much better than I dreamed. I'm buzzing with the possibilities for how my future will look, but I'm desperate to check whether Rav has replied yet. The company has arranged for me to stay overnight at the hotel so, after my meeting, I go straight to my room to check my emails.

Nothing.

All this time, I've been holding on to this hope that Rav hasn't replied because he's been too busy and hasn't had a chance to read my email. But it's been one and a half weeks. There's no logical reason for him not to have seen it and replied by now.

Unless I've hurt him too badly and he doesn't want to be with me anymore.

Well, I'm not giving up on him. I need to tell him the truth about how I feel and then everything will be in his hands. I'll even break my rule and fly back to England mid-project if I have to.

But what will I do if I've destroyed any chance of us having a future together?

Immediately I pick up my phone to call Rav. I know Suriname's only a few hours behind England and he'll still be at work but I can't wait. I need to know.

It goes straight to voicemail. I try phoning again – at least I can hear his voice on the recorded message.

Then I remember that Rav has call waiting. There would be no reason for my call to go straight to voicemail unless his phone was off and he would have no reason to turn it off during the working day.

My heart beats faster. What if something's happened to him? I call Kesh.

He isn't pleased to hear from me. Rav must have told him we'd ended our relationship.

'You broke his heart, Annika,' he tells me, curtly.

'I know,' I whisper. 'I need to speak to him though. Do you know where he is?'

Kesh sighs. 'All I know is, if Rav isn't answering his phone there'll be a good reason for it. Just give him space. You owe him that.'

I disconnect and toss my phone on the bed. Kesh is right. There is a good reason for Rav not answering – he doesn't want to speak to me. He told me he loved me and I threw it back in his face. Why should he forgive me?

After an hour trying to relax in my room, I give up and go downstairs to read by the pool.

I find a lounger in the shade and get comfortable but I can't concentrate on my book. I keep thinking about what Kesh said, that I have to give Rav space.

I know he's right; I *should* give Rav space. But what if he uses it to put distance between us and decides to move on with his life with no room for me in it?

Like a pre-teen with her first crush, I phone Rav again, wanting to hear his voice even if it's only pre-recorded.

The phone rings through this time. I hold my breath waiting

for the call to connect. Concentrating on my phone, I almost miss the sound of a ringtone playing the melody from a Bollywood love song nearby.

My ringtone. The ringtone Rav has for me.

I get up from the lounger and follow the sound. My breath whooshes from my body, then my heart rate accelerates erratically. It can't be. I blink, not believing my eyes. He can't be here, can he? My imagination must have conjured up a Rav-shaped mirage.

I move in his direction. The man sees me coming. His face breaks into a wide smile. I shake my head, still not sure I can trust what I see.

'I didn't expect to see you here,' the Rav mirage says.

I gasp. 'You didn't expect to see me? Wha … what are you doing here?'

'I came to see you.'

'Why?'

'So we can have an open and honest conversation.'

'Why?' I repeat foolishly.

'There are things you didn't give me a chance to say.'

I cock my head. 'And you flew all the way here just to say them?'

'Yes.'

I swallow, still having trouble processing the truth before my eyes. 'Did you get my emails?'

'I did.'

'And you didn't think you could say what you needed over a video chat.'

He shakes his head. 'No. Can we talk?'

I clench my hands to my sides, desperate to touch him. To make sure he's standing in front of me asking to speak to me.

'Annika,' he says.

I shake myself out of my stupor. 'Yes, of course, we can talk.'

He grins. 'Shall we get a drink at the pool bar?'

I follow him as if in a trance, still not believing he's here. I don't know why he's come, but I'm not letting him leave until I've had the chance to tell him how I feel and to beg him to give us a chance. He must want that; surely, he wouldn't have flown halfway across the world otherwise.

Moments later, I'm sitting under a parasol at a table opposite Rav. He's really here. In Suriname. There's so much to say, and yet I'm lost for words.

'You're looking well,' Rav says after we've ordered refreshments.

'Thanks, you too.' To be honest, he looks thinner but that could be my imagination.

'I wasn't expecting to see you here. I thought you'd be on site.'

'I had a meeting. I'm back tomorrow.'

'Must be serendipity we bumped into each other.'

It's unbelievable. Fate rather than coincidence. 'How long are you here for?'

'That depends on you.'

'What do you mean?'

'I haven't booked a return ticket.'

'What? Why not?'

'Because we have things to discuss and I don't know how long it will take.'

Rav doing something without a fully developed plan is so out of character.

'What about work?' I ask.

'Greg can handle things until I'm back.'

I clear my throat. 'You said we have things to discuss.'

What we need to say feels too private to talk about in public, and yet going to one of our hotel rooms would be too intimate.

'Do you want to take a walk?' I suggest, thinking it could help the conversation flow more easily if we're not looking directly at each other – help me at least.

'Sure.' He stands up then comes round to pull out my chair, taking care not to brush against me.

We walk past the pool towards the tropical gardens.

245

'Have you heard from Mr B?' I ask.

Rav nods. I hold my breath. His mouth breaks into a grin. 'We got it. He accepted our proposal.'

I throw my arms around him. 'Congratulations. I'm so pleased for you. So happy.'

'Thanks. It means a lot to our employees. It's a relief.' He hasn't let go of me completely, so I take a step away.

'I hope it makes having me as your fake girlfriend worth it.'

He looks embarrassed. 'The truth is, I never needed a fake partner, not really.'

I scoff. 'What?' This can't be true. 'But what about our arrangement? Why did you reach out to me in the first place?'

He slowly moves his head up and down as if weighing up what he's about to say. 'I wanted a chance to get to know you better.'

'I don't get what you're saying. You didn't need my help for your business?'

'It didn't hurt. Rupert is the kind of old-fashioned businessman who feels more comfortable doing business with people in committed relationships. But if you hadn't mentioned your need for a fake suitor or if you didn't agree to the proposal, Greg and I would have worked out a way to convince Rupert on our own merits. It was a helpful deception but not essential.'

'So you were just doing me a big favour?' I don't know what to do with the information. Something about the business never made sense to me, but I assumed it was because I wasn't part of the corporate world.

'I was getting something out of it too.'

'What?'

'I told you, I wanted the chance to know you better. I've always wanted to. I tried to talk to you at those doctor parties but I never found the courage when you were always in demand.'

I shake my head, still not believing that's true. 'Well, at least you managed when we bumped into each other at the hotel.'

'You were on your own. If I crashed and burned nobody would be around to see. But so I didn't totally embarrass myself, I pretended to think you were Shakti.'

I laugh. 'And is that why you asked to sit with me? To get to know me better? I've always wondered why.'

'Yes. I've known for a long time that many people used to compare themselves to me. I didn't like it and I didn't ask for it. And I know you saw me as some kind of—'

'Nemesis,' I interrupt.

'Exactly. But that perfect child you claimed I was, who got the scholarships and the good grades, isn't *all* I am. It's not *who* I am. I wanted a chance for you to get to know the real me.'

'For what purpose? You knew I wasn't interested in settling down. Did you think I would change my mind, simply because I spent time in your company?' I say with a laugh.

'No! Well, not to begin with. I meant what I said – marriage wasn't part of my plans for the next few years. But your need for a fake suitor sounded like a good opportunity for me. One I couldn't pass up. I thought we'd spend some time together, enjoying each other's company and hopefully, be friends. I wasn't expecting anything more.'

'But things changed?' I prompt him.

Rav gives me a gentle smile. 'You know I'm in love with you, Annika.'

Many phrases aren't important. But a few phrases can mean *everything* to someone – that make the difference between an ordinary world and one filled with dreams and possibilities. When Rav told me he was falling for me before I left for Suriname, it was the wrong time for me to hear it. I was trying too hard to pretend what we felt wasn't real.

But for the past few weeks, hearing him tell me he's in love with me is all I've longed to hear.

'I love you too, you know,' I tell him quietly and simply.

He gasps. Then his smile widens. I've never seen anyone with

247

that look of complete happiness before – I'm sure my expression mirrors his. He gathers me to him and bends his head to kiss me thoroughly, passionately. As if he needs me to breathe. The way I need him.

Chapter 27

Hours later, we're lying in bed, dissecting our relationship, talking about the past.

'When did you know you loved me?' I ask.

Rav plays with my hair as I rest my head against his chest. 'I'm not sure there was one single point. In some ways, I feel like I've always loved you.'

I chuckle. 'Always? We've known each other since we were at primary school.'

Rav grins. 'Okay, maybe not always. Although you've often intrigued me. I tried to get to know you at the parties. There's something about you.'

'The way you describe me at those parties, that "something" was rude and obnoxious.'

'I never told you,' Rav says with a playful tone, 'but those are the first two criteria for my future wife.'

'Be serious, Rav.' I give him a light tap, although my heart accelerates at him mentioning 'wife'. We still haven't started discussing the future yet.

'For a long time now I've felt some unexplained connection to you. It was never a big deal, though – I was still convinced my life plan was the right one.'

'Married at thirty-five. Kids straight away.'

'That's right. Falling in love with you was not part of the plan. But by the first dance practice, I knew my plans were totally derailed.'

'That early?' I'm shocked Rav has been feeling this way for so long.

'I know it wasn't the same for you,' he says, tapping my nose. 'I was your nemesis. You never saw me as a potential boyfriend.'

'I've always thought you're attractive.'

'But nothing more.' He sounds disappointed.

I bite my lip and shrug. 'But it's better nothing happened when we were younger, don't you think? I wasn't ready at that time to accept a real relationship. Travel and freedom were too important to me. I needed to do some growing up.'

'Then I'm glad we waited.' Rav reaches down to kiss me. 'What about you? What made you realise you cared about me? Was it the distance?'

'Oh, I knew before I left England. I tried to convince myself that how I felt was temporary although I now know I was just trying to protect myself from getting hurt. But I needed the time away to figure things out. To know for sure it wasn't only sexual attraction. To know with certainty, I'm completely in love with you.'

At my words, Rav covers my body with his. It's another couple of hours before we order room service and think about getting out of bed. There's still a lot we need to sort through. We have time. Rav has officially taken two weeks of annual leave, although he tells me he was prepared to stay in Suriname until I agreed a relationship between us is possible.

We both know that saying we love each other aren't the last words, but just the start of some major conversations.

After eating, Rav sits in an armchair, and I sit on his lap. Our discussions don't have to be across a table from each other – we're going to approach the future from the same side. The side that wants our relationship to last.

But we need to be honest about what is possible.

'So,' I begin, 'I guess the first question is what do you see for our relationship? Do you want me to return to England?'

Rav laughs, then shakes his head before kissing me fully. 'No, Annika, I don't. I know how you feel about your work and settling down. I'm not asking you to give up anything.'

'Then how ...'

'I can adjust my plans around you.'

I frown. 'But then you're the one making the sacrifices. I wouldn't want you to resent me.'

'That's where you and I have always differed in our thinking,' he replies, pressing a kiss to the top of my head. 'It's not a sacrifice if it's something that I want to do. It's a choice.'

'Even if it means giving up having the wife and family you want?' I ask, curious to know how far he's willing to give up things he's planned for years.

'A wife and family was something that was expected of me. And to be honest, I never challenged that expectation. I never had the same pressure you did. It only became clearer to me when my parents were interrogating you.' He twists a lock of my hair. 'Besides, I hope, given time, I'll persuade you that being my wife doesn't mean settling down.'

'So you'd be happy being married to someone who isn't in the country for half the year?'

'If that someone is you.' He deserves a kiss for that, so I give him one and we quickly become distracted before he gently moves me a little further away. 'Once this deal with Bamford goes through, I'll have the freedom to travel. The fact you're working in a different country doesn't mean we have to be separated.'

'You mean you'd follow me?' I can't believe he's suggesting that.

'I'd join you where I could. Besides, what's my alternative?'

I shrug. 'To follow your original plan to start looking for a wife.'

'But she wouldn't be you,' he says earnestly. 'So I couldn't give her all of me. And that wouldn't be fair to anyone.'

251

Before I left England, Rav asked me to take a step towards him and told me he would cross the rest of the distance. Coming to Suriname, telling me he'll travel with me, proves he means what he said. I need to let him know I'm ready to take a step too.

'You don't need to travel with me,' I tell him.

'I want to. Yes, there will be times when we have to be apart, but we'll make it work long-distance. At other times I can stay somewhere close to where you're based. I don't mind.'

'And I appreciate that, but that's not what I mean.' I'm bursting to tell him my news.

'What do you mean?'

'I've been ready for a change in career for some time now. I met a director from one of my client companies today to see whether there was any more troubleshooting work, similar to what I was doing over the summer but with some travel abroad. And they're prepared to create this new role of supervisory coordinator for me. I'll have to go back to being an employee but I'll be a trouble-shooter for a variety of projects, which means I still get to work abroad. It won't be for months at a time though, more like weeks. We won't have to do long-distance that often.' My words trip over themselves in my eagerness to get them out.

Rav stares at me, not blinking. I was expecting more of a reaction, to be honest.

'I can't ask you to make that sacrifice,' he says.

'You didn't ask me to. It's like you said. It's not a sacrifice if I choose to do it.'

'But you love your work. What you do is important.'

I beam at him. 'And I'm still going to be doing that work. Like I said, I was ready for a change, ready to try branching out. And I'm not giving up anything. I'll still being working abroad.'

He looks at me intently. 'Are you sure this is what you want? I've told you I'm prepared to travel with you.'

'And I love you for offering. Perhaps you can still come with me when I need to go abroad. Believe me, I'm not making this huge sacrifice. I'm still going to travel and do work I love.'

'But as an employee. You won't have the same freedom when you're not on a project.'

My heart is ready to burst at how lucky I am to have someone like Rav – someone who understands me so well. 'It's going to be fine. Over the last few months I've been reprioritising what's important to me. And I'm ready to have a permanent base in England. Besides, my decision isn't all about you,' I say, playfully pushing against his chest. 'I want to spend more time with my family too. This summer, I realised how much I enjoy being around them. Ironically, they're no longer pressuring me to settle down. They'll be over the moon that I'll be buying a house in England. Although maybe I should hold off finding a house until we decide …' I break off, suddenly embarrassed in case I'm being too pushy.

He brings my hand to his lips. 'Yes, we should probably decide together where we're going to live. I don't mind looking outside London if you want to live closer to your parents. Perhaps in the Oxford area.'

Touched by yet another example of Rav's thoughtfulness, I move my hand from his lips to behind his head, bringing it closer to me.

'Does that mean you're not against marriage or a husband?' he asks slowly after we break apart.

'Not if that husband is you,' I reply with a grin. Then I get serious. 'And one day, if we want children, if we're lucky enough to have them, then we'll …'

'Then we'll find a way to make it work so you can still do everything you want to.'

I nod, believing anything is possible for the two of us.

'All right,' he says, 'I think this sounds like we need to start making new plans for our future.'

'Absolutely,' I reply with a laugh because Rav wouldn't be Rav without his plans – some things don't change. But so much has.

Who would have thought, back in March, when I blurted out my need for a fake suitor to my childhood nemesis, that I would find the one person in the world who is perfectly suited to me in such a real way?

A Letter from Ruby Basu

Thank you so much for choosing to read *The Love Arrangement*. I hope you enjoyed it! If you did and would like to be the first to know about my new releases, follow me on Twitter, Facebook and my website.

I hope you loved *The Love Arrangement* and if you did I would be so grateful if you would leave a review. I always love to hear what readers thought, and it helps new readers discover my books too.

Thanks,

Ruby Basu

Twitter – @writerrb01
Ruby Basu | Facebook
Home (rubybasu.com)
Instagram – authorrubybasu

She's here for the perfect Christmas escape ...

Sharmila arrives in Pineford for the holiday of her dreams, gifted to her by her dear late friend Thomas. But she's in for a surprise because Thomas has left her with one last request: if she completes his Christmas wish list, her chosen charity will receive a big donation. Or so she thinks.

... He's there to reclaim his family's legacy

Little does she know, she's set to inherit Thomas's estate, much to his nephew Zach's disbelief. Now he's come to Pineford to do everything he can to stop Sharmila from fulfilling that list and let his family's legacy be left in the hands of a stranger.

When Sharmila and Zach meet, sparks fly, and they find themselves unexpectedly growing closer with each passing wish. But just as Sharmila feels her heart opening up to Zach, she learns he's been keeping a secret from her. Can she forgive him and get the happily-ever-after she's always wished for this Christmas?

Acknowledgements

Thank you to my editor, Mel Hayes, for your incredible feedback as well as your understanding and support. Thank you to Charlotte Phillips for giving me the gorgeous cover of my dreams. Thank you to all the online writing communities I'm part of, too many to name here. Without these groups writing could be a lonely pursuit.

I'd also like to thank Joanne Grant, who helped me get my writing mojo back when I desperately needed the motivation.

Thanks to my amazing husband, Gareth, for being my sounding board and for always being my biggest cheerleader; and to D and E, who keep me grounded.

And finally, I should acknowledge my own childhood nemesis. Although you probably don't know who are.

Dear Reader,

We hope you enjoyed reading this book. If you did, we'd be so appreciative if you left a review. It really helps us and the author to bring more books like this to you.

Here at HQ Digital we are dedicated to publishing fiction that will keep you turning the pages into the early hours. Don't want to miss a thing? To find out more about our books, promotions, discover exclusive content and enter competitions you can keep in touch in the following ways:

JOIN OUR COMMUNITY:

Sign up to our new email newsletter:
http://smarturl.it/SignUpHQ

Read our new blog www.hqstories.co.uk

𝕏 https://twitter.com/HQStories

f www.facebook.com/HQStories

BUDDING WRITER?

We're also looking for authors to join the HQ Digital family!
Find out more here:

https://www.hqstories.co.uk/want-to-write-for-us/

Thanks for reading, from the HQ Digital team